WHERE BIG TREES FALL

WHERE BIG TREES FALL

Jeff McClelland

iUniverse, Inc.

New York Lincoln Shanghai

Where Big Trees Fall

iUniverse, Inc.

For information address:
iUniverse, Inc.
2021 Pine Lake Road, Suite 100
Lincoln, NE 68512
www.iuniverse.com

ISBN: 0-595-32508-4 (pbk)
ISBN: 0-595-66616-7 (cloth)

Printed in the United States of America

To Carla, may you find the love you seek. To Susan, who taught me what love is, and what it isn't.

Contents

▼

Acknowledgement

My thanks to Greg McClelland, Margaret Marquis, Kay Hoffman, and Jan Gibson for reading and helping to edit my story. Thanks to Mike Altman, my PSA at iUniverse, and to iUniverse for all their help to make this book a reality. Thanks for all your help.

Timber, tall timber as far as the eye could see. Tall trees that reached through the sky and climbed high to touch the stars. The giant trees lived in the land, filling the soil of the earth with their roots to hold them in place. The trees stood as though they would never be removed before their time. Their time was a millennial life cycle from the germination of the seed to the decaying of the mature tree. It represented life at its fullest in seasons of giving and receiving.

The people who lived among the big trees knew that the trees gave life. The giant cedar tree was honored and worshipped by these native people, who, like the big trees, had a long history of being rooted in the land. They would go on and on fearing no disease or end, for as far as they believed, they were healthy and would last as long as the big trees they lived among.

Along came other men, great men, giant men, and men rooted in the pursuit of profit. These were the timber barons who made millions. Along with them came more men, strong men, determined men, men rooted in their faith and determined to farm and raise a family, and they worked hacking out a hard living in the land where big trees fall. And as the big trees fell, so did the people who called this land their home.

This is their story—the Natives, the settlers—the timber barons, and the loggers—lest someday their memories are lost.

CHAPTER 1

▼

THE JOURNEY

In the year 1893.

"When will I have those feelings of falling in love?" Victoria asked.

Her sister, Rachel, combed and ran her fingers through Victoria's hair as they rode in the carriage. "You should have already fallen."

"I don't know what love really is," Victoria said as she watched in a hand held mirror.

"Love is love—what is there to know?"

"I know I haven't felt it from a man yet."

"Oh, you will soon," Rachel said laughing.

Victoria laughed with her sister and then sighed. "Is love only a thought, a feeling, or is it a long journey down an unknown path?"

"I am sure you will find your answers soon sister."

Victoria desired to fall in love as every other young woman, yet love seemed as far away from her as Scotland is from America. These thoughts soaked her mind as she rode through the soft misty rain to the old stone church in the middle of the village. It's here that sixteen years ago Victoria was baptized as an infant. Here, she would be submerged in marriage to Mark Southerland.

Mark was ten years her senior. He was an honorable man, and he spoke often of his love for Victoria. Still, she questioned that love, and her lack of feelings of love for him. It overwhelmed her soul as if the floods of doubt would never recede. "I don't know if I really love Mark."

"Does mother know that?" Rachel asked.

"Yes, I told her a while back, but she assured me that my love would grow given time."

"Do you think it will?"

"Six months have passed and even though I have spent much time with Mark, there are no fires burning in my heart."

"What are you girls whispering?" their mother asked from the front of the carriage.

"Talking about love mother," Victoria said.

Victoria liked Mark. He was kind, considerate, and at times could show affection. Yet, at other times he had a temper that would scare her. His appearance didn't excite her senses. Mark Southerland had a medium build and worked on a large belly, which he accredited to his mother's fine cooking. He had dark brown hair and stood five feet seven inches. He wore a mustache that he was proud of, and which Victoria wished he would shave off. His parents had given him a comfortable life, and he desired to give the same to Victoria.

Victoria stepped out of the buggy making her way into the church. The stones gave off a chill as she walked inside, which made her look at her own heart wondering if in time Mark could become the love of her life. Victoria's father stood next to her. "I want what is best for you. Mark will provide a good life for you. In many ways I wish I were in his place—you will be happy."

"I do hope so father. Yet, I feel as though he thinks of me as an object and not as a woman who has feelings and thoughts of her own."

Her father reached up and moved his hand across Victoria's mouth. "Smile dear, men and women have their places in society. Yours will be at the side of your husband to follow his will and his desire. Like your mother before you—you have to put your desires and wants to rest."

"But father! I have…"

Her father reached over covering her mouth and then pulled down her veil. "You must not be seen."

"Mark has seen me a hundred times."

"It's tradition—accept what has always been. Life is better that way."

"It won't be easy father, but I will try."

Those were the only words she could find to say. She didn't want to upset her father, as she desired his approval. From under her veil she forced a smile as she continued down the hall.

After the wedding Victoria and Mark would board a ship for America. Victoria was leaving behind her whole life, her parents, her friends, and her sister

She knew that she couldn't tell him the truth. "Of course Mark, very happy," she said.

He wrapped his strong arms around her as they drifted off to sleep.

In the morning Mark and Victoria boarded the ship bound for America. It was the first ship of any kind that she had been on. She thought her mother and father were right in saying that she was one fortunate girl to have such an opportunity.

"We'll be staying in the second-class passenger cabin," Mark said.

"I don't mind."

"I wanted to save as much money for when we are ready to purchase property."

Victoria smiled at him. "I understand—I don't expect everything to be the best."

They walked into their room and looked around. It wasn't as nice as the room they shared the night before, but it was comfortable.

The fresh salt air smelled pleasant to Victoria as she walked on the deck looking at the coast. She knew that she might never see this land again. She wished that her sister could have been there to see her off, for of all her family, it was her sister that she would miss the most.

As the ship began to sail, she watched as the land slowly disappeared—just as the sun does at sunset. Mark stood at her side, holding her hand and looking towards the open sea. She wondered what thoughts were running through his mind, what thoughts he had about leaving his family and starting a new life in America. "What are you thinking about, Mark?"

He didn't answer her. His eyes were fixed in a distant gaze across the ocean dreaming of things to come. Victoria looked at him with anxious eyes. "Mark, talk to me—tell me what's on your mind."

He turned to her smiling. "We'll have a good life in America, Victoria."

"I do hope so—I hope our dreams are fulfilled."

"Stay with me and they will be. At the end of the week we'll be in America and there is so much that we will be able to do."

✳   ✳   ✳   ✳

The day they landed on Ellis Island in America, the sun shone bright through broken clouds. Victoria couldn't believe that she was in America. It always seemed so far away as if it would take years to arrive there. Mark smiled as they walked off the ship. Feelings of joy ran through him as he took pleasure in being back on land after their long trip.

Victoria didn't know where they'd end up living; all she knew was that Mark wanted to go out West. She had a few fears about all the stories of Indian savages attacking settlers, yet she wanted to meet an Indian and find out what they were really like. Mark assured her that the Indians were no longer a threat to the white settlers. "Whatever resistance the savages put up has been put down," Mark said.

It took all day standing in lines to enter America through immigration. There were so many people from so many different countries. The people talked in their own language—it was a confusing place. After they finally made it through immigration they were back on a boat headed for New York City.

Victoria could see the tall buildings reaching into the sky rising out of the mist to touch the rays of sunlight. She touched Mark on his arm. "It's a beautiful sight to behold. I wish my sister could see it all."

"She might see it one day," Mark replied.

"I will write and tell her about everything I see and feel—I want her to know what I think."

"Sometimes you think more of her than you do me."

"I miss her."

Victoria looked at Mark, and again questioned her heart, asking if she could fall in deep love with him. They first met when she was seven and he was seventeen. Their parents were friends who lived and farmed near each other. Mark was a hard worker, and running his father's farm left him without much time for courting.

When, at the age of twenty-five, his mother told him he should find a woman that would make a good wife, all the decent ladies his age were taken. He set his eyes on Victoria and asked permission of her parents to court her. By showering her with gifts and attention, he hoped to gain her love. Victoria's parents loved Mark more than she did, and they encouraged her to marry him. Mark understood this, but was sure in time Victoria would come to feel true love for him.

Two months and two weeks after they had arrived in America Mark and Victoria stepped off a train in Seattle. A gray sky welcomed them with a light mist of rain. The mist reminded Victoria of Scotland. The trip took its toll on both Mark and Victoria. They had traveled across the heart of America and saw many different things, and people.

Mark, desired to be a gunsmith by trade, and thought that the Northwest would be a good place to make a start in the business.

They picked up their belongings and went to find a hotel. Upon finding one and being shown to their room Victoria helped Mark unpack some of their things. Then he went out to see if he could find work, knowing what money they had would soon run out.

The booming town of Seattle stood before him as he stood on the street. "This place is different than any place I have ever seen," he said, as he looked at all the buildings.

Mark couldn't have pictured it any other way from the things he had heard. The buildings were rustic with some made of wood, and others made of brick. The men on the streets wore strange-looking pants that appeared as though they could stand up and walk on their own. Mark smirked and thought how uncomfortable they must be to wear. It truly was a different world.

The hotel sat one street up from the waterfront. Victoria stood in the window watching the ships coming in and out of the harbor. It was a busy place. It was Saturday and the streets were full of men who looked as though they hadn't taken a bath in months. Victoria counted eleven saloons on the main street and watched the men fill them as soon as they walked into town.

Victoria thought about how lucky she was to have a man who didn't spend his time in saloons and other such places. Mark was a man of integrity and she knew that someday he would have a high standing in whatever community became their home. She unpacked some things, and settled down on the bed falling off to sleep.

Mark began his search for work—there must be something he could find to do in such a large city, he thought. He was willing to take any job to make money. He had only enough money to buy some land and a few supplies to build a house. He needed to make more money before they started dipping into what they had named their dream money. As he walked by one of the newer brick buildings, he saw a job posting.

WANTED: GOOD MEN WHO ARE WILLING TO WORK

*The company
of McMaster and Waite Lumber are looking for men to work
in their mill or logging camps in the Skagit Valley near the
new town of Clear Lake. The pay is top rate and the working
conditions comfortable and clean. There is plenty of land for
sale so married men are encouraged to apply and to bring their
families. Opportunities abound—so come start a new life in the
timber industry. There is no better place to work and raise a*

family than in the pristine forest of Northwest Washington.
For more information inquire within at the front desk.

Mark stepped toward the door and grabbed the handle. The thought of working in the forest sounded interesting. He always loved the outdoors whether he was shooting or working and knew it was good for the soul. "How hard can it be?" he said as he opened the door.

Inside men stood around talking as he walked toward the front desk. He wondered if they were thinking of going to the Skagit Valley to find work in timber. He walked up to the desk where a man sat reading the paper. "Excuse me, but I am interested in the posting I read outside."

The man raised his eyes from the paper. "What do you want to know about it?"

Mark thought the question was strange. He smiled at the man. "I want to know how I get to that place and get a job."

The man looked Mark up and down, sizing him up. "How old are you?"

"Twenty six," Mark replied.

"Kind of old—are you married?"

"Yes, and I'm looking to make a good life for my wife and some day my children."

"Good, you're the kind of man Mr. McMaster's looking for. Wait here."

The man rose and walked toward the back of the office. Mark thought this man could use some lessons on how to be friendly. He looked around the room as he waited. The man came walking back to the desk with another man. The other man reached out his hand. "Hi, I'm Joe McMaster."

Mark reached out to shake his hand. "Glad to meet you, Mr. McMaster."

"It's nice you're interested in working for me, but it's hard work and long hours and I'm looking for men that are dependable and willing to stick it out for the long run."

Mark knew that he needed the work, and that he didn't mind hard work, but he didn't want to work in the timber for life. He needed a way to make good money so he could open his own store and become a gunsmith, and this new area with a new town sounded like a good place to start.

"I'll be a good worker for your company."

Mark felt uncomfortable, so he didn't talk all that much. Mr. McMaster noticed his accent. "How long have you been in America?"

"Almost two months."

"Are you from Scotland?"

"Yes, I am," Mark replied.

"That's where my father and mother were from. We moved to America when I was four years old."

Mark felt good that he was talking to a man who had a homeland in common with him. "What town are you from?" McMaster asked.

"In the country just outside of Glasgow."

"I don't remember much about Scotland, but my parents were from Glasgow." McMaster studied Mark. "What do you want to be in this new land?"

Mark stood tall and smiled. "I want to open a store and build guns."

"That's a good dream. You must like to hunt."

"I do."

"In the mountains where I log there are more animals than anyone could ever shoot in a life time. Cougar, bear, deer, elk, and mountain goats just to name a few."

"I would like to have the opportunity to see that place and work for you," Mark said.

McMaster wrote on a paper and handed it to Mark. He pointed toward the harbor. "On Monday morning a boat leaves Pier Two at eight for the town of Mount Vernon. It will cost one dollar for the trip, which includes meals and a berth. I expect to see you there."

"I'll be there, and thanks for the job."

"I look forward to seeing you."

McMaster came to Clear Lake in 1893. He purchased a shingle mill from the Day brothers and a large section of land east of the lake. Before coming to Clear Lake he had spent his time searching for gold up in the Yukon. While returning from that area, he was sitting on the deck of a ship noticing the big trees along the shore that extended all the way down the Pacific coast. He had walked by them, over them, and around them, but it wasn't until he saw them from the ship that he realized they were green gold.

He set out to enter the timber business and make his fortune. His motto was, "Seek the best, and forget the rest."

That was the order he gave to the workers. "Fall only the trees that are sound in the heart, straight as a plum line, taller than the sky, and fatter than the last soiled dove the men had been with. Leave the garbage standing." In the mill he would tell the head sawyer, "Not to waste your time trying to save the edges of the log. There are many more logs waiting to be milled, so cut the heart and move on."

McMaster was a tall man and intimidated people with his height. His company fast became a force in the industry, and he needed more men to have it grow.

Mark was one of many who were coming to the Northwest seeking wealth. Some came to open stores, some came to farm, and some came to search for gold. The Pacific Northwest had its own kind of gold, called timber, and there was plenty. Some of the largest trees in the world were growing for over a thousand years in the valleys and mountains in the territory of Washington. They had lasted through storms, fires, winds, and rains. They stood tall as though they would never fall.

Mark couldn't wait to tell Victoria about his job. He hurried back to the hotel and ran up the stairs to find Victoria sitting by the window looking at the rain falling on the buildings and streets outside. She was happy to see him, and as he walked toward her, she could tell by the look on his face that something good had happened. "I've good news, Victoria, I've found a job in a small town north of here in the timber industry."

She smiled. "How far away is it?"

"About seventy miles."

"When do we leave to go there?" she said as she unpacked a bag of clothes.

"We'll be leaving Monday morning on a boat that leaves Pier Two at eight. Until that time, we should get plenty of rest, for there is much work ahead of us."

"I'd better not unpack everything then," she said. "We should go get something to eat before it gets late."

Mark nodded as they headed out the door.

CHAPTER 2

▼

THE NATIVES

The Skagit valley was home to the Salish Indians. They consisted of a few different tribes. Out by the sound were the Swimnomish and the Samish. Inland were the Skagit and the Nookachamp tribes. Most of the time they were at peace, but at other times they would wage war with each other. It would sometimes happen that the inland tribes would unite to fight the Swimnomish tribe that lived by the sea. The fighting usually would be over one man killing a man from another tribe or disputes about hunting grounds or honor.

In times of peace all the tribes would meet to have Potlatch. Potlatch was a festival that would last many days. There would be eating, story telling, dancing, drum playing, and trading. The chiefs would sit in the longhouse by the fire, while the others would be outside wondering what was being discussed. Sometimes an incident would happen between men or women from one tribe to another at these gatherings, which would lead to an end of the Potlatch and set the tribes warring against each other again.

If the tribes had all banded together to fight the encroachment of the whites, they could have slowed the settlement down. The warring between themselves, the fear of the white man's army, the white man's whiskey, and the offer of money for the Indian's land combined to ruin any effort to resist.

The Swimnomish and Samish agreed to a Treaty in 1855, and the United States government included the Skagit and Nookachamp tribes in this treaty even though their chiefs were not present at the signing. Therefore those two tribes always contended they were not "treaty Indians."

The local natives had lived around Clear Lake and the Nookachamps Creek for as long as they could remember, since the beginning of time. They called Clear Lake *Shaishliet,* which means, "Whose waters reveal the depth of the soul."

A few hundred yards from Clear Lake sat another lake, and the Natives named this lake *Kashamut,* which means, "Whose waters hide secrets." None of the settlers could pronounce the Indian names. They just called the lakes Clear Lake and Mud Lake.

The smallpox epidemic of 1855 took its toll on the Natives and they never recovered. Their tribes went from two thousand down to a couple hundred. With the whites came more disease and a steady supply of whiskey, which brought more death to the Natives, and few were left when the town of Clear Lake was founded.

In the summer months, the Indians fished and hunted in the upper mountains and meadows. In the winter they would return to their *Nook-aw-chap* camp. The word meant, house on high ground. Their camp was alongside a small creek that would often flood throughout the winter, being a main tributary of the Skagit River. Thus the name of the creek became Nookachamps.

The encroachment of the whites onto their land didn't alarm the local Indians around Clear Lake. They liked trading with the whites and learning about them. They became fascinated with Isaiah's cedar tree house. He was one of the first settlers in the area. They would come by and look, but they would never enter for they heard from Mr. Turner that Isaiah Cultas was a great Indian fighter on the Plains. They feared him some, but not enough to keep from stealing things he left outside his house.

Shortly after Isaiah arrived with Caleb and built his house he began to be fed up with the Indians and their sassy ways. Having returned from Seattle on a trip to buy a few needed supplies, he found his saw, his ax and a few buckets missing. He learned while in Seattle that there would be a total eclipse of the sun in two weeks on a Thursday at 12:30 pm.

He went to the tribe and faced the chief. "If thing are not returned in thirteen days I will call on my God, and cause a great darkness to come upon the land."

The chief laughed as did the rest of the Natives that heard Isaiah. The chief waved his hand for Isaiah to leave. Every day he would walk down to the village and tell them the same thing. "A great darkness will come upon the land unless you mend your ways."

On Thursday at about ten in the morning the Indians started to show up around his place. They brought whiskey to drink as they were jesting and laughing, making fun of Isaiah. Isaiah went out and pleaded. "Change your ways and I will turn back the darkness."

The Natives laughed and made fun of Isaiah. Before noon all the Indians in the vicinity stood around Isaiah's house. The sky was clear and the sun shone brightly down through the trees and into the meadow on the north side of the hollow tree house. At twenty past noon Isaiah came out of his house. "I've warned you, now face your judgment."

He retreated into his house, and the moon passed in front of the sun. At first the light started to fade slowly, but in a few short minutes darkness fell upon the earth. Fear overcame the Indians, and they started wailing and crying for mercy and for Isaiah to stop the darkness. They didn't want to hear any more of his *cultus-wa-wa* which meant bad talk. He came out of his house. "Fear not, for if you are truly sorry, I will go and intercede for you and bring back the sun."

He again retreated to his house and waited for the sun to reappear before meeting the Indians again. His waiting added to the suspense and made a great finishing touch.

From then on the Indians never bothered his things again, and Isaiah was called *Hea-Shau-Tyee,* which meant, "He who knows the Great Spirit."

They had the same respect for Caleb since he was Isaiah's grandson. Shortly after the eclipse incident Caleb became sick and Isaiah asked the Natives for help. Nookachamp Rose was sent and healed Caleb. Rose started visiting Isaiah and Caleb and they became good friends that lasted through the years until his death.

The Natives were seldom seen in town except for a few that would sit on the main street and watch everything. They were never welcomed in the places where whites shopped, and they were encouraged to join their brothers out on the reservations. They fast became strangers in their own land.

CHAPTER 3

▼

THE SETTLERS

The year was 1877 when two brothers, one being Robert Pringle and the other William Pringle, were given a section of land directly from the government. That same year they arrived at the shores of Clear Lake and became a few of the first pioneers to settle in the area.

The first recorded white man to settle near Clear Lake was Mr. Turner. He lived in a small cabin about a mile west of Clear Lake. His neighbor, Isaiah Cultas lived on Cultas Mountain, but no one knew for sure the exact time of his arrival. Isaiah was feared by the Indians and left alone by the other settlers. "Isaiah is a real crazy man," Turner said.

The town of Clear Lake had small beginnings. The Pringle brothers worked at clearing four acres of trees and stumps. They lived in two huts built out of cedar boards. Soon after their arrival, the Babcock brothers settled near the Pringles, which brought a total of four huts to Clear Lake. The Day brothers showed up and settled on the northeast side of the lake.

The settlers cleared an old Indian trail that led to Mount Vernon and used this to get supplies. With the trail came more settlers. The Whitings procured four cleared acres from the Pringles and built a house overlooking Mud Lake. Soon to follow were the Isaacsons, the Bartls, the Smiths, Mrs. Josephine Green and the Hammers.

The trail was made into a road, but it was still an all day event traveling to get supplies from Mount Vernon.

As the town grew the demand for goods and services increased. Lumber was needed to build houses and other buildings. The Day brothers had been spending months working on building a sawmill on the shores of the lake. They were going to run the mill with a water wheel.

The day came when all things were finished and in place. John Day opened the gate that held the water back. The water flowed down the flume picking up speed. It hit the paddle wheel and started turning it. The wheel picked up speed as more water rushed down the flume. Michael Day waved his arm high in the air. "It's working!"

John came running down the hill and jumped around with his brother. "We have the first sawmill in the area. We're going to be rich!"

"Now we only have to figure out how to move our finished product."

"We'll ship it by wagon to Sedro."

Later that day the first log was milled into lumber on the shores of Clear Lake.

The people of Clear Lake came to town that evening to celebrate the opening of the sawmill, and another new building in town. Not a single person was absent as Mr. Smith stood on the porch of his new hotel along with Mr. Beddall. "This building represents the future of our great town. May we some day be the largest town in the state."

People clapped as Mr. Smith cut the ribbon hanging between the beams of the hotel. People crowded inside to tour the rooms and eat at the restaurant. "Surely a glorious beginning for this great place," Smith said.

The town grew at a steady rate over the next few years, and the mill was sold to McMaster.

McMaster wanted more timber so he set out to lay claim to the forested mountains east of Clear Lake. He climbed up Cultas Peak with his guide. "We're at the top sir," the guide said pointing to the valleys below.

McMaster viewed the mountains and surrounding hills, and the deep lush valleys filled with green gold for as far as he could see. "I don't know if any man could ever log all of this land in a thousand years," McMaster said.

"I have walked these mountains for years. There are a lot of trees, but I suppose they could all be cut down some day if there were enough men," the guide said.

"How many hours to that peak over there?" McMaster asked pointing to Deer Peak.

"About six hours at my pace, and about twelve hours at your pace," the guide responded.

"Some day soon Caleb you will be under me. I'm going to own all this land, and I'm going to log it all."

The guide looked at McMaster and shook his head. "I don't think so. I'm a free man and will never be under anyone."

Caleb's grandfather raised him from the age of seven. Caleb lost his mother and father soon after he was born. His grandfather's last name was Mclearen, and because of the trouble he had back east he wanted to change it to something new. When he arrived on the mountain above Clear Lake and made his home, the Indians started calling him *Cultas-ma* because they thought he had to be bad to live on Cultas Mountain. Cultas was the Indian word for bad. Mclearen liked the name and took it hoping it would keep the Indians from stealing his things. He gave the last name to Caleb. "This boy needs a new start in this land."

Caleb stood over six feet tall and had a muscular build. He had eyes of blue and light brown hair. He was strong as an ox and spent most of his time in the mountains. He learned what to eat and not to eat. He could track any animal and sneak up on any unsuspecting person he wanted. Nature was in his blood. He could walk thirty miles in a single day, and he possessed courage having few things to fear. He was seventeen when his grandfather died, and he lived alone in the old hollowed-out cedar tree that he and his grandfather had made into a picturesque home.

The tree was twenty-three feet through at the base and held that width for thirty feet up. A door at the base opened into a large kitchen area where Caleb had placed his new stove. The walls were two feet thick and had various carvings on the inside, done by his grandfather. On the far end of the kitchen was a ladder going up to the second floor. Up there was a big open room with two bunks against the east wall. Three windows were cut into the tree, one facing south, one facing west, and one facing northwest. Caleb returned to his house. Only two other people had been in the tree house. One was Nookachamp Rose, as she would visit Caleb's grandfather often. She was one of the few Indians that he trusted.

On the floor were furs from all different animals, bear, cougar, deer, and others. There was also a third floor that most people didn't know about. A ladder led up between the bunks to a room with one large window facing west. From this room Caleb could see the waters of Puget Sound on a clear day. Caleb had furs on the floor and a table against the south wall. On the table was the only book that Caleb and his grandfather had. It was the *Bible*. From this book Caleb learned to read and write. He also learned simple math, which was more than most boys his age living in the frontier knew.

As McMaster and the guide walked through the mountains surveying the land and trees, men worked falling trees near Clear Lake.

McMaster and Caleb arrived at the edge of the clear cut where the men worked. They watched a tree fall destroying everything thing in its path. Thud! Snap! Boom! All the sounds made McMaster flinch as the tree came to a rest on the ground. Dust rolled up into the sky. "I'm glad I'm not doing that," McMaster said.

"You can't run fast enough to save your life—better to have young men doing that work."

"Boy you don't know the first thing about logging."

"I can fall a tree, but I'd rather see them standing."

They watched as two fallers worked on a huge tree. It started to fall, as the one faller yelled, "Timber…"

The bucker didn't hear the loud call as the fallers jumped off their springboards running for safety. The tree, two hundred feet tall, balanced on its cut base. The fallers looked up and saw the wind blowing the top, keeping it from crashing to the ground. The wind blew stronger as it finally pushed the tree in the opposite direction than the fallers intended. They took off running as the tree fell towards them.

The bucker poured another splash of oil onto his twelve-foot cross cut saw. He hung the bottle back on the side of the tree. He climbed up on top of the log and reached for the bottle. He grabbed it and then he saw a flash of green in the sky. He looked up as the tree came crashing down on him with a loud roar that drowned out his screams. He was sixteen.

The fallers saw branches and dirt flying up in the air as the tree hit the ground with a loud crash. There was nothing they could do for him. It was life and death in the woods.

C H A P T E R   4

▼

A NEW HOME

On Monday morning Mark and Victoria packed everything they owned onto the steamer *Alki*. The boat was nothing special, except that unlike other boats that Victoria had seen, it had a flat bottom. More men than women were on board, which was understandable given that women were not going to work as loggers. They were shown to their berths and discovered that there were more people than berths.

After putting their things away, Mark started talking to some men that were standing by him. Victoria decided to take a walk around the ship and have a look. She found the dining room, which wasn't as she had pictured. It looked as if it would be cramped, eating with everyone on board. She took joy in knowing that this trip would only last one day. She saw one of the crewmen standing on the bow watching the water.

"The dinner area looks as if only a handful of people can eat at one time."

"Ma'am women and children are served first according to captains orders. After that the men and after that the crew."

"Does it bother you eating last all the time?"

"Not at all, the food is cold, but at least it's food."

She walked on the upper level of the ship holding an umbrella. From the time she arrived in the Northwest it had rained everyday. However, it wasn't a real rain but more of a continual mist. It wouldn't soak a person in a few minutes, but over the course of the day, one would end up drenched.

The ship pulled away from the pier. They were finally on their way to what would become their home. Except for the trees, the landscape reminded Victoria of Scotland. The ship *Alki* sailed through Puget Sound, hugging the edges of various islands and peninsulas, making its way north. Neither Mark nor Victoria had seen such beauty. As the day wore on, the clouds parted and rays of sunlight shone down on the water. The warmth felt good to their bones as they stood out on the deck of the ship.

Their eyes worked to take in every sight. They looked to the north, and out of the clouds appeared a snow-capped mountain. They had never seen a mountain so high and white in the middle of June. Out in front of the ship were four Orca whales swimming, rising out of the water and disappearing over and over.

Victoria walked up to Mark as he stood near a group of men. "Look at the beach," she said. "Everything seems perfect as if it hasn't been touched by man. It's as though I am in a dream."

Mark stepped away from the men. "Perfection is what men strive for, not what nature is."

Victoria pointed at the beaches, the mountains, the trees, and the whales swimming near the shore. "If God made paradise, this is it."

McMaster walked up to them smoking his pipe. "Won't be long before we're there." McMaster said.

"Tell me about the town of Clear Lake."

"In 1890 Jacob Bartl platted fifteen acres of the Pringle claim that he secured, and established a store and a post office. He became the first postmaster in April of that year. That set Clear Lake on the path to becoming a town."

"Are there any accommodations?"

"Yes. In 1891 the first hotel was built and owned by Alexander Smith. In the same year the Day brothers, Michael and Will, built the first shingle mill. Five years later the Day brothers sold the mill to me. The town is just beginning. We will be the ones to make its future. And a great future it will be."

The sound of a horn startled them. They made their way around to the front deck and found the ship at a stand still. The clouds cleared out of the sky and most of the passengers were up on the deck enjoying the sun. Mark knew that the engine of the ship wasn't running and became concerned that something was wrong. "Why isn't the ship moving?" he asked a crewman.

"It'll be another hour before high tide. Then the ship will move up the river."

Mark looked down into the water and could see bottom. "It's really shallow. Even if the water rose two more feet would that be enough?"

The crewman threw an anchor over the edge. "That's why the bottom of this ship is flat. It's because we have to travel up the Skagit River for a few miles, and the river is shallow, so a flat bottom keeps us from getting stuck. To be safe we'll wait for the tide. Sometimes in late summer that's the only time we can make it upstream."

Mark and Victoria nodded their heads. "How far up river do we travel?" Victoria asked.

"About eight miles—really can't go any further up river in a boat this big."

"Why not—seems like a big river to me," Victoria responded.

"There are log jams the size of cities in the river that haven't been cleared yet. There used to be one before Mount Vernon, and it took the residents three years to clear it all out."

"It seems impossible to believe that many logs are in the river."

The crewman pointed to the mountains of green. "Lots of logs from those mountains that get washed into this river."

Mr. McMaster joined them again and pointed toward the northeast. "See that mountain with the big crater on the side of it?"

Mark and Victoria nodded as they looked. "Clear Lake sits at the base of that mountain. At one time the town was going to be called Mountain View, but that name was already taken by some other place in the state, so they named the town after the lake."

After an hour of waiting the steamer *Alki* started up river. Every once in a while a large log would come floating down, and the ship would have to maneuver to avoid being hit. Both Mark and Victoria looked at the big trees hugging the shore. It was the first time that they had seen trees that large so close. When the trees ended, they saw homestead farms scattered along the shores of the river. In the fields of some of these farms were tree stumps the size of small houses.

After some time, they saw a small village on the bank of the river. Few buildings were standing as smoke rose from the black ashes. Men lined the shores watching the ship pull in. McMaster stepped off the ship and looked at the men standing near the river. They were covered in black soot and smelled of rotten smoke. "What the hell happened here?"

"The town burnt last night. Three Indians got a hold of some whiskey and got drunk in a back alley. They made a fire in a bucket to keep warm. One of them must have kicked it over and burned the town down."

"Damn Indians," one of them said.

McMaster shook his head. "People have to learn to keep those Indians on the reserves. They're nothing but trouble."

Victoria and Mark looked over the remains of the town of Mount Vernon. Beyond the burnt buildings was a deep, green, dense forest.

McMaster looked at the forest behind the town. "We're lucky it's been raining a lot or the fire could've spread into the forest."

The crew unloaded Mark and Victoria's belongings. Joe McMaster walked over to some men that stood near the shore. "Take their belongings and put them on that wagon teamed with horses. These are my guests and treat them kindly."

Mark helped the men load his things. "How long will it take to get to Clear Lake?" Mark asked.

"Four hours, if everything goes right."

When they were loaded, they started their trip into the dense forest.

Victoria looked at the huge trees watching the trail as it wound through the forest. The trail was wide enough for one wagon. McMaster rode up along side of Mark and Victoria. "This trail is a big improvement from a year ago."

"How far is it?"

"It's about a ten mile trip one way. It's easy going now, but it used to be an all day event."

"How's that?" Mark asked.

"The trail was narrow and the Nookachamps Creek had to be crossed, which wasn't hard unless water levels were up. As more people moved into the lake vicinity, the trails were widened so that a horse-drawn wagon could travel on the path. Then, the people of Clear Lake worked together to build a small bridge over the Nookachamps Creek, which opened more opportunity for the growing town."

"Will we encounter any Indians on our way?" Victoria asked.

"No, not likely. Most of the Indians have died—only a few are left—we're busy rounding them up and moving them to reservations. They have never really bothered us whites—spend most of their time killing each other. They won't be with us long—even the ones on the reserves will die—if not from disease—whisky and killing one another."

"That's a sad description. Why not teach them proper things, and let them stay in their homes?"

"They don't belong with whites—I wouldn't want them mingling with any of my blood."

"It seems a shame to make them move from their homes," Victoria said.

"You will quickly learn about them—learn how they live. Then you will understand. There are not many people around here that sympathize with Poor Lo."

"Poor Lo?" Victoria asked.

"Poor Lo is another name for the local Indians. I don't know where it came from, but it describes their condition perfect."

As the party made their way through the forest, it looked as though they were traveling through a big cave. The trees were so tall and the branches so thick that they blocked out most of the sunlight.

Moss, which smelled musky, grew like hair on the trees. The path wasn't straight, as it wound around the big trees. Mark looked at the huge trees. "How do you fall such large trees? It seems to me that it would take all day to fall one."

"It's hard work, but with the proper tools it doesn't take long at all."

"Looks plenty hard and dangerous to me."

"You won't be falling trees for a long time. You will start at the low end of the stick."

McMaster laughed. "Just a grease monkey for a while."

Mark didn't respond. He had no idea of what McMaster meant.

They arrived at the bridge that crossed the Nookachamps Creek, and stopped to let the horses have a drink. In the clear water of the creek they could see trout on the bottom, hiding in the rocks. The men led the horses down to the bank of the stream, letting them drink. Victoria sat resting on the edge of the bridge when a young man came walking by. He had been in Mount Vernon and was returning home with a few things he purchased. On his back sat a cast-iron stove, and he looked as if he were having a hard time with his load. Mark and Victoria were amazed at such a sight. His muscles gleamed from sweat as he walked. He turned his head and looked at Victoria and Mark. "Hello," he said.

Mark nodded at him with a smile. "They make mules to haul things like that," McMaster yelled.

The young man kept walking as he looked back at McMaster. "It's not the stove that gives me the problem. It's the twenty-five pound sack of flour inside that keeps moving from side to side that makes this hard to carry."

Victoria smiled and watched as he kept walking toward Clear Lake. Mark shook his head as he watched him. "Who is that young man—does he work for you?"

"He's Caleb Cultas, and no, he doesn't work for me or anyone else that I know."

"What does he do for work?"

"Caleb makes his living by panning for gold, and selling Cascara bark, and items like that. He makes so called magic potions from things in the forest and sells them around town. He guided for me when I first visited this place. He knows this mountain better than anyone.

"You seem to know him—is he your friend?" Victoria asked.

"No, not a friend of mine. He's a friend with Indians—since he doesn't have many white friends. He lived with his grandfather until that old man died a couple of years back. He prefers to be alone most of the time I think."

"Why would you say that?" Mark asked.

"Everyone around town knows him. He's a different type, kind of a simple man. I don't see much future for the boy—keeps to himself. That's why."

"What's Cascara bark?" Victoria asked.

McMaster let out a laugh. "It's bark from a native tree. It helps a person have bowel movements. Besides that the wood is worthless."

"I can see people needing help with that sometimes," she responded. "Where does he live—in town?"

"No, he lives by himself up on the mountain that bears his last name. I hear his house is inside an old hollow cedar tree. I've never seen it, but I hear it has two floors."

He shook his head as he finished talking. "You have to be crazy to live in a hollow tree."

"What kind of magic potions does he make?" Victoria asked.

"Potions that he says can heal sickness—plants and roots mixed to help him make a few pennies. Whitewash if you ask me. If this were Salem, he would be burned at the stake for being a witch."

"I would like to learn some of those things," she said.

Mark gave a stern look to Victoria, and then looked at McMaster. "You have to excuse her—she is young and doesn't know what's real and make believe sometimes."

Both men laughed as a look of disappointment came across Victoria's face. "I know what's real—nothing wrong with wanting to learn things."

They finished watering the horses and continued along the trail. An hour later they crested a hill and the lake came into view. A beautiful sight to behold, Victoria thought. She saw the crystal clear water reflecting the mountains above which rose four thousand feet to touch the sky. The mountains were covered in shades of green, changing to shades of silver near the top. To Victoria it was as if millions of trees were waving their arms, sending their scent down on the breeze greeting those who reside in paradise. "What a wonderful place to make a home and raise children," she said to Mark.

He smiled as he took in the landscape. "Truly, this is a wonderful place."

The small town was nestled among four hills sitting at the base of Cultas Mountain with the rest of the Cascade Range as a backdrop. The town had Clear Lake on the east side and Mud Lake on the west side. Between the two lakes sat a few houses, a store, a post office, a couple of saloons, and a hotel.

The horses stopped in front of the hotel and a few of the men helped Mark and Victoria unload their things. They would need to make arrangements to stay there until they found a place of their own. Everyone made them feel welcome, which made them happy.

Mr. Smith, the proprietor of the hotel, came out to meet them. "Welcome to Clear Lake."

"Thanks," Mark said.

The men hauled their belongings up on to the porch. "Where do you want these things Mr. Smith?" One of them asked.

"Put them up in the upper room—it's the best."

Mr. Smith walked inside with them and showed them to one of the best rooms. In the room stood a wood bed made of maple. The grain was beautiful—polished to a clear shine. The floor was made from Douglas fir without a single knot in any of the boards. The closet was lined with Western Red Cedar, making the room smell fresh and clean. The hotel was natural looking without a single painted board. From a distance, the hotel looked rustic, but once inside, the wood appeared to be living. Mark and Victoria unpacked quickly so they could go out and make their way around the town and see it all.

Across from the hotel stood a wood shack that operated as the schoolhouse. They walked south toward the mill, passing houses, shacks, and various places of business. The main road ran right down to the mill, which was situated on the west shore of the lake. Logs floated in the water waiting their turn to be milled into lumber. Across the lake, they saw a line of wagons each with one log. The wagons dumped the logs into the lake. The logs made a terrific crash, and a huge splash rose into the air as the logs hit the water. Victoria pointed at the log dump. "It's a wonder they managed to get such huge logs onto the wagons."

"Looks like hard work to me," Mark said.

"I can't believe those men walking on the logs in the lake," she said as she reached down and felt the cold water.

"I wouldn't want to fall in that lake."

"What are they doing?"

"Looks like they're working the logs to the mill," Mark said.

East of the log dump, they heard a loud noise coming off the hill. Their eyes focused on a log flume that ran straight up the mountain. A roar like the sound of thunder led the way for a log the size of a locomotive that came flying out of the flume. It hit the water and sent spray three times as high as the logs that were being dumped by the wagons.

The sun shone through the spray, making rainbows that evaporated into the warm air. A few minutes later another log came flying out of the flume, sending another splash of water into the air. The logs hitting the water sent waves across the lake that hit the shore where they were standing. Victoria held onto Mark as they watched the logs fly out of the flume. "I think I'm going to like this place," Mark said.

"I agree it's going to be a nice place to call home."

They both dreamt of what they wanted their lives to become. Mark wanted to be successful, a man of stature, a man who was noticed and heard just like the logs. Victoria wanted to be a mother, and a teacher, she wanted to create a place of comfort; she wanted to love and be loved, just like the waves that were lapping at their feet. This place was going to be their home, their life, and their dream. "I wonder what kind of work I will be doing tomorrow?" Mark asked.

"I don't think you will be cutting the big trees down. But whatever you do, you will do it well."

"I was told to be at the log dump at five in the morning."

"That's early—though not much different than working on the farm."

McMaster saw them standing near the lake and walked up to them. "It's a nice sight—those logs coming off the hill."

"Yes, really amazing," Mark said.

"In couple of years we will have all the big trees near the flume logged," he said as he smoked his pipe.

"Do you extend the flume up the mountain?"

"No, we are busy laying railroads to get at the timber."

"There isn't a railroad here."

"In the next few weeks the railroad will be completed from Seattle to Everett, then north to here. Until that time the shingles and lumber milled here are loaded onto wagons, ferried across the Skagit to Sedro-Woolley."

"There has to be a better way to move product," Mark said.

"When I purchased the mill, Clear Lake received its first locomotive, and railroads are being built along the existing skid roads to reach the timber. In the woods bulls are being used to get the logs to the landing to be loaded onto the tracks to be trailed to the log dump. I plan on trying horses soon. Then I plan on getting some new steam donkeys—I hear they are working out well down in Humboldt, California."

"Steam donkeys?"

"A machine that takes the place of the bulls. That's the future of logging."

"How do you get the logs on the wagons?" Mark asked.

"They are rolled on by leverage."

"How about on to the tracks?"

"When the logs get to the landing they are rolled onto the tracks and long iron spikes called "dogs" are pounded into them. Chains are used to hold one log to the other to make up a run. An average turn consists of five to ten logs. Since I've taken major control of the logging and mill, I've purchased another locomotive to get the logs out of the forest. Wagons will be history. I am working on the idea of a railroad from Clear Lake to Mount Vernon. This will be the route I'll use to ship the finished product."

Mark nodded as though he understood everything McMaster said. "I have business to tend. Good day," McMaster said.

They watched him leave. Victoria shook her head. "That man is sure long winded."

CHAPTER 5

▼

GREEN GOLD

Mark arrived at the log dump a few minutes before five. Men stood next to sets of railroad wheels held together by long logs. One of the men pointed at Mark. "You're new—jump up on the disconnects."

"Disconnects?"

"Yes, that's what they're called unloaded—disconnects. When they're loaded they're called connects—real simple."

Mark shrugged his shoulders and jumped up and sat down. He wasn't dressed like the others, and it concerned him. They all seemed like a sober bunch of men. No one was talking, none of them laughed, and each man had a serious look on his face. From behind him came a loud, boisterous, obnoxious voice. "All right, you timber beasts, you most miserable men! Get your soft asses on the cars. It's time to face your punishment."

The obscenities kept coming from the man's mouth. Mark turned to see who was in such a wretched state as to be talking in such a manner this early in the morning. As the two locked eyes, the man gave Mark a hard, cold stare. "So you're the greenhorn McMaster hired in Seattle. I bet you won't make it a week before you quit or die. The trees give life, but they can take it away just as easy."

Mark didn't know what to think about the miserable man. A worker sitting next to Mark reached over and nudged him. "You've just met the bull of the woods, Ol' Hammer. Don't take anything he says to heart unless it's about how to do your job. He yells obscenities at everyone all day long, and when he gets home he yells obscenities at his wife. He's the master of profanity—he can stand on a stump and swear and cuss and curse for six hours straight and not say the same word twice."

As the man spoke to Mark, Hammer could be heard bellowing, "Today better see more trees on the ground, you worthless no good dogs."

Hammer came to Clear Lake to start a farm. Farming didn't work out, so he looked for another way to make a living. He was the first man hired by the Day brothers. When McMaster bought the company he placed Hammer in charge of all operations. Hammer got the job done, and McMaster was pleased. Ol' Hammer stood five feet three inches. He was a little man with a big voice and scary beady eyes. Most men didn't respect him, but many feared him.

The train pulled away from the log dump running up a grade of eight percent. It was the steepest part of the trip. The railroad wound through logged over areas climbing higher in to the mountains. Hammer cussed and cursed the entire trip, hardly taking a breath as he found every word, term, or phrase to belittle and humiliate the men. He appeared to receive much pleasure and enjoyment from hearing his own words. "Does that man ever shut up?" Mark asked.

"Nope, he just keeps going all day long," Doug said as he smiled.

It was nice to finally see a smile. Mark stretched out his hand. "My name is Mark Southerland."

"Mine is Doug Draper. Nice to meet you," he said shaking his hand. "Here's a word of advice—stay alive—stay alert at all times—listen to the men who've been in the woods for a long time—and never, and I mean never stand in the bite."

"Thanks, this is my first day. Do men often die while working in the woods?"

"Not every day, but we lost a man yesterday. He wasn't paying attention and a log rolled right over him. Yep, left him flat as a hot cake. Kind of nice he wasn't married and didn't have any young'uns. The ladies in town are likely giving him a decent burial today."

Doug said this with no emotion—as if it didn't bother him that a man had died.

Mark pondered the things Doug said. The ad he read didn't say anything about the daily chance of dying. He didn't come all this way to be killed in the forest. He committed himself to take Doug's advice and stay alive. "What's the bite?" Mark asked.

"It's the inside of the undercut of a tree, or an inside position of a set of wire rope. One breaks and it could slice you in half. Just always stay out of the bite, or it will get you every time."

"What's wire rope?"

"Rope made from tightly wound steel wire. A great invention for logging in these woods—only bad thing is it can cut you in half if you get in front of it."

"I wouldn't like that to happen," Mark said.

"If you have trouble just look for me. I've been in the forest a long time and I can help you stay alive."

Doug Draper came to Clear Lake to work for McMaster. He traveled from Wisconsin where his family logged for years. Hearing of the big trees out west, he left his home and his love. Doug had an athletic build. He was six feet in height and had muscular arms. He was handsome, with blonde hair, brown eyes, and a warm smile. In the woods he was a faller, the most dangerous job and one of the highest paid. He was the master of two tools. One being the double bladed ax and the other a ten-foot crosscut saw also known as the "Misery Whip." The fallers of the Northwest invented the double bladed ax to speed up their time in falling trees, and there was no one faster at swinging that ax than Doug Draper.

Other fallers liked to work with him because of his strength; he could run a crosscut saw like no other. While some called it a whip of misery, Doug could make music with it. To him it was a partner that he enjoyed. He held the record for falling the most trees, all over four feet through, in a single day. To the men he worked with, he was a loner. He was a friend to many but close to no one.

The train came to a stop in a clearing from which many trails led away into the forest. On a couple of the trails there were teams of oxen all yoked together. Hammer came over to Mark and looked him in the eye. "Today you'll be the grease monkey. It'll keep you alive for a day or two. Besides, you'll learn why you are just a beast."

Hammer handed Mark a bucket full of black, oily, greasy, slimy paste. A small wood-handled tool stood in the middle of the grease as if it were cemented in the bucket. "You stay ahead of the bulls and slop grease on the cross logs so the large logs can glide easy. Now you better keep ahead of the oxen, or your worthless body will become fodder."

Mark walked down the skid road with the bulls following behind. Hammer walked behind the bulls with a large stick called a goad. With it he would goad the bulls along, screaming, bellowing, and cursing them to eternal damnation. With the goad he cracked the backs of the bulls to keep them moving. Mark stayed ahead of the bulls, slopping grease on the cross logs. Hammer stopped bellowing for a moment and walked up to Mark. "What the hell are you doing?" he yelled.

"Putting grease on the logs like you told me to do."

Hammer cried out with a long, whining growl. "You don't have to put grease down 'til we have a turn of logs. Are you stupid or something?"

Mark shook his head and stopped putting grease down on the cross logs. "This is my first day, and the directions you gave were not that clear."

Hammer raised the goad over his head. "If you don't watch your words this may be your last day!"

Mark looked at the goad and stepped back. "I only want to do my job well."

"Well, then get to work and stop wasting my time."

They walked down the skid road heading for the tall trees. Broken trees, scrub brush, and dried moss lined the side of the skid road. "This is mighty ugly land," Mark said.

"Maybe ugly to you, but it's beautiful to me. The only good tree up here is a tree on it's way out of the mountains. We need to cut these things to let some light get to the earth."

"Looks as if getting the light is killing more things than helping."

"Greenhorn—you have much to learn about the woods."

They pulled up to a fresh cut tree that stood twelve feet at the butt. Hammer circled the bulls around and lifted a chain a couple of spikes off one of the bulls. "Don't just stand there and watch me—help me damn it."

Mark ran over and took the chain and followed Hammer to the tree. "Now pay attention carefully—I only want to show you once. If you can't learn it you're no good to me."

"I can learn anything," Mark said.

Hammer pounded the spikes through the chain and into the tree. Mark wrestled with the chain as he pulled it toward the back rigging of the bulls harness. "Looks as if you worked around animals before," Hammer said.

"My whole life."

After they finished hooking up the chain Hammer grabbed the goad and gave a strong hit to the back of the lead bull. The bulls all pulled as the log started to move along the cross timbers of the skid road. "Now run ahead and slop grease down on the ties—if you don't keep up I'll run you over!"

Mark ran down the skid road slopping grease as fast as he could. It was ugly work.

By mid afternoon the sun broke through the clouds, shining down on the men as they worked. Thirst took a grip on Mark's throat. From the top of the ridge he could see the waters of Clear Lake, making him yearn for a cool taste of water. Next to Clear Lake he could see Mud Lake, and even that dark ugly water looked good. "When do we get some water?" Mark asked.

mosses, and huckleberries. From the creek the land rose up to a small hill over-looking the town. She wondered why no one had bought this place. She fell in love with it and became excited about telling Mark of her find. She walked around the grounds thinking of how she would make everything look. It would become their personal paradise.

*   *   *   *

After work Mark arrived back at the hotel and threw himself onto the bed exhausted. He never worked so hard in his life. Victoria brought him a glass of water, sat down next to him and rubbed his back. Mark enjoyed her touch. "I went for a walk today and found a remarkable piece of property."

"Did you walk by yourself?" Mark asked.

Victoria continued to rub his back. "Yes, I'm a big girl, I can take care of myself."

Mark felt the strength in her hands as she kneaded them into his back. "I worry about you. There are so many things out there that can harm you. Wild animals, depraved men, who knows what may befall you. I only want you to be safe."

It was nice, she thought, that he cared so much for her safety. Knowing what he wanted to hear she said. "I'll stay close to town unless I'm with you. Now, do you want to go see the land that I found?"

Mark nodded his head yes, and rose taking Victoria by the hand. After a long walk they arrived at the property. It was the same place she stood hours before. She crossed the creek and pointed to a flat spot on the ground. "This is where the house should go—this is where the barn should sit. I will make the garden here, and plant an orchard on the side hill over there," she said pointing.

Mark looked over the site. "You have a lot of plans for a woman."

"I have great plans. I want it to be a park like setting. Our own paradise to raise our children."

Her heart was flooded with excitement as she spoke. Mark didn't walk around much. He stood still and surveyed the land. "This will make a great farm."

"It will be beautiful—this is where fairies live."

Mark looked at the big trees, the creek, and kicked the ground to see if the soil was any good. He walked up the hill as Victoria followed. "I don't believe in fair-ies, and neither should you."

For what Mark saw wasn't the same as Victoria. When she saw the trees, she saw magnificence, grace, and splendor. When Mark saw the trees he saw capital, financial gain, and prosperity. She saw the trees standing; he saw the trees down.

"This is fine land, Victoria. With the monies we've saved, I hope we have enough to purchase it."

They walked the rest of the property, looking, touching, and dreaming of the things they would do. In their minds they could hear the sounds of children playing hide and seek in the forest, splashing water on each other in the creek, running up to the house for evening dinner. Their hearts seemed united on the same common goal. This was the land of dreams. As they made their way back to the hotel Mark stopped and looked back at the property. "Come Saturday, we'll make an offer to purchase this property."

They both fell off to sleep that night smiling, and dreaming of great things to come.

*   *   *   *

As with the property that Victoria and Mark were considering, the whole valley was covered in trees and brush. It was no small task to clear ground for a house, let alone enough ground to farm. After falling the big trees, the remaining stumps were as big as houses. With the use of fire, dynamite, axes and saws, men would work for hour upon hour to rid the soil of wood. Oxen and horses were pressed into labor to help pull the mammoth roots from the soil.

There was so much wood that millions of board feet were burned each year. In the 1880's there were days in the valley when the sunlight couldn't find it's way through the thick clouds of smoke. Once the trees and stumps were out of the way, the ground produced abundant crops, the soil being some of the most fertile in the world.

Some people would only take the time to remove the trees and brush, and plant grass or other crops between the stumps. They were called stump farmers or stump ranchers, and they were looked down upon as a lower class of farmer, not having the time or money to remove the stumps. Cattle or hogs were used to clear the brush out around the stumps, which made it easier to move through the thick maze that nature created. All in all, the land was being tamed, and Mark was bent on taming his own property, while Victoria wanted to keep it wild.

*   *   *   *

Mark worked the rest of the week, rising early to ride the train up the mountain, slopping grease on the cross logs, listening to Hammer run off at the mouth all day. Returning to the hotel exhausted he would find dinner waiting for him—eating and then falling off to sleep.

It was Saturday and that meant it was payday. At the end of the day all the men came down to the mill office on the main street in town. Mr. McMaster walked along the line of men handing out wages in gold and silver coins. Mark noticed that no man reached for his pay, but waited until Mr. McMaster moved his hand toward them to give them their money. As McMaster made his way down the line, one young man reached for his pay. McMaster slapped his hand, and scowled at the young man. "Never reach for my money again! I'm the one who gives you work, so you receive pay when I give it, not when you demand it."

The man stood motionless, stunned by what he heard. Mark thought, didn't the man work? Isn't he owed for his labor? Didn't he have a right to reach for his pay? Was he just another beast, told when to rise, when to walk, and when to rest? McMaster treated him more like a slave than a free man who chose to work for him.

When McMaster reached Mark, he gave him his pay. "Mark meet me in my office in five minutes."

The other men made their way out of the building, some heading for home, some to the saloon, and some to other towns to spend their money. Mark walked into McMaster's office. "Have a seat," McMaster said.

As Mark sat down, McMaster looked up from the papers on his desk. "I've heard how hard you worked these past few days. I like men that work hard—there's a good future for them, just as there's a good future for you. Do you think you could run a team of horses to yard logs out of the woods?"

Mark thought for a moment and nodded his head. "I worked with horses on my father's farm back in Scotland. I'm sure I could do a fine job for you, Mr. McMaster."

"That's why I'm asking you. Most of these men here only know logging. I figured you would know horses."

"I do, and you will not be disappointed."

McMaster stood up from his chair. "Today I purchased eight horses, big horses. I think that they'll pull a turn of logs faster than bulls. I've hired Mr.

Isaacson to haul feed to them just as he does for the bulls. I expect you to take good care of them."

"I will, Mr. McMaster, I will."

"Call me Joe from now on—enough of this formality."

McMaster started to walk out the door, he turned back looking at Mark. "There's a pay raise with the new job."

Mark rushed to the hotel to tell Victoria about his new job. He was glad he would no longer be the grease monkey. He thought that he'd continue to work hard and aspire to moving up in the company. With his success, he would be able to purchase the property he and Victoria desired.

CHAPTER 6

▼

THE LAND

Mark and Victoria made their way to Mr. Cheasty's office. Mark had his life savings with him and some money from his recent work. He had been frugal with his money knowing he would need as much as possible to purchase land. They walked into the office and put the money on the table. The land sold for fifty dollars an acre. Mr. Cheasty signed the papers and gave them the title. "This is fine land you have bought," Cheasty said.

"Why hasn't it been logged?" Mark asked.

"It wasn't worth the money to run tracks out there. The trees are mostly Hemlock—a few cedars, and a few firs. The mill just wanted to sell it. It might be worth logging some day if the trees grow more."

"I'll log it myself someday," Mark said.

They left the office and went to town. With the money they had left over they bought a canvas tent and a few other items and tools from Beddall's Mercantile. This would be their home until Mark could build a house. It was summer and it would be like camping.

Victoria stood outside Beddall's store looking at potted apple trees. Mark came out of the store with the tent. "What are you looking at now?"

"I want an apple tree to plant."

Mark rolled his eyes and shook his head. "We don't need an apple tree yet."

"I know, we need two so they pollinate."

"I don't have money for that right now."

"Isn't it our money?"

Mark didn't respond. Victoria lifted two of the trees out of the bunch and set them on the side. "I'm getting them. We will have apples next fall and you will thank me."

They walked toward their property holding hands, filled with joy and happiness. Once there, they would wait for a wagon from town to deliver their goods. There was much to be done before winter came, and they knew their days would be full, working on their property.

The wagon arrived and Mark unloaded it. He looked at the stack of items. "Well, it's not going to get all set up on it's own."

"I'll help you," Victoria said as she picked up a rake.

It wasn't long before they cleared enough room to set up the tent. Mark made some furniture out of various twisted pieces of wood. They were rustic, but they would serve their purpose for a time. After the tent was set up Victoria took the shovel and grabbed the two apple trees. She dug two holes twenty feet apart and planted the trees. Mark watched her from the front of the tent as he sat in a chair he had made. She walked over to him. "What do you think?"

"They need some sun light to grow."

"When we take a few trees down for the house they will have light."

"Yes, they will have plenty of light."

Mark stood up and grabbed an ax as he walked toward the creek. "Come with me. I have to decide which trees to fall."

She was surprised at what Mark said. She didn't say a word but followed him up the creek. He took the ax and started to chop at a tree, taking off some bark to mark it. She didn't say anything, but just watched him mark tree after tree until he had about a hundred trees marked. When he finished with his last tree, Victoria looked at him. "I thought we'd only cut down enough trees to make a house and to make room for a garden. I didn't think we would cut down every tree."

"You thought wrong. These trees will more than pay for this property."

With determination in her eyes, she stood next to one of the big trees. "This property is already paid for, and you have work, and we already have more than what most people have."

Mark stepped toward her and spoke in a firm resolute voice. "Listen, Victoria, I'll fall these trees, and I'll sell them to the mill, and I'll put this land into pasture. I will!"

She'd seen Mark act this way before. When he set his mind to something, and he felt he was right, it was going to be his way. She had her desires, her wishes, and she thought about standing up for them. She thought her sister would argue with Mark, yet she couldn't bring herself to fight with Mark. She desired peace in their relationship. "You know what's best," she said.

Mark focused on the trees and what they would bring, and he couldn't see that he had crushed Victoria's heart. She walked back to the tent, went inside and started cleaning.

The argument with Mark brought to the forefront all the emotions that she'd been holding inside. Leaving her home and family, the long trip to America, the long trip to the Northwest, all came flooding out of her in tears. She stopped cleaning and curled up on her bed grabbing at her heart, feeling intense loneliness, terrible loss, and misunderstood. She remembered how her sister would come and brush her hair when she had been crying. She would brush with long even strokes. Victoria could feel her calming touch, and hear her sister's voice. "Do as you desire, and pursue your dreams."

Remembering brought a smile to her face. It was as though she could feel her sister sitting next to her on the bed running her fingers through her hair. Sighing, she closed her eyes and fell off to sleep.

✳   ✳   ✳   ✳

Mark looked forward to working with the horses. He wanted to get as many logs as possible to the landing to prove his worth. It was his goal to move more logs in one day than any man had done before with oxen. He met Mr. Isaacson at the log dump early Monday morning. Isaacson had the horses reigned together ready to head up the hill. They followed an old dirt trail that ran next to the railroad tracks. When they reached the logging site, Isaacson handed the reigns to Mark. "I'll be up to feed the horses every morning and evening. Take good care of them—I don't want to have to fix them at all."

"I will take good care of them."

"Be sure to pick their hoofs every day. A lame horse is no good for nothing."

Isaacson finished and rode off the hill. Mark took the horses and went to his first log. With a couple of dogs, he chained the log in a bridle grip and attached the line to the horses. He gave a loud yelp and the horses started to pull, their muscles straining to get the log in motion. The horses lowered their heads with their hooves digging in the duff, pulling with their strength. The log started to move, slowly at first, but it picked up speed until the horses were in a rhythm, moving the log down the skid road.

By the end of the day Mark made more turns than any of the teams of oxen did before. He led the horses to a makeshift corral where they would wait for him until morning. Mark checked the shoes on each horse when Hammer came walking up. "Is everything fine Mr. Hammer?"

"Yes, you did really good today."

Mark stopped picking at the shoes and looked at Hammer as if he couldn't believe what he heard. "Thank you. Those are kind words."

"Hell, if every man worked as hard as you do—we'd have half of this mountain logged in a couple of weeks."

Those were good words to hear considering the source.

Isaacson showed up with the hay for the horses. Mark helped him throw the hay into the corral next to a small stream that ran on the edge of the fence. The horses could get their water out of the creek. When Mark was satisfied that all things were in order, he headed for the tracks."

Mark climbed up on a log lying on the tracks waiting to be trailed to the log dump at the lake. Some of the braver men would ride to town sitting on top of the logs. The logs sitting on the tracks were all brought to the landing by his team of horses. One of the men sitting on the log looked at Mark. "How's the grease monkey today?"

Mark raised his hands showing that there was no grease on them. "This man is no longer a monkey."

The men laughed. Mark smiled enjoying his new position.

Like it was for Mark, it has always been the goal of man to find a more efficient way to do any kind of laborious task. Anything that can make a job easier, or more profitable, inspired men to come up with an idea to bring about the desired results. Oxen, the great beast that brought wagons west, were first used to haul the logs out, but they were not the smartest of animals pressed into service for men. They had to be constantly goaded and prodded to work. They were strong but slow. Horses are strong and fast. Horses are social animal and they want to please their handlers. No goading was needed to make them move, just a loud yelp. It wasn't long before horses replaced the oxen as the beast of burden in the woods.

$$* \qquad * \qquad * \qquad *$$

Victoria spent the morning picking wild blackberries in a logged-off area just south of their property. Wild blackberries were some of the first plants to find their way into logged off sites. She filled her pot with the tiny berries, wondering if she ate more than she saved. From the other side of the hill, she heard singing in a language she had never heard before. She walked toward the singing, not sure of what she would find. It was the voice of a woman, an older woman. She crested the hill and saw the Indian woman she had met in town. Nookachamp Rose turned around and gazed at Victoria. Rose smiled as she waved. "Come here, my new friend."

Victoria made her way down the hill. Rose sat down and motioned for Victoria to sit next to her. "I see you are picking berries," Rose said.

"Yes, we don't have these where I come from."

"You will find all that you need here—it's always been that way for our people. That's why I sing."

"What were you singing?" Victoria asked.

"I was thanking the Earth for giving me these berries to eat. It's a song of harvest. I've known it since I was a young girl. My grandmother taught me."

"It sounds beautiful. I wish I could learn to sing like that, but I don't have a voice to sing."

"Only some people have a singing voice, but like me, everyone can sing from their heart. We all have a song. Why fear what you can't do—why not do the things you can?"

"I've never thought of that."

"Much life is wasted not thinking, or thinking things that lead to nothing."

"I wish I were allowed to pursue what I wanted."

"Just because a tree is rooted in one place doesn't mean it can't grow to be the most magnificent tree of all."

"I don't understand," Victoria said.

"You're here—with your husband. It's where you've been planted. That doesn't mean that you can't become all you want. Chase what you desire like the cougar chasing after a deer—catch it."

Victoria smiled, wanting to know more about these things, and more about Rose. She looked at Rose seeing the years of sun sparkle in her eyes. She wondered about Rose. "When did you learn to speak English?"

"Many summers ago a white man settled close to here, and one summer his grandson came down with fever. He tried everything to make him better, but white medicine wouldn't work. He found me by asking others if they knew anyone who could help. My people come to me when they're sick. I can heal sickness—I can heal hurts of the heart. I learned your language from him."

"Did the young boy get better?"

Rose picked a leaf off a plant that grew on the ground. "Yes, I took roots and leaves for medicine and made him a drink. I prayed over him for a day. When he woke, he was better. I stayed and waited for him to become strong. During that time the white man was kind to me and helped me learn your words. He was a good friend, I was sorry to see him go on to the next life."

"Why don't I see more of your people around here?"

Sadness rushed over Rose. "When the white people came, they brought a bad sickness that killed most of my people. A sickness we could not heal. I was a young girl and watched my family and friends die. Most of my people are dead, but some are left that live close. The others live out on the reserve."

Victoria listened to the story Rose told, and enjoyed learning about Rose's life. She yearned to know more. "Do you really know how to make people well? And can you really see the future as some say?"

Rose reached out and picked up a stick and started drawing on the ground. She drew a picture of a plant. "When bodies become sick there are many plants that can make them well. But the big trees are being killed and it's becoming harder to find plants that heal. Many of them need the cover of the big trees."

Rose stood up and motioned to Victoria. "Follow me, I'll show you things you should know."

They walked into the forest and Rose stopped beneath a few tall trees. The smells changed from those that were out in the clear cut. The forest floor and canopy were alive with all kinds of plants, insects, and birds of every type. On the ground was a plant with little broad heart-shaped leaves. Rose picked one up, gave it to Victoria. "This plant has many uses. The berries heal hunger, and the oil from the leaves can heal sores on your eyes. Put the leaves to a cut and they will help it heal faster. This plant only grows in the shade of the deep forest, and soon it will be gone if there are no trees to protect it. It will go the way of my people—back to the ground."

Victoria listened with fascination to the ideas and thoughts that Rose shared. She continued to walk with Rose down a worn path through the big trees. Along the way Rose told her of all the plants and their many uses. "You need to learn these things for your children. The earth has everything we need for our lives. It's given to us by *Tyee*."

"Who is *Tyee*?"

"He is the Great Spirit that gives life—he made everything."

"You mean God?"

"To whites he is God, but the name he gave us is *Tyee*."

Victoria let out a long sigh, inviting Rose to share more. "I have always wanted to be a teacher," Victoria said. "What I learn I desire to share with others."

Rose smiled. "We all teach—just some in different ways."

As they walked they came to a fork in the path that was divided by one of the biggest trees Victoria had seen. She stopped and looked up to find the top, but only saw branches hiding the sun and clouds. She walked around the base of the tree, counting as she took each step heel to toe. "One, two, three...forty."

The tree was over forty feet around. Rose met her as Victoria finished counting. Rose reached out and touched the tree. "This tree is the Tree of Life. It gives us clothing, shelter, tools and wood for canoes. You can make medicine from this tree—it's everything. From the time we're born to the time we die the Tree of Life provides all. If you stand with your back to the tree, you will receive power."

Victoria stood with her back to the tree. She closed her eyes as she felt a warm rush. "I can feel it running through my body."

"I know you can—*Tyee* is in everything."

"I am learning this."

"*Tyee* shall return to our land someday in a great canoe made from the tree of life. Our babies are clothed in its bark when they are born, and our dead are put in Tree of Life canoes for their trip to the next life."

Rose kept on talking about the tree as if she were worshiping it. "Soon there will be no more trees such as this one. They will be gone—gone like my people. Gone until *Tyee* restores everything."

Victoria looked toward the top of the tree, listening to Rose. "Right now I feel as though I could never learn enough about these things."

"Learning never ends—even after you pass you learn."

"I will teach my children all these wonderful things someday."

Victoria sat down in a bed of ferns and picked a leaf off a large sword fern. "Is there any use for these ferns?"

"Yes, in the early spring before the fronds appear, you can eat the shoots to cure hunger. There is a use for everything in the forest."

Victoria put the fern to her nose and smelled it, and then put it to her mouth tasting it. She spit it out with a disgusted look on her face. "I don't know if I could eat some of these things, no matter how hungry I was."

"Oh, if you listen to the tree spirits, they will guide you to do right."

"Spirits?"

"Yes, spirits live in the trees, live in the rocks, and live in the life of the forest. They live in the cougar, the bear, the fox, and the raven. You need spirit eyes to see them, but anyone can hear them—they are all around us even now. You need to learn how to see differently."

She listened, and thought that maybe they were just like the fairies that live in the hills of Scotland. "I believe what you say, Rose. I think I've seen them before, where I come from."

"Not many people can see such things."

"How do you see all these things?" Victoria asked.

"You need to look at what others don't. Look beyond what you see with your eyes and learn to see with your heart. Then you will see all there is about life."

Victoria put her head back, staring up into the branches, dreaming of the things she could imagine about life and love. She stood up and looked around to find that Rose had disappeared; she looked down the path wondering where Rose had gone.

The forest made its own sounds. Victoria walked through the thick moss and listened to her feet as they hardly made a sound. She heard fir cones hitting the ground as they fell from the trees. She looked up and saw a squirrel running on a branch and cutting the cones. "You're a busy worker," she said.

The squirrel chattered back and the sound was lost as it traveled through the trees. The trees muffled all the sounds that she or the animals made. She walked back out into the clear cut and could hear the birds. They were over a half a mile away, but the sound carried having nothing to absorb it. She could see the difference between the forest and the clear cut. They both had different lives.

She gathered up her berries and headed home.

Once she was home she decided to walk into town to get some sugar at Beddall's store to add to the berries she had picked. She stopped by the lake to watch children playing in the water. Some of the boys were standing on logs that were floating in the lake. The waves would rock the logs, as the boys would see who could stand the longest. She could see the large burner pouring out a hazy light smoke that dissipated as it rose into the sky. She walked past the mill toward Beddall's store. She walked inside. "Hi, Mr. Beddall," she said.

"Hello young lady."

"Do you have some nice material?"

"I have many new rolls that just arrived a couple of days ago. Let me show you."

She followed Mr. Beddall to the back of the store. He pointed to a wall filled with rolls of material. He watched her as she browsed the material. "Have you met many of the people around town yet?" he asked.

"No, not with everything that has to be done in moving to our property and all. I've been visiting with Rose somewhat; she's the only person I've had any chance to talk with."

"That old Indian woman is strange. Indians do nothing but sit around and drink too much whiskey. I'm sure you can find better people to visit with if you'd get out more often."

Beddall's words surprised Victoria. "She seems really nice to me, and I don't think she drinks whiskey. She knows about a lot of things, and to me she's a great person to visit."

Mr. Beddall shook his head, letting out a grunt of disagreement. He figured it was no use in trying to convince Victoria of his view of Nookachamp Rose. Victoria sensed his disapproval and feelings. "I need a pound of sugar please."

He packaged the sugar up for her and she paid for it. "Thanks for your service." She started to walk away and turned back around. "I think you could learn a lot from Rose. Have a good day, Mr. Beddall."

She walked out and headed home to wait for Mark.

As she walked home, she thought of the things she'd read back in Scotland about the Indians. They didn't hold true with the Indian woman she met here, for Nookachamp Rose was no savage. She was no warrior, nor a human that gets pleasure from killing. She believed that Rose was a woman of peace, of kindness, of love. It was wrong, she thought, to judge people without knowing them. She would continue to talk with Rose no matter what people thought. The right to choose her friends was something she was going to stand up for. She smiled, as she knew she was seeing with her heart.

✳   ✳   ✳   ✳

Mark worked hard learning everything he could about the timber business. He looked forward to every Saturday for his pay and spending Sundays working on his property falling trees.

The first Sunday he fell three big cedar trees. He split them into lengths of up to twenty feet long and an inch thick. It amazed him that he could make planks without the use of a ripsaw, the grain of the cedar tree being so clear and fine. It was choice wood to work with. At the end of July, Mark had enough boards and planks split to build a house.

CHAPTER 7

▼

HOME

The summer heat wave set high temperature records. It hadn't rained in twenty days and the forest was parched. Victoria would spend every morning carrying water from the stream to water her apples trees. She had built a fence around them to keep the deer from eating them. The sounds of the forest changed with the heat. The soft feel under her feet turned to hard snaps. She poured a second bucket of water on one of the trees. "I wish it would rain," she said to Mark as he sat near the tent.

Mark nodded his head. "I wish it would also. McMaster fears the loss of timber, and has ordered all logging operations halted. He says fire might sweep through the whole forest."

"That wouldn't be good."

"No, there would be no work."

Victoria put her bucket away. "You can use the time to build our house."

"That's a good idea, I'd rather be working, but logging won't resume until there has been ample rain to limit the possibility of fire."

"The time off will be nice for us. I bet most of the men like having time off," Victoria said.

Mark shook his head as he carved on a limb. "The feelings of my co-workers vary. Some like the time off, and others need the work. I just hope it doesn't last long. I will build our house. I just wish I had help."

Mark spent a few days rounding up all the materials he would need to build the house. Mark thought it would be a month long project. On a Friday near the end of August, Mark worked laying out foundation blocks cut from cedar rounds for the start of his house. As he worked he heard what seemed to be a large crowd of people walking up the trail toward his place.

The sound grew louder, and soon he saw many of the men with whom he worked coming with tools in hand. Doug Draper, who led the crowd, walked up to Mark and reached for his hand. "Since the day you bought your property, you've been talking about building a house. And since we're not working I talked the men into coming up and helping you put your house together. Later this afternoon the ladies in town will be bring up supper for everyone."

Mark tried to hold his emotion inside. The help of these people made him feel that he was looked upon as an American, not as a foreigner. It was something he never expected. "Thanks, I sure could use the help, but I don't know if I can repay you all."

Doug smiled and put his hand on Mark's shoulder. "You're a friend—you won't owe any of us a thing."

Victoria came out of the tent when she heard all the voices. Mark came over to her. "My co-workers are going to help build our house."

Victoria covered her mouth and started to cry. "You're kindness I will never forget," she said to the men. "I have grown tired of living in the dirt, and I haven't felt right in pushing Mark to build since he works so hard every day."

Doug walked over to her and gave her a hug. "We all just want to help you."

The men, under the direction of Doug, started grabbing planks and nails and laying them out. By the time noon rolled around, four outside walls were up and trusses for the roof were being set. Victoria kept busy running back and forth from the stream, getting water for the men. They would drink some of the water and the rest of it they would use to wash the sweat off their foreheads.

Victoria watched the men work. "When are the men going to take a break?"

Mark stopped sawing and looked around at the men building his house. "Should we take a break men?"

Doug walked over to Victoria and Mark. "If Hammer were here and heard those words he would curse you for a year straight with out stopping."

Mark and Doug laughed. "We will finish your house. Our break will be when evening comes and your house is complete. Until that time we will work."

Mark went back to sawing as Doug held the board for him. "That's a fine wife you have there Mark."

"She's young, and has much to learn. I'm working on making her a fine wife."

"I don't think there's much work needed."

Mark smiled at Doug and looked back at Victoria. "Yes, she is fine."

At the end of the day the basic structure of the house was complete. The floor, walls, shake roof, front porch, and doors were done. A few details were left for Mark and Victoria to finish on the inside, but the house was livable. Mark stood with Victoria, gazing at their new house. It was about six hundred square feet and looked like a large wooden box. But to them it was their castle, a dream come true. This was their new home.

The ladies arrived just as the men were finishing the last bit of shake roofing, bringing hot dishes of every imaginable taste. Deer steaks, baked beans, dandelion greens, bear meat, and other foods that Mark and Victoria had never experienced before. The dish that surprised them the most was squirrel stew, but they just couldn't bring themselves to try it.

As they finished eating, some men made a fire with the leftover scraps of wood. A couple of fellows started playing their fiddles, and people began to dance around the fire. Warmth came to the hearts of Mark and Victoria. They looked around at everything and knew this was their home and these were their friends. They joined the others in dance until everyone slowly began making their way home.

Victoria gathered up some blankets from the canvas tent. "Mark, come with me. We'll sleep in our new house."

They went straight for their new bedroom and laid the blankets on the floor. Mark moved close to Victoria, embraced and kissed her. In a few short minutes he made love to her and fell off to sleep.

She watched him sleep—seeing a smile on his face. She was happy for him—she was learning to love him—yet she had some yearnings inside her that she could not describe. She wondered what those and feelings were, she didn't understand them. Those thoughts made her think of her sister, and she decided that in the morning she would write and let her sister know how everything was going. She fell off to sleep dreaming, of past times, of running through the hills of Scotland with her younger sister chasing her.

Since Mark and Victoria had arrived in Clear Lake, it hadn't rained, though they heard from all the locals that it did nothing but rain. Mark and the rest of the men employed in the timber were hoping for rain to come soon because they were anxious about getting back to work, but McMaster knew his entire livelihood rested in timber that wasn't burnt. He would love for the men to be out bringing in the logs, but common sense ruled. He knew if just one spark were to fly into the brush, it could burn over a million board feet of timber in a short time. The risk was too great to chance working.

Mark spent his time preparing for winter. He sawed small logs for firewood, and adding finishing touches to their new house. Victoria walked out to where he was sawing wood and sat down, watching him work. "When are you going to start a business making guns?" She asked.

He stopped and wiped his forehead and looked at her. "Maybe I'll make a gun next week if I can find the right parts. I'm enjoying my work in the forest. Mr. McMaster seems to like me, and I'm sure if I work hard I can quickly move ahead in his company."

"I thought your dream is to make guns."

"It was, but not now."

"I only want you to be happy no matter what you do."

He smiled at her and continued sawing. It was the last time he would think or talk about becoming a gunsmith. Victoria stood as Mark looked at her. "I'm going into town to get some vegetables for dinner."

He put down his saw and wiped his forehead. "I'll go with you. You never know, something could happen to you."

"I walk to town by myself almost every day when you're working—nothing will happen to me."

Mark frowned. "You know I don't like it when you do that. Just stay home and wait for me to accompany you."

Victoria shook her head as she walked into the house to get her things.

They made their way to Beddall's store. A few of the men that Mark worked with were standing outside of Buster's saloon and pool hall. Doug saw them walking by and came out to greet them. Doug was becoming a good friend to Mark, and since meeting Victoria he'd taken a liking to her. He stepped close to them and started walking. "What brings you two into town?"

"Victoria's going to get some things for dinner," Mark said.

As they were talking, Doug stared at Victoria. She could feel his eyes on her, which made her feel uncomfortable. She drew closer to Mark to show Doug that she was not available. Mark however was oblivious to what was going on. Victoria sensed that Doug was interested in her from the day the men came to work on the house. He would take every opportunity to talk to her and sit by her. At first she thought it was kind of nice to be noticed and pursued, but only to a point, a point she could not exactly define.

When Doug met Victoria desire consumed him. He stood on the boardwalk watching her as she walked with Mark. She was young and beautiful, pleasing to look upon. Doug thought if he worked at being closer to Mark, he could gain an inroad to Victoria. "Why not?" he said, looking at his reflection in the store window. "What young girl or woman wouldn't like a man such as me making advances toward her?"

Doug had an ego to fit right in with his looks and charm.

As in the other logging towns and camps in the Northwest, women were in short supply. Asa Mercer, a few years previously, had shipped a number of women from Boston out west to Seattle to satisfy the men living and working there. Clear Lake, like every other logging community, had its lack of lady folk. As the communities grew, women were soon to follow: some married, some single looking for husbands, some single looking for profit. It wasn't long before Clear Lake had its first brothel.

Soiled doves, as the ladies were called, were there to take away the longings and loneliness of the men who worked the woods. Doug was known to fancy such places. "It gives me added strength," he would tell others.

A few months after the Southerlands arrived in town, Jezzy Orlander opened her house. It was conveniently located near the log dump where men came off the hill after working all day. Jezzy was named after her mother's favorite Biblical character, Jezebel. "Jezzy has done me proud," her mother said.

Now Jezzy wasn't the most beautiful woman to look upon. Most of the men that came to visit preferred to have the lights kept low. It was always said among the men that the sight of Jezzy made a strong case for fidelity.

Jezzy was five feet tall with a medium build and blonde hair that was always pulled back whenever she went out. She was loud, always made her presence known and could drink most of the loggers under the table. All of these traits made her hated by the married women and a friend to most of the single, lonely, and deprived men. The other women in town talked constantly about her, yet none of those women would take the time to talk to her.

*   *   *   *

Mark walked into Beddall's store, browsing over different items. Victoria quickly followed behind him, trying to lose Doug. Mr. Beddall came over always anxious to make a sale. "May I help you with something?"

"Yes, I need some new pants," Mark said.

He looked at some cotton jeans, but Mr. Beddall waved his arms pointing to some jeans down the isle. "You don't want those ones—you want some tin pants."

He reached up on the shelf and pulled down a pair of pants made out of canvas. He unfolded them and handed them to Mark. "When the rains come, these pants will keep you dry. They look uncomfortable, but they'll last a long time. I'll even throw in a extra can of wax."

Mark looked at the pants, holding them and running his hands over the knees. "I don't know if I can move in these pants."

"Every man wears them in the woods. Tin pants are the unspoken uniform of the logger. You're not a real logger until you wear these

"Mr. Beddall could see that Mark was undecided. "You'll get used to them and come winter, you'll thank me for selling them to you."

Mark smiled. "Then I'll take them."

Victoria picked up what she needed for dinner; they paid for their things and headed back home. As they walked outside they ran into Doug. He glanced at Mark and then stared at Victoria. "Would you like to join us for dinner?" Mark asked.

"Sure would—been a long time since I had a good home cooked meal."

Victoria glanced at Mark. "You should've asked me first before inviting him over. I didn't get enough food for three people."

"We can make do. He's my friend."

The extra work in cooking didn't bother her. It was the way Doug was acting toward her, and having him around would just encourage him more.

The rains came in the second week of September. On Sunday afternoon the sky clouded over. The clouds flew in from the west, forming out in the Pacific and drawing up moisture to release on the Cascades. Victoria saw high clouds while walking down by the creek. As she made her way up to the house, the clouds grew dark and thick. Mark sat on the porch watching Victoria. "That's a welcome sight."

A few scattered sprinkles made wet spots on Victoria's dress. Before she made it to the house the light faded and the skies opened up. "This is wonderful," she said as she danced in the rain.

"Get inside before you get drenched!" Mark yelled.

"It's been so long—I never thought I would enjoy seeing it rain."

It rained all night and when Mark awoke the next morning he could hear the rain on the roof. He put his tin pants on and ate some breakfast. He grabbed a heavy coat before he headed outside. "I hope it doesn't rain all day."

He made his way down to the log dump to catch a ride up the hill. All the men had forlorn looks on their faces, even though they were going back to work. Mark sat next to Doug. "Why the long look on everyone's face?"

"Because it might not stop raining until next July, and working in the rain makes things twice as hard."

"Next July, huh? That's a long time for it to rain."

"Get used to it—we may not see the sun for days—hell, maybe even weeks. If you stand in one place long enough, you may even get moss growing on you."

Mark laughed, and then heard the only man that seemed to be happy about the rain. Ol' Hammer loved the rain. He was smiling and singing. "Oh how wonderful to have rain…"

He could be heard on every disconnect. "Why are you men so sad about the rain?"

No one responded. "We're all back to work and you are all in misery. Open your eyes and see the wonderful rain."

The only time Hammer was happy was when others were not.

Mark's new tin pants repelled the rain, not letting one drop penetrate into the fabric. The horses were in the corral waiting for him when he arrived at the landing, where it seemed to be raining harder than in town. He bridled them together, and then headed off to the timber. The dust on the skid roads had turned into sloppy mud in which the horses moved slower than they had in the dust. Mark knew this day would drag on, just as Doug said. He whistled at the horses for them to pick up speed, but he knew they were already giving him all they had to offer.

The day wore on as the rain kept falling. His production of logs scaled about half of what it was in the days before the rains came. It seemed that even he himself was going slower. The rain not only slowed him physically, but mentally. It hit his mind continually with each drop, washing away optimism and flooding it with discouragement. Each step became a chore, each dog that needed to be pounded into place, each chain laid and hooked to the horses, everything was in slow motion. It made the day seem a hundred hours long, as if it would never end.

$$*\qquad*\qquad*\qquad*$$

Victoria sat inside watching the rain fall outside her window. The small stream grew deeper and wider as the rain fell. Out on the edge of the clearing, she saw Rose walking toward her house. Victoria opened the door expecting to see Rose drenched. She stared at Rose standing on the porch perfectly dry. Victoria looked at the clothes she had on. They were not the ones she had seen her wearing before. She wore a hat and a beautiful coat made out of cedar bark. They did a fine job of keeping the rain off of her.

Victoria closed the door as Rose entered. She helped Rose take off her hat and shoes that had a beautiful design on them. They were made out of cedar bark like the rest of her clothes. Rose saw her admiring the shoes. "I can teach you how to weave the bark into many wonderful things."

Victoria smiled with approval, desiring to learn. "What brings you here on this rainy day?"

"I haven't seen you around lately, and I'm wondering how you are."

Rose looked around the house, enjoying the smell that the cedar gave off.

"Would you like something hot to drink?" Victoria asked.

"Yes. That would be nice."

Victoria went to the stove where a pot of water boiled. She made some tea and gave it to Rose, who took a sip. "Sometimes the rains stay for days. Sometimes the river floods all the way to Clear Lake."

"That river is three miles away! How does it reach all the way here?"

"When I was a girl, the floods came and made the whole valley look like one big sea. My father brought me to a place above where the town sits—it was all under water. It'll happen again, but not this year."

"Will my house flood?"

"No, the river never comes up this high. Only once was the ground covered. My people were safe in the great canoe—which came to rest on Sauk Mountain. That mountain is a sacred place for my people—so is the big rock south of here."

Victoria smiled, listening to Rose's account of the flood. She was not interested in correcting her saying that it was Noah's Ark in the great flood. She understood that people interpret events in different ways, and she knew Rose was just recounting a story told from generation to generation by her elders.

Rose had a serious look on her face. "The next time the earth needs cleansing, it will be with fire, not water."

"When will that be?"

"Before I die—I saw the fire when I was a girl. My grandfather said that's when my eyes will be set free. He told me when I was young that the Great Spirit gave me eyes to see things that are not."

"Have people always said that about your eyes?"

"Yes, I was born on the shores of Mud Lake while my mother was gathering reeds. My mother was alone and weak, she fell and dropped me in the muddy water and I passed to the other life. The eagle saw my spirit and flew down and picked me out of the water and set me down next to my mother. She kissed my lips and I passed back to this life. My eyes never came back fully—they are from the other side and that's why I see the things I do. I always wanted to see the earth clearly, but my eyes are blurred, and I see what others don't."

"You seem to get around with out much problem," Victoria said.

"I follow not only what I can see—but what I see inside. Everything is my friend—they're my guides."

Victoria sat listening to everything Rose said. She felt a connection with Rose—she could understand the things Rose spoke about, things that touched her.

"Do you talk to others in town much?"

"No, they won't listen. I am Indian, and the whites are not interested in things they cannot see or feel."

"Yes, I find that a lot of my people are like that," Victoria said.

The rain fell and Victoria thought of Mark working out there all day. She gazed off through the window over the creek past the tall trees. Rose walked over and stood by her. Rose reached out touching Victoria's shoulder. "Your husband will be fine working in the forest unless the trees whisper his name. If they whisper his name—have him quit—oh, please, have him quit."

Her voice was urgent.

"I don't understand," Victoria said.

"You'll hear it, I'll hear it, and Mark will hear it. You'll know, your heart will know—you'll feel it deep within you. The spirits live in the trees. They see things before they happen."

The words sank into her soul; she understood. She knew what to do if she heard the trees whisper Mark's name. Rose finished her tea and put her shoes on.

"I have to be going—many things left to do today."

"Thanks for stopping over. Please come again."

Victoria watched Rose disappear into the misty rain.

*   *   *   *

Mark made slow progress in the sloppy deep mud. He thought of working inside, of being dry and working next to a warm fire. He returned for another log when he heard a faint cry for help. He left the horses and ran toward the place where a bucker had been working on a tree over twenty feet at the butt. He didn't see him but could hear a weak voice saying, "Help me, help me."

He looked and saw nothing, yet he kept hearing the voice of a man coming from under the massive log. He ran around to the other side and saw the man gasping for air with most of his body trapped under the weight of the log. The man saw Mark and tried to reach for him. Panic grabbed Mark as the thought what to do. "I'll help you, just wait here."

The man murmured. "I don't think I'm going any place."

Mark ran back and grabbed the team of horses. He led them over to the log and quickly pounded in two dogs and hooked the chains to them. He let out a yell and the horses started to pull on the log, their hooves splashing in the mud, reaching deep for traction. They pulled the log off the man. Mark ran over to the log and knelt down beside him. The man reached for Mark. Mark slid his arms under him and held him close to offer him comfort. Mark knew there was no nope for this poor soul. He had seen the man riding the disconnects every morning up to the site but didn't know his name. He looked at Mark and spoke in broken words. "I'm too young to die."

He took a shallow breath as if he couldn't take another. "I don't want to die."

Mark held him—he could see that his legs were crushed with bones and blood covering the ground. He knew the man was going to die. "What's your name?" Mark asked.

"Steven."

"Are you married, Steven?"

"Yes, and I've three children."

Steven looked up at Mark and breathed his last. Mark didn't let go of him. He had never seen a man die, let alone held a dead man before. Steven was alive a minute ago, and now he was gone. Life had disappeared.

The rain washed the blood into the ground, making the scene look clean. Clouds rolled over the hill and through the trees. The fog closed in around them like a shroud. In less than an hour the earth would swallow up any evidence of a death except for the lone lifeless body being carried out to the connects for his last ride off the hill. This was no sweet chariot, but a long lonely ride back to town.

After a few minutes Mark laid the man down and went to get help. He saw Hammer making a turn of logs at the landing and went running over to him. "A man has died and I need help getting him out."

Hammer looked at Mark with disdain and started his ramblings. "What do you want me to do? Cry? I don't care if he's dead—he ain't doing us any good now. He should have been more careful. Now get back to work, and the next time you come to the landing without a turn of logs, you'll be fired. When the day's done, I'll send some men up to help get the worthless beast out."

Mark shook his head as he headed back to his horses, grieved with how Hammer had responded to him. He thought that Hammer was all talk, and underneath that talk was a man with some heart, but he was now convinced that Hammer had no heart. Somewhere along his life, he had lost it. What a pity, he thought, to go through life with no compassion, no forgiveness, or no mercy—with no heart. What does a man have left? Only his work and the misery he can bestow on others who cross his path. "Some people are dead long before they will stop breathing—just like Hammer," Mark said as he grabbed the reigns.

Mark took the lead and gave a yelp and the horses started to pull the log down the skid road. It would be two more hours before the day was done and Steven would be on his last ride out. The log Mark pulled was on its first and last ride out. It was dead, yet it was going to provide some type of life to someone. It could be a roof, a door, siding, or maybe even a music box. In the forest it was life for a life, and death for a death.

With each turn of logs Mark would look over to see if somehow Steven had come back to life. The wind picked up, rustling the branches of the trees. Mark stopped and listened because he thought he heard another voice. All he heard was the wind in the trees. He pulled up to another log and pounded in the dog when he thought he heard someone say the name Steven.

He turned around, figuring it was Hammer playing a stupid game with him, but no one was behind him. He hooked the chains up to the log and again he heard a voice say, "Steven."

He became frightened, looking over his shoulder and to his sides. Maybe the fairies that Victoria always talked about were in the forest playing games with his mind. He worked to convince himself that the death didn't affect him, and that it was his mind playing with him, nothing more. As he pounded another dog into a log he saw a man, dressed in the bark of a tree, standing on the edge of the clear cut.

Caleb wandered out of the forest over to Steven's body. Mark walked over next to Caleb. "What do you want here?" Mark asked.

Caleb looked at the body then back at Mark. "I heard the trees whisper—I came to see if I knew the man."

"What are you talking about?"

"Things that some men will never understand."

"I can understand any thing."

"The forest has its own life. The forest has lived in unity with all creatures for hundreds of years, but now a creature is destroying it. If you listen you can hear the forest whisper and cry with each tree that is removed."

"Nonsense!"

"As I said, there are some things men will never understand."

With those words Caleb left and disappeared as fast as he had appeared.

At the end of the day they put Steven's lifeless body on the back connect unknowingly next to the log that had killed him. The train blew its whistle and headed off the hill. There wasn't one man with a smile on his face except for Hammer. He was in a happy mood standing on the connects. "Smile, you wretched beasts—it could have been any one of you today."

Death was on the connects, reminding each man that it could have been any one of them. If only they didn't have to see it on the connect. Mark sat next to Doug as they listened to Hammer. "I'd like to jump up and push that man right off of this train," Mark said.

Doug nodded his head. "Yes, my anger burns at him sometimes, but it's best to be like the rest of the men and forget about death."

"Yes, forget about death, forget I am wet to my bones, forget that it will be raining tomorrow, and forget that I have to do this all again."

"Maybe tomorrow it will be you or I on our last ride out of the forest. I pray that it will never be that way," Doug said.

The train whistle blew as it rounded a curve. Mark held on to the cables holding the log. "Victoria is at home preparing a nice hot meal for me. There I will find comfort—there I will find rest."

Mark smiled as he thought about dinner, and Doug closed his eyes and dreamt.

As the train arrived at the log dump men started jumping off the connects and heading to their homes. Hammer sent for the undertaker. Mark thought about how Steven's wife and children were going to take the news. It was something he never wanted his wife or children to go through.

Mark walked into the house and sat down at the table. "How was your day?" Victoria asked.

"It was wet."

"Maybe tomorrow it will be sunny again."

Mark drew a heavy sigh looking at Victoria. "A man died today—in my arms."

Silence filled the room. Victoria felt sorry for him but didn't know what to say. She walked up and kneeled down on the floor and put her head on Mark's lap. He was staring out the window. "It's a bad feeling when you can't help a man who's dying. I wish there were something I could have done. Strange thing is that after I started working again, I thought I heard someone calling his name in the trees. I looked around but didn't see anyone; it was as if the trees were speaking his name over and over. Then that young man we saw carrying the stove on his back showed up and talked about strange things in the forest."

Victoria looked intently into Marks eyes. "Mark, if you hear the trees whisper your name, please run, quit, and come home. Rose said when the trees whisper your name, death is certain, so please, if you hear your name, come home."

"You need to stop believing in fairy tales. That old Indian woman is going to fill your head with more tales and things that only scare you. She sounds like that young man. A man died today because logging is dangerous work. He didn't die because of some Indian fable. You should make some other friends and stop talking to that old woman!"

Victoria wiped tears off her check. "I can choose my own friends, and I will."

Mark took a deep breath. "What are you crying for? There's nothing to cry about—you're safe, and with me."

Mark rose to his feet. "I'm going to bed. Tomorrow will be another wet day in the woods."

He felt as though he didn't have the patience to listen to Victoria cry. He didn't understand women and wondered if he ever would. Life was life, he thought, and she had better learn to accept it as it comes.

*   *   *   *

Victoria knew that living on the other side of the world was going to take some getting used to. She was prepared for that. What she wasn't prepared for was how difficult it would be. Day after day the homesickness intensified. She longed to see Scotland, but especially missed her family. She had never been more than twenty miles from her house in all her life. And now she found herself thousands of miles away. Many nights she would cry herself to sleep.

She received letters from home occasionally, telling her of any news. But what she really wanted was to spend time with her family. Knowing that this wasn't possible was breaking her heart. At times she was inconsolable. "Sometimes I forget how young you are Victoria, but I know that you will learn to love this place in time."

It troubled Mark to see her so sad. He didn't know what to do on those days, as nothing seemed to make her happy.

Victoria enjoyed wandering the surrounding hillsides looking for berries and other edibles. It was on one of these day trips that she came upon something that both delighted and surprised her. There, peeking out of the overgrowth was the remnants of a ramshackle cabin. Winding itself up what was once the front porch she found a rambling rose, straining up through the broken wood and branches that surrounded it. She moved to it and pulled the crimson petals to her face. She closed her eyes and the scent took her back to Scotland, and her mother's garden.

She wondered who would have planted this rose bush, and what happened to them. She began to untangle what she could and using a piece of tin she found nearby, she scraped at the dirt to free the roots. She would take this treasure back down the mountain and care for it. When Mark arrived home that night she was delighted to show him her rose bush. She planted it on the sunny side of their house, positioning it so that she could see it from her kitchen window. Victoria looked forward to watching it grow.

As the days past the bush thrived and Victoria would often cut the blossoms for her kitchen table. When the flowers were spent she would crumble the dried petals into a pot and steep them in hot water. She poured the liquid into a small jar and each day would dab a bit behind her ears. The scent pleased her. It not only reminded her of Scotland, but also made her feel pretty.

Victoria's birthday was coming up in a few days. Mark wasn't the type of man to spend hard earned money on frivolous things and he was having a difficult time trying to think of something to give Victoria as a present. Mark didn't understand why the plant made her so happy. It seemed like such a small thing to him. However it warmed his heart to see her smile. It also gave him an idea. He had seen something a few weeks before and he now thought of a nice present for Victoria. He set off one morning on a quest to find her gift. Mark hiked up the mountain, carrying a shovel and small box. As he reached the top he found exactly what he was looking for.

All over the mountainside alpine heather was growing, he knew that Victoria would love to surround their new home with these little bushes. Although not as fragrant as the Scottish heather found in the fields of their homeland, it was a beautiful plant. Wanting to do what he could to fill the void in her heart, he began digging them up, till the box that he had brought was overflowing. Then he carried his bounty down to the cabin, turned over the soil and pressed them firmly into the ground. They made a wonderful display and he could hardly wait for Victoria to arrive home to see her face.

Not too long after he completed his project he spotted Victoria walking down the path toward the house. He went outside to greet her. "Happy Birthday darling, I hope that you like your gift."

Her eyes moved slowly over the newly planted heather. "Oh Mark, where on earth did you find them?" she said, as tears began rolling down her cheeks.

"In the alpine, I thought that you would enjoy having them close to you," he said.

He picked a flower off one to show it to her. "Why are you crying?"

"Only because I am so touched Mark, they are wonderful and so are you. Thank you so much for doing this for me."

She found that she really enjoyed tending to her small garden. It was a soothing pastime that made her happy. Mark was pleased that he had found something to make her smile.

CHAPTER 8

▼

THE WAR

After four days of rain, the sun came out. A fresh grave in the cemetery reminded Mark of the dangers of logging as he walked to the log dump. There were some flowers sitting next to the cedar board bearing the name of Steven Johanson, born in 1869, died in 1894, a loving husband and father.

As Mark took his seat on the disconnects, Hammer sat down beside him. "It's a war out there. It's us against them."

"Them?" Mark asked.

Hammer pointed to the mountain of green. "Them, the trees. Us or them—one or the other has to die. If you let your head down or your guard down for just one blink of an eye, they can grab you and steal the life right out of you. It's a war, always remember that—remember that we are always at war with nature."

"There are people that don't believe that," Mark replied.

"Radicals they are. People bent on keeping us in the dark ages."

Mark nodded in agreement, and Hammer smiled. "Look at the Indians—they thought they were at peace with nature—living with things instead of having dominance over it. Now we are dominating them. That's the way it works—it's nature or us."

Hammer stood up and looked at the men arriving late. "My grandma could make it here before you bastards! I am going to dock your pay—you no good worthless dogs."

Hammer picked up a branch and swung it at one of the men. "It's dry again so get your ass moving—more trees all you crying crows."

Mark was happy that the rain had stopped. Work was more enjoyable when things were dry, and he was glad that Hammer had taken a liking to him.

Mark learned everything he could about the various jobs and tasks to be performed in the forest. He wanted to know it all. First there were the timber cruisers. Their job was to scale the trees to tally the board feet. They made the decision, after seeing the trees and the layout of the land, whether there was a "logging chance." A logging chance was the term used to decide if there would be profit in a logging operation, which depended on the number of board feet and how difficult it would be to get the trees out. They needed to know how far they were from a mill and the going price per thousand board feet. They were well paid when the profit was right.

Next came the men who built the roads into the woods. It could be a skid road, a railroad or flumes or chutes. Flumes were filled with water and chutes were dry. The logging companies would use whatever method was easiest to get the logs out of the forest. They used oxen and horses and later locomotive power, which came at about the same time that Mark arrived in Clear Lake. The steam donkeys replaced the ox and the horse, and the engineer and the operator replaced the bull whacker. Jobs were constantly changing as logging techniques advanced. Mark viewed them all, wanting to learn all he could.

∗   ∗   ∗   ∗

Each day Victoria busied herself working in and around the house. She would have every thing prepared for when Mark would return. Mark walked in the door and sat down at the table. Victoria set a cup of tea in front of him. "How was work today?"

He took a drink. "There was sun today—it was good. What are we eating tonight?"

"Potato with eggs."

Mark leaned back in this chair and watched as Victoria served him. "I may not work as hard as you do every day, but I do work hard to do things around here and you never comment about them."

"It's what should be done—and you have no idea how hard I work."

"I would like to know."

"I work up on the mountain, but I doubt if you would dare make it up there to see."

"I just wish you would see all that I do around here for you. It makes me sad that you don't."

"There is no need to be sad."

There was a knock at the door. Victoria looked out to the porch and saw Doug. "Your friend is here," she said.

Mark jumped up and welcomed Doug in. "Bring us something to drink," he shouted.

As Victoria walked into the room Doug's eyes smothered Victoria. She gave them both a cup of tea and returned to the kitchen. The men spent most of the evening visiting, with Doug taking every chance to say something to Victoria.

The following week on Thursday morning she got up soon after Mark left, and started to prepare a meal. She made sandwiches, some cut vegetables, and a cake. She packed them into a basket and headed out the door. She walked through town and started up the hill towards the logging operations.

The hill was steep as she struggled with the basket. She stopped and sat down next to the tracks. She saw the town sitting among the hills scarred with clear cuts. She had been in town a short few months and the landscape had already changed. The land went from beautiful to ugly with each tree that came down. She heard movement behind her. "Hello friend," Rose said.

Victoria smiled as Rose and Caleb came close. "Hi," she said. "What are you doing out here?"

"Caleb and I are going to get some mushrooms in the dense forest. We saw you and Caleb thought we'd help you carry your basket. It looks heavy."

"I am doing fine," Victoria said.

"Let us help," Caleb said. "I know where your husband is working—you'll find him faster."

Rose pointed up the mountain. "It's a long climb to where Mark is."

Caleb picked up the basket and all three of them started to walk up the mountain. After a couple of hours they crested a small hill where Mark worked leading his horses down the skid road. Caleb handed the basket to Victoria. "I am sure your man will love having a meal brought to him."

Caleb and Rose left as Victoria made her way down to Mark. He saw her and stopped his horses. "What are you doing up here?"

"I brought you lunch—things that you like."

Mark looked confused. "Why?"

"You said I don't know how hard you work—I thought I would come see."

"It's not lunch time—not for another hour."

"I'll wait then we can have lunch together."

Mark mumbled as he gave a yelp to the horses. Victoria walked up the skid road toward the standing trees. Next to the clear cut was a small stream. She spread out a blanket in the moss, and prepared the food for Mark.

On his return trip he saw her sitting next to the stream under a giant fir. He stopped his horses and walked over and sat down next to her. "Now do you see how hard I work?"

Victoria looked at Mark. He had lost a lot of weight. His body was in the best shape she had ever seen. She reached out with a cloth and wiped the sweat off of his forehead. She felt his arms and how strong they had become. "You are becoming a very handsome man Mark."

"What? I wasn't handsome before?"

"That's not what I mean. Your body is looking nice, and I like that."

Mark smiled. "Thank you. All this running up and down this mountain takes all my strength."

"I do see how hard you work. I will never again think that logging is easy."

"Now you see things correctly."

They ate their lunch and enjoyed the time together. After they ate Mark went back to work, and Victoria returned to town.

Victoria would visit town often. On her walk there she would converse with everyone she met along the way. Most people seemed friendly enough to her, but some of the older ladies in town appeared cold. She thought maybe it was because she was young and new to the community, and that in time she would be welcomed into the social circle once the ladies came to know her.

Victoria arrived home and looked at the apple trees she had planted. The leaves were falling to the ground. She knew it would soon be winter. She walked inside and emptied her basket. As she worked she heard the door of her house open. She was startled, not knowing who would enter without knocking. Standing in her kitchen, Victoria saw seven Indians walking into her front room. A couple of them sat down, while the others remained standing, not saying a word as they stared at Victoria.

In a nervous but welcoming voice, she greeted them. "Hello," she said, while she peeled potatoes. They didn't acknowledge her, but continued to watch. She was frightened but kept working, not knowing what they wanted. There were two men, three women, and two children. She thought maybe they were hungry and offered them something to eat. They shook their heads no and continued to watch. After some time, they all left, not saying a word, leaving just as they had entered.

She was afraid to tell Mark what had happened when he arrived home. She was sure the visitors meant no harm, and she thought it best not to have him worry about her during the day and decided not to mention the incident. It could become one more thing to make Mark upset at her, and she didn't want or need that.

A few days later Rose arrived at Victoria's house, and with her were some of the same visitors from the previous visit. Victoria was relieved to see Rose with them and welcomed them into her house. All but Rose took the places they had occupied a few days earlier. Victoria whispered in Rose's ear. "What do these people want?"

Rose smiled. "They know you've been visiting with me, and they're interested in what makes you different from other white people."

"Why do they think I'm different?"

"Because you visit with me—to most whites we're dirty and you view us the same as you, and I told them you're *Ha-lea-chub*."

"What does that mean?" Victoria didn't attempt to repeat the word, knowing she would never be able to pronounce it.

"You're like the great white mountain to the north. It's covered in snow all year long, and will awaken with fire when her desire becomes great. They are here to see if what I say is true of you."

"How will they see that?"

"They already believe that you're like the snow on the mountain because you were not afraid when they entered your house the other day. So now do your work, and let them watch and soon they will go. They are as curious of you, as you are of them."

Victoria did some cleaning, and while she prepared a stew for dinner, her visitors sat and watched. Every once in a while she would look up and smile at them; they would stare at her, not showing any response. Rose had long left and Victoria felt comfortable with her visitors, knowing they meant no harm. She wondered if any of them spoke or understood English.

Looking out of her window, Victoria saw a few dogs that belonged to the Indians raising havoc and chewing on her apple trees. She pointed out the window. "Can you keep your dogs away from my apple trees, please?"

In her voice was no disrespect, no anger, only a pleasant request to have the dogs kept away from her trees.

The Indians went outside and called the dogs over to them and proceeded to beat the dogs to death. Victoria went running outside trying to dissuade them but to no avail. The Indians took the dogs and threw them on a stump pile that

Mark had gathered up to burn once it rained enough. One of the oldest men pointed at the dogs. "They were no good dogs."

Victoria worried that they misunderstood her and felt nervous over the incident that had taken place. She wished Rose were there to explain why they did that to their dogs. The Indians didn't return to the house, but headed back to where they had come from. She was relieved to see them go.

Over the next few weeks, Victoria's house became a stopping place for every Indian that passed through the area. The local Indians dropped by and entered her house to watch her work. She became friends with many of them, helping them learn English and the white man's numbers, and at the same time she learned their language. They would never call her Victoria but *Ha-lea-chub*, and would smile with pride as if knowing her were a great pleasure.

As in all small communities, word travels fast about the things that others are doing. So it was no surprise that everyone in Clear Lake knew about the visitors Victoria entertained. Mark soon heard and anger burned within him.

He arrived home early from work, storming into the house. "How many savages were in my house today?"

Victoria didn't act surprised as she answered. "I had a few visitors—and they're not savages—they're like you and me."

"You and me? Look at yourself. You're not brown or red—you're white and I want you to stop being friends with those people."

"You're right they are people—I don't know why you're so upset? They don't hurt me and I enjoy their company—I learn from them."

"You can't learn anything from them—they can't even read or write—they only drink whiskey and then think they see spirits."

"Mark, you are not speaking kind words."

"They are inferior and I order you to stop seeing them. So help me I'll start shooting them if I see them around here."

Victoria's eyes filled with tears. Mark was satisfied that his point was made. He was king of this place and his word was law.

"Why Mark? Can't I choose my friends? Do I choose your friends? What if I told you I don't like Doug? Would you stop seeing him?"

"No."

"Then let me make my own choices. I won't do anything to hurt you."

Mark grabbed his coat and went outside and started cutting wood.

It rained on and off for a couple of months. Mark became accustomed to the weather and kept his mind set in a positive mode. On payday McMaster called all the men together to show them a new machine he had purchased. The men gathered on the north side of the mill in the holding yard where sat a large steam boiler and drums on a wooden sled.

"It's a 12x14 skidding donkey. This is the wave of the future, men. This will replace oxen, horses, and make the turns faster. We won't need a grease monkey, but he will become the fireman, keeping the fire hot for the operator of the steam donkey. Oh, the marvels of steam," McMaster said.

The men all looked at the machine in wonder, they touched the drum, and tried to figure out how it worked. Mark was impressed; building moving parts of this machine wouldn't be much different than building a gun with all its moving parts.

Most of the men left with their pay. Mark stayed, and walked around looking over the steam donkey. He pulled levers and read gauges. McMaster watched Mark from his office window and smiled. He rose and went out to talk to him. Mark didn't even notice McMaster walking up behind him; he was intrigued with the machine. "You think you can run this steam donkey?"

Mark looked up, excited at the thought. "Given some time to learn it, I'm sure I can."

"Well, how about you start learning to run it Monday morning. Then you can teach two other men when the other two steam donkey engines arrive."

"When do they arrive?"

"Within the next month—the timber is getting further from the mill, and I'm going to have to start up camps away from town to keep the men close to the trees. With three steam donkeys running, I can have three sites at one time pulling in more logs than ten teams of horses or bulls."

McMaster smiled as he talked. Mark could see the dollar signs in McMaster's eyes. Taking advantage of McMaster's smile, he asked, "Do I get a raise in pay for running this new machine?"

McMaster kicked the dirt as he thought it over. "A dollar more a day for now—maybe more later if things go well."

Mark jumped off the donkey and shook McMaster's hand. "Thanks, I won't disappoint you."

"You'll do fine—I know you will."

"What are you going to do with the horses?"

"We need to keep a few horses for the haul back line, but the rest we'll sell to the locals or shoot for meat."

Mark didn't like the idea of killing horses. He loved the animals and didn't want them to be hurt in any way. If they didn't sell, he would turn them loose. No one would know.

"Would you like to join me for a drink at the club?" McMaster asked.

"Yes, I would," Mark said.

They started off for the Clear Lake Club. It was just a fancy name for a saloon. Sam Huggins named it the Clear Lake Club in hopes that the ladies in town would think that their men were attending to good things instead of just drinking. No women were allowed inside, but they all knew that inside the men played cards and drank.

Jezzy was the only woman allowed inside the other saloon in town. It was called Buster's saloon. She was considered one of the men. The two saloons in town served two different groups of people. There was one saloon for the more distinguished men in town and one for the average men. The only differences between the two were the kind of men that made the establishments their second homes. Mark felt privileged to be a guest of McMaster at the Club.

Doug sat inside Buster's having a drink watching the ladies dance and watching the street out the window. He saw Mark walking with McMaster into the Club. He got up and started walking toward Mark's house.

Victoria was inside preparing dinner when she looked out and saw Doug walking up to the door. Her heart fell and fear grabbed at her. She knew Mark should have been home an hour ago. She was apprehensive when she answered the door, expecting the worst. Doug smiled. "How are you today?"

"Fine, where's Mark? Is he all right?"

Doug could see the concern on her face. "Yes, Mark's all right. He's down at the Club having a drink with the boss."

Victoria sighed with relief hearing that Mark wasn't hurt, but was disappointed that he was spending time at a saloon instead of with her. She knew Doug's intent in coming to tell her where Mark was spending his time. Doug walked right into her house without being invited, which was getting to be a common thing—sometimes she didn't mind, while other times she did.

He sat down so he could see the path leading to the house. She walked into the kitchen and started doing dishes, hoping Doug would get the message that she didn't have time for him. He rose, following her into the kitchen. "How do you like your new life here in America?"

"It's nice. Mark is a wonderful man who's working hard at giving me a good life, and I love him."

Doug looked directly into her eyes as she spoke; she knew that what she said didn't dissuade him at all.

He moved closer to her. "Why do you try to convince me that you love Mark? Does he love you, or does he tell you that he loves you? I'd tell you—I'd give anything to have a wife like you."

"You'll find a good wife some day—Mark waited ten years for me."

Those were words Doug didn't want to hear. He hated it every time she spoke of her devotion to Mark and how wonderful he was. Yet, he would not let it be a discouragement to him, and Victoria could see that it didn't slow him down. She was torn between trying to be nice to him for Mark's sake, and her uneasiness of how she felt around him. She needed to convince him to stop pursuing her, because there was no way she could ever give herself to him. She found herself in a difficult situation and one that she wished she didn't have to deal with.

Victoria hoped that he would realize that she was not interested. Doug thought that if he could just keep spending time with her, she would come to desire him. Arrogance had many times helped him overcome more difficult problems than winning over a married woman's heart.

Mark came home after his drink with McMaster at the Club. Walking into the house he smiled when he saw Doug inside waiting for him. He wanted to talk to him about the new steam-powered donkey that McMaster purchased. Victoria came out of the kitchen to meet Mark. Mark looked at her then back at Doug and thought it will be nice to have both his wife and best friend at his table. "Victoria, make sure you set a place for Doug. We have much to discuss."

Doug smiled, knowing that Mark didn't see his true intentions toward Victoria. Feelings of guilt were far from Doug, for there was nothing wrong with craving another man's wife, because he thought he could give her much more than Mark. Doug thought that in life all is fair game, even another man's wife.

Victoria listened to the men talk as she worked in the kitchen. As Mark and Doug chatted, Doug continually stole looks at Victoria every time he caught sight of her. She felt resentment toward Mark for not seeing Doug's intentions. It hurt her heart and made her feel unsafe. She yearned for Mark to see Doug's evil ambitions and come to her defense. She longed for Mark to see not only the obvious forces that could hurt her, but the hidden forces also. She knew that she couldn't let Doug see the contempt that she felt for Mark, or he would pursue her relentlessly. She had strong feelings inside, but how could she express them without causing contention. The torment she felt waged war in her soul.

The month of December brought a constant cold downpour that never seemed to stop. Mark sat under a tin roof on the donkey engine, happy that he wasn't working out in the weather. The rain had no effect on the steam donkey.

Mark proudly learned how to use it to its best advantage. This new machine doubled production after the first week

By the end of the week a few horses were sold, and the other's turned loose. Mark missed them, for they were his partners. He treated them kindly and bonded with them. They would do what he asked of them; they trusted him. Now he was at the controls of a machine that had no life apart from him. It was alive only when fired up, dead when shut down. Lacking a mind of its own—Mark was total master.

The donkey engine had two drums. One for the mainline, and the other for the haul back. The mainline ran out the skid road to a block, which was a large pulley weighing eighty to a hundred pounds. On the end of the mainline sat the carriage, which held the cables that hooked to the logs. The haul back was connected to the back of the carriage. It ran through a first block and then a second block, then back to the second drum. The mainline could be pulled out to get a turn of logs and pulled back to the donkey, all with action from the levers. The mainline was double the size of the haul back. It was the workhorse.

The fireman, who filled the burner so steam would generate power, was a young man of seventeen years. His name was Charles Boyd. He worked hard to keep the fire going for the donkey. It was one of the lowest paying jobs in the woods, yet he needed to start somewhere, and work his way up. He quit school to help support his family after his father had been killed by a falling tree. He was the sole wage earner for his mother, five sisters, and one younger brother. He was small, being only five feet, but his arms were as big as his thighs. McMaster told him, "Never let the fire go out," and he hadn't failed since taking the job. He'd cut a cord of wood within an hour after arriving on the site, and then would stand by the wood and smile at Mark as if he had won a game.

Mark worked the levers as he looked at Charlie. "Enjoying your new job?"

"Yes," Charlie said.

"Do you want to go back to school?"

"No"

"Going to work in the woods all your life?"

"Yes," he said as he threw another log in the firebox.

"Can you say more than yes or no?"

Charlie smiled. "No."

Mark laughed. "I didn't think so."

Mark felt sorry for the boy and thought he should watch out for him in the woods as well as keep him away from the men who would lead him down the wrong path.

Mark enjoyed his new job. There wasn't much walking, and it kept him out of the rain for the most part. He was by a hot fire when it became cold. The only job he thought was better was being an engineer of the locomotive. Running back and forth up the mountain hauling logs to the log dump.

He pulled a lever to bring in a turn of logs. Out of the corner of his eye he caught sight of a young man sitting on a huge stump, watching him. He knew he'd seen him before, and remembered it was when Steven died. He kept working, but every once in a while he would check to see if he was still being watched. Charlie saw the young man also and kept an eye on him. The young man sat on the stump, a cedar hat on his head, chewing on a piece of grass, watching the workings of the donkey engine.

At noon Mark shut the donkey down to eat lunch. The young man jumped off the stump and walked toward Mark and Charlie. He walked all around the donkey, looking it over, shaking his head. Mark and Charlie sat eating their lunches watching him look everything over. Mark looked at the visitor. "If you want work, you have to go down to the office to apply."

The young man looked at Mark, still shaking his head. "Nope, don't need any work. I've plenty of things to do."

"Then what do you want?" Mark asked in a demeaning tone.

"Looking at this new fangled machine. Could be problems—yep, lots of problems. Bring something into the forest that doesn't belong—could be problems."

"You don't know what you're talking about."

"I may not know all that you know, but what I do know—I know, and I know this could be a problem," he said with a big grin on his face, which made Charlie smile also.

"What's your name?"

"Caleb Cultas. What's yours?"

"Mark, and this is Charlie."

"I know Charlie's family. His sister was sweet on me when I went to school a few years back."

Saying those words brought Charlie's memory back. "Yes, I do remember you. You always sat in the back of the class and didn't say much, and you only attended for a week or so."

"Yep, didn't need that school—learned everything I needed to know from my grandfather. He taught me to read and write. And he taught me that things in wrong places can be problems. It's usually not what is seen that destroys, but what is unseen. Yep, big problems."

"Will you shut up about the problems?" Mark said, shaking his head.

Caleb walked back over to his stump and climbed on top again and sat down. Mark looked at him, thinking the boy was strange. Just as McMaster said the first day they saw him carrying that stove. "What are you going to do now?" Mark asked.

"Sit here and watch you. Watch for a problem and let you know when I see it."

Mark felt as though he was arguing with his younger brother just as he did back in Scotland. He finished his lunch and went back to running the donkey. Caleb sat on the stump and watched for almost an hour and then jumped off, walked up to Mark and said, "I see the problem."

With those words he walked off into the woods, fading from sight. Mark wondered to himself what the problem might be. He shook his head, smirking inside, thinking that Caleb would get along really well with that old Indian woman Rose.

CHAPTER 9

▼

THE CAMP

The snow came in January. Victoria watched it fall through the branches and land on the ground. The snow lying under the tall trees was safe from the sun and sometimes wouldn't melt until spring. Mark was extremely happy that he was close to the firebox on the donkey. The temperatures didn't rise above freezing and production in the forest slowed down.

McMaster was unhappy about the low production and ordered a company meeting to be held Friday after work. After all the men assembled in the mill yard, he gave them the news. "Logs are getting too far from the mill and it makes more economic sense to build a camp above the lake between the first hill and Cultas Mountain."

A few of the men grumbled.

"I have already hired men to erect the building and am in the process of hiring cooks and servers to work the camp. You will all be living in camp from Monday morning 'til Friday night. If anyone doesn't like the arrangements, he can find a job someplace else."

Work on the camp started the following Monday. Most of the men working for the company didn't mind the idea of living in a camp during the week. They would be close to work, have their meals cooked for them, and have a dry place to sleep.

In less than a month, the camp was completed. It consisted of one cookhouse with dining room for seventy-five men, and two bunkhouses each with forty bunks that were double stacked on each other. In the middle of the bunkhouse stood a wood stove to supply heat and boil water. There were a few lanterns to give light for reading, or card playing which was a more prevalent pastime.

In the camp office were maps and time cards. Next to the office stood the tool shop that also housed the filer's room. Filers were important to the logging operations because production would slow down without sharp axes and saws. The filers were the unsung heroes of the woods.

On the east side of camp sat the largest outhouse Mark had seen. It was a ten seater, and each seat had a dividing wall so that a man could have his privacy.

Men moved into camp the second week of January. It was a cold month, snowing most days, and when it wasn't snowing, it was raining. The men always stoked up the fire in their stove before they left for the timber so there would be coals when they arrived back at camp. At bedtime they would fill the stove to capacity, but some nights it wasn't enough to keep them warm.

It took only days before the bellowing began. There were many complaints about the cooking, the sleeping conditions, and the long hours away from home. Every man seemed to wallow in misery. As usual Hammer seemed to enjoy seeing the men in such a state. He, of course, being the camp foreman, had his own private room away from the infestation of lice and vile vermin that took up residence in the bunkhouse. Sometimes it was hard to tell the vermin from the men, Mark thought.

After a hard day's work, the men would often sit down to dinner in wet clothes and try to enjoy the carnage, called a meal, put before them. Doug sat down to eat and looked over what was set before him on his plate. He couldn't distinguish whether it was real food or sawdust mixed with rawhide baked to a rock-hard texture. He stood up and shouted at the cook who was dishing out this concoction. "What in the hell are you feeding us? My dog wouldn't eat this stuff if he were starvin'. I ain't going to work anymore until I get some real food here!"

What he said made sense to most of the men at camp. They all stood up and started shouting. "We're not working until we get better food, and that means breakfast in the morning," Doug said.

The workers cheered.

Hammer stood up and waved his arms around till everyone stopped talking. "No, need for everyone to get upset. There will be better food tomorrow after work. I'll promise you that."

While some men bellowed about the food, other men hovered over their plates as if Doug were asking them to throw it away. For some this was a great meal, better than what they would've made themselves. Those men felt it was best to sit down and shut up before they lost it all and had to fend for themselves. Hammer's words calmed the crew, and they went back to eating.

Mark didn't like the food that night, but he didn't complain about it. His thoughts drifted off to Victoria and the delightful meals she would make. He thought about how his mother was the best cook of all. He looked at Doug and pointed at the food. "Sit down and be happy that you have food and a place to work! The food will get better. This is only the first week of camp."

"Yeah, but I still don't like it."

"Well, stop your ranting and eat. Then we can go play some cards."

After dinner the men made their way to the bunkhouse. Mark took off his shirt and tin pants and hung them on a wire that ran across the space between the two sets of bunks. The fire burned hot in the stove, but the heat dissipated fast.

When Mark climbed into his top bunk, he could see his breath as he exhaled. Doug walked over to stand near the stove. "I thought we were going to play cards?"

"It's too cold," Mark said.

He pulled his blanket over himself and thought of being with Victoria. He missed being next to her, and having her warm body next to his. He missed her hands touching his back as he fell off to sleep. He knew that come Friday he would be back beside her again. A question forced Mark out of his thoughts. "Have you been with a soiled dove?" Doug asked.

All the men in the bunkhouse looked at Mark as they waited to hear what he was going to say. The room fell silent as they stared Mark down. "No," he said.

Doug laughed, as did the rest of the men. "Last time I was in Seattle I was with the most beautiful dove I have ever seen," Doug said.

"I was with her also," another shouted.

For the rest of the night the men talked of the soiled doves they had visited. The ones they liked the most, and what kind of woman they would dream of that night.

One of the men looked at Doug pointing at him. "I have seen you leaving Jezzy's place."

"No, I have never set foot near her place," Doug said.

"Oh yes you have," the man said, as others started to laugh.

"I think you're blind."

"No, you're blind to be able to climb into her bed."

The men all laughed as Doug looked for an escape. "How could you have seen me there? Only if you spend your time there also."

They all turned their eyes on the man. "Yes, I visit her place often—why not? Everyone needs lovin'."

For the next twenty minutes everyone either admitted or denied to have set foot in Jezzy's place. It made for good entertainment as each of the guilty parties tried to exonerate himself.

Mark stretched out in his bed as he listened to the stories and lies being told by the lonely-hearted men. What more was there to life? Work all day in the forest with rain beating at you incessantly for low pay. Sit in a bunkhouse filled with men who were as lonely and miserable as you. To think of the woman you love, or to dream of the one you wish to love were all that most of these loggers had left at the end of their long, weary days.

Doug hung his head over his bunk and looked at Mark. "Tell us Mark, what's Victoria like?"

Again all eyes turned toward Mark as they waited for his answer. Most of the men had seen her when they were helping Mark build his house. Others had seen her around town, and some hadn't seen her at all. Mark had a smile on his face. "She's nice—really nice."

"Is that all you're going to say?" Doug asked, prodding him on.

"She's young and has much to learn, but she's nice and that's all I'm going to say."

All the men started to laugh, as Doug kept asking more questions. Mark laughed with them, taking no offense at Doug's prodding or the men's jests.

Doug laughed along with them, but inside his contempt grew toward Mark. He really wanted to know what Victoria was like; it was she and not another that he dreamed of when he fell asleep. His contempt for Mark grew not out of hatred for the man, but because of the ignorance and naiveté that Mark displayed concerning the motives and intents that Doug had toward Victoria. In Doug's heart he repeated, "What a stupid man." Those were his thoughts as he drifted off to sleep.

Mark listened to the last voices fade to silence. He thought about the good friend he had in Doug and the others he was growing to know, how things in America were better than he imagined, and how he saw nothing but good in store for years to come. These thoughts rested his heart and put him to sleep for the night.

*   *   *   *

Victoria didn't like being alone during the week. She couldn't sleep well, waking at every sound. Her eyes were often tired when she woke up in the morning. She would look forward to Friday nights when her husband would return. Not too long after Mark started living up at camp she found herself feeling ill when she woke in the morning. Her stomach was upset and she felt that she was coming down with a sickness. On these mornings she would have to force herself out of bed to get on with her chores. After she got up and started to do some things around the house she found she felt much better.

One day, she was still lying in bed, when she heard Rose singing outside. She heard a knock at the door. "Come in Rose." Victoria yelled.

Rose opened the door, walked in and looked around. "I'm in my room Rose."

As Rose entered, Victoria raised her hand motioning for Rose to stop. "Better stay back—I think I might be ill."

Rose smiled and reached out to hold Victoria's hand. "You're not sick in a bad way—you're with child. I heard the deer speak of children."

"If I'm with child, Mark will be in good spirits when he hears of it," Victoria said as she climbed out of bed.

"I'll also write my sister and tell her the good news—and my mother—oh—there is so much that needs to be done."

It was as if her face illuminated the whole room. She twirled and danced into the kitchen, stopping to put water on to boil for tea. Rose's heart was glad for her, for Rose had never given birth.

"I'll help you—give you medicine from the earth to ease the pain in birth. I'll help you when you're weak—I'll be your strength."

Tears appeared in Victoria's eyes. The warmth and love she experienced from Rose was overwhelming. The things she'd read back in Scotland about the savages that inhabited the west—the killings—their barbaric ways—their inferiority compared to whites—was nothing near the truth when it came to the Indian woman Rose. This was her friend.

Victoria thought about the Natives and their land. Had it occurred to the white men that arrived in the Northwest that the Indians, like themselves, would try to defend their land? All the places the settlers arrived from, whether Scotland, France, England, Germany, or any other place in the world, had at one time or another defended their right to keep the land where they lived. Why would these aboriginals be any different? Yet the same men who at one time fought invaders to keep their land, thought nothing of the Indians who fought to keep theirs. People are the same no matter where you live, Victoria thought.

*   *   *   *

Mark was tired as he rode the last train to the log dump late Friday. It was dark and the men who were with him all sat atop the logs on the connects. The air was cold as the train pulled the loaded connects down the hill, but it was better than walking the long distance to town.

Upon arriving at the log dump, some men jumped off the train and headed straight to Jezzy's house. McMaster made the trip to the camp and paid the men before they left for town. With money in hand, they had lots to catch up on after being in camp all week. Mark made his way home. He walked through town past the mill and up the hill to his house. Victoria met him outside the door, all smiles.

"I've something to tell you, Mark."

"And what is that?" Mark asked, uninterested.

"We're going to have a child."

Mark looked at her, surprised, as a smile crawled across his face. She said it again. "We're going to have a child—isn't this wonderful?"

"Yes, it is—I do hope it's a boy."

"I just want a healthy baby—it doesn't matter if it's a girl or boy."

Mark wrapped his arms around Victoria and gave her a kiss. He was going to be a father; he couldn't wait to tell Doug and the others he worked with.

*   *   *   *

McMaster increased the size of the mill and logging operations, which helped the town of Clear Lake grow. Next to the mill office McMaster had a company boarding house built, because so many of the men and boys who came to work for his company were single, or had left their families back on the homestead. It would cost him less money to have them stay at his own place than to pay Mr. Stevens for rooms. He would actually make money by charging the men for their stay at his boarding house.

McMaster planned to have the men that lived in or near the town of Clear Lake work in the mill. The others he would hire to work out in the forest. There he could keep them in the camps, fed and housed away from town.

*   *   *   *

After a few weeks of living in the camp, Mark began to really hate camp life. Lice and fleas took up residence in the bunkhouses. The stench of damp clothes drying, and the wet conditions in the woods themselves were almost unbearable to even the foulest man in camp. One of the older men had taken to sleeping in an old hollow cedar stump to keep away from the vermin and the stench. Mark wished he could move in with him, but he knew there was only room for one.

Mark would stretch out in his bunk at night with a blanket he had brought from home and scratch and slap at the vermin until he fell asleep. He would get up in the morning and head to breakfast. In camp the men were now being fed well. Sleeping conditions could be bad, but it would be the end of the camp and McMaster's company if the men were not fed well.

Mark told every man in camp that he was going to be a father. Most of the men were happy for him, but some weren't. "You poor bastard," Hammer said.

Doug pretended he was happy for Mark, but inside he burned with jealousy.

Mark fast became a respected man in camp and in town. He was a friend to everyone who meant something and even to those who didn't. Men would confide in him about their personal lives, knowing he was someone they could talk with. Of the men who lived in camp, he was one of the older ones, as most of the men were in their late teens or early twenties. Mark, being almost thirty, was looked upon as one of the old men. It always made him laugh when someone only four years younger would call him gramps.

Mark was a friend to all, and he wanted to have high standing in the community. He trusted those around him that he considered friends, but he didn't trust men that wandered from place to place and didn't have work. He couldn't understand how Victoria had chosen to be friends with savages. He didn't trust the natives, he didn't trust Rose—he didn't know that he had much to learn about trust. He would often remember the words Caleb spoke while watching the steam donkey. "It's usually not what is seen that destroys, but what is unseen."

Mark operated the donkey engine on the same site that Doug worked falling trees. With a new man as bucker, they were setting records for getting logs out of the woods in a single day. The new man was a big Swede of only nineteen. He had worked in the woods before, and came to the Skagit Valley looking for better pay. McMaster looked at the size of the man and hired him on the spot. His name was Ivar Svenson, and he was over six foot four and weighed over two hundred-fifty pounds. This man was all muscle with no fat and few brains.

On the first day he walked into camp with his brindle at the end of a ten foot cross-cut saw, fear struck the hearts of the jesters of the camp. They sized him up and knew that if they teased this new man, they might get a good whippin'. Mark befriended him and so did Doug. Mark and Doug both knew Ivar would be a good man to have on their side.

Ivar walked into the bunkhouse and put his brindle down on a bunk by the door. He didn't want that bunk, for it was already taken. He was just going to look for an open bunk and didn't want to carry his brindle up and down the narrow aisles. The man whose bunk he had set his brindle on, ran and grabbed his own things and moved them to an open bunk.

Ivar looked down at the man. "I am not chasing you out of your bunk—I'm only looking for a bunk that's empty. I can move my brindle."

"That's fine, I need a new bunk anyway."

"What's a brindle?" Mark asked.

"It's a bed roll with everything we own—a traveling logger has to have one," Ivar said.

The other man found an empty bunk. "I found me a new bunk—you can keep that one."

He wasn't about to upset Ivar in any way. Doug could sense that Ivar wasn't a violent man and that he was just a boy in a big body. Yet he wasn't going to let the others know this, so he could use it to his advantage.

Doug laughed, watching all the men going out of their way to keep from upsetting Ivar. The only men that didn't were Mark and Hammer. Hammer called him Sasquash, after the Indian legend, because his feet, Hammer said, "could span any gully they would encounter on this mountain."

It was true his boots were the biggest in camp, but no one else dared to comment about his feet.

When it came to bucking logs, there were none faster. He could run a ten-foot cross-cut saw as if he were cutting through butter. He would spend an hour after dinner sharpening his saw even though the company supplied filers. "I can do a better job than they could ever dream of doing," he said.

*   *   *   *

Victoria spent time looking at some new material that had arrived in Beddall's store. She was working on making clothes for her expected child. As she dug through the pile, a woman came up and grabbed the top roll of material.

"I need that," Jezzy said as she pulled it close to her.

Victoria smiled at her. "I didn't want that one, so you may have it."

Jezzy laid the material back down and looked at Victoria. "I guess I don't need that one either. Which one do you need?"

"Why do you ask that?"

"Because the one you want is the one I need."

Victoria looked at the rolls. "I need them all."

Jezzy let out a laugh. "You got me. You know I won't buy them all."

"I know, I didn't think you could."

Jezzy reached out her hand. "My name is Jezzy, what's yours?"

"Victoria, and it's nice to meet you."

Jezzy sized Victoria up and down, wondering if this young woman knew who she was. "Do you know who I am?"

Now everyone in town knew Jezzy, and what she did since she had the only brothel around. "Yes, I know who you are, and I know what you do," Victoria replied.

"Then why are you talking to me? Don't you know I might soil you?"

"No, I may get dirt on me, but it can wash off—anything can be cleansed—even the inside of a person."

"Sounds as if you have been talking to that Indian woman Rose."

Victoria smiled. "Yes, I have"

Jezzy reached out and felt Victoria's stomach. "You've been doing what I do." She let out a loud laugh, as Victoria felt a bit embarrassed.

"In a way I've been doing the same thing as you, but I'm married and in love, and that's different."

"Listen, you may think it's different, but we all make them pay somehow. Whether they pay with money or good deeds—they all pay."

A couple of women watched them talk, and whispered between themselves, which made Victoria feel uncomfortable.

"Would you like to come to my place for tea?" Victoria asked.

Jezzy's eyes lit up. She had never been invited to another woman's house before. She knew most women hated her because of her life style. Yet, here was a young woman who was married and asking her over. "Yes, I would," Jezzy replied.

They left without buying anything and started walking together toward the house.

"Why are you being nice to me? Don't you know everyone will be talking about you?" Jezzy asked.

"I find you interesting, and I'd like to get to know you better. Besides they already talk about the company I keep—why not give them something else to talk about?" she said laughing.

Arriving at the house, they went inside and Jezzy took a seat by the window. Victoria made some tea and worked at keeping up with all the questions Jezzy asked.

"Do you think less of me because of my work?"

Victoria started to answer but Jezzy cut in. "Have you ever been with another man other than your husband?"

Victoria smiled. "No."

"Do you want that?" Silence hung in the room. "Well, do you? Come on, you can tell me."

"It's not right to desire other men in that way," Victoria responded.

"I'm not asking whether it's right or wrong—I'm asking what you want."

"I've never really thought of it before. So I guess not."

Jezzy chuckled while looking into Victoria's eyes. "You guess. You're telling me that you don't know what you think about that? You're telling me that you don't know how you feel inside? Come now, I think you know yourself better than that. Every woman at one time or another wants another man. We're just afraid to admit that."

"I'm in love with Mark, and he's the only one I desire."

Jezzy hung her head and watched her feet as she kicked the floor. "Love— what's love? I've loved many—yet have I been in love? Maybe, maybe not."

"When were you in love?"

"I'm in love every night. Sometimes four of five times a night."

"I don't believe that, Jezzy."

"Well, I pretend to be, and that's what a lot of women do. They pretend to be in love. I see a lot of the women around here pretending to be in love with their men, but they're just surviving and getting through this life, hanging on to some kind of dream."

"Having a dream is good."

"Yes it is, but there are differences between dreams and reality."

"I dream of always being happy and that is real."

"I've seen you with your husband, and you don't look all that happy most of the time, either. Now that I think about it, it's not only women that pretend. I have a certain logger that comes to my place and is only happy if I have a woman that looks like Victoria Southerland—I didn't know who this Victoria was until today."

"Who would ask such a thing?"

"A young man named Doug. He comes into my place and all he wants is a woman that looks like you. Do you know him?"

"Yes, he's a friend of my husband."

"Oh, interesting," Jezzy said. She lingered waiting for Victoria to reply. Victoria had a shocked looked on her face and was in deep thought. "The way I see things is that you and I aren't much different. We both pretend—the only difference is that you pretend with one man and and I pretend with many," Jezzy said.

Victoria pondered those words as she looked into her own heart. What did she feel? Did she pretend? Was she really in love? These thoughts took hold deep in her soul as she wrestled to find answers.

"Now you're thinking about whether I'm right. I can see it in your expression, in the way you hold your cup. It's all right, dear, he won't know you're pretending. Men just want to be made to feel a certain way. Have relations with them, and they'll believe anything. Scream, let out a little laugh, say oh God, oh God, and men think they're the greatest."

"I'm not pretending Jezzy, I have learned to love Mark," she said.

"I pretend, and so do the girls who work for me, and so do a lot of women around town. The husbands tell me more than they tell their wives."

"Mark would never go to a place like yours."

"You're probably right, some men never will."

Victoria wondered what made a man secure in a relationship. When did his heart question the love of his wife? What made her secure in Mark? Would she question his love for her? Jezzy made her think about things she had never addressed.

Jezzy sipped her tea, savoring the taste. She drank more like a man than a woman, which made Victoria laugh. "No, hold the cup this way," she said to Jezzy.

Victoria showed Jezzy the proper way for a lady to hold a cup. Jezzy adjusted her grip. "Now, do I look lady like?"

They both laughed, and enjoyed the new friendship that was developing between them.

*   *   *   *

Mark slowly became accustomed to camp life. He had his friends with whom he would play cards in the evening after dinner. McMaster had a strict rule about no whiskey in camp, the men fearing for their jobs quickly learned to follow his rules.

Mark struggled to get comfortable in bed as he listened to the rain falling on the roof. "Is the rain ever going to stop?" he asked Doug.

"Yep, next summer sometime I reckon."

At times it would pour for days on end. Then the sun would peak through the clouds only to disappear moments later. Mark would rise in the morning to the sound of rain bouncing on the cedar shakes. He would be soaked by the time he made his way to the mess hall. Inside he took his usual place next to Doug and Ivar. The three spent a lot of their free time together. They were becoming good friends as well as one of the best logging teams for McMaster's company.

It would be raining as they made their way into the forest. It would rain on them as they worked. It would rain on them at lunch. It would rain on them in the afternoon. It would rain as they made their way back to the camp. It would rain and rain and then rain some more.

Wet and musty were the smells that crawled out of the bunkhouse along with every variety of vermin imagined by men. It was a fight of survival between the loggers, the lice, the fleas, and the bugs. Most of the time the vermin won. Hammer hung a sign over the door to the bunkhouse. "Vermin with Vermin." He used the words to curse the men every chance he got. It was as if he sat around thinking of new ways to belittle the men everyday.

At the end of each week, the tempers of the men would become short. The virtues of patience, kindness, and brotherly love were not qualities to be found in the logging camp bunkhouse.

Mark took a seat near the stove, removed off his wet socks and hung them to dry. The warmth of the fire felt good as he raised his feet over the small stove. His toes were wrinkled from being wet all day. He sat back and let out a soothing murmur as the heat surrounded his feet, warming them.

The bunkhouse door opened and in walked Glen Preston. He hated himself, and because of that he hated everyone else. No one liked working with the man because of the way he treated others. He never had anything good to say about anyone or anything. Most men thought he was the son of Hammer, and would laugh at that thought. Preston looked at Mark as he stepped toward him, raised his foot and pushed Mark off the stool he was sitting on.

"This is my place, you little shit!"

Mark looked up at him, not saying a word. Then he stood up looking Glen directly in the eye. He could feel anger and hate rising up inside him. He clenched his fist and stood his ground. Glen stood with a wicked smirk on his face. "Go ahead, hit me—come on, hit me—I'm looking for someone to kill right about now—just give me a reason—hit me!"

Mark was not much of a fighter. He wanted to hit him, he wanted to humiliate him, and he wanted to crush him. Yet, he was over matched by the size and strength of Glen. Mark turned away, making his way to his bunk, knowing that all the men were watching to see what was going to happen. Mark could feel their eyes on him as he walked—eyes of those that saw him as wise, and eyes of those that thought saw him as a coward. He heard a few men laugh. Silence filled the room as Mark turned and started back toward Glen. Doug jumped up and grabbed Mark. "Don't do it. He isn't worth it."

Glen pushed Doug away from Mark and raised his fist. "Let him fight his own battle asshole!"

Ivar stood up from his bunk and walked over to Glen. He looked down. "Do you have a problem?"

Glen didn't say a word as he looked up at Ivar. "I think it best that you leave now," Ivar growled.

Glen looked Ivar up and down and then turned and walked out the door thinking, another time. Mark helped Doug up off the floor and then patted Ivar on the shoulder. "Thanks Ivar, you kept me from getting a good beating."

The men went back to talking and playing cards. They had all seen fights over nothing before and this was no different. Some of the most entertaining fights came during the card games. The dim light provided by kerosene lamps would barely allow the men to see the color of the cards or their kind and this was often a bone of contention in the bunkhouse.

Mark, Doug, and Ivar sat by the stove watching their socks dry. "All three of us should have just beaten the hell out of him," Doug said.

Ivar chuckled. "I could take him myself. I don't need any help."

Doug laughed. "The only thing you've ever hurt is a tree. You've never been in a fight, have you?"

"Once, when I was young. I hit a man and I thought I killed him. My father was mad and told me to never fight again, but I will if any man bothers my friends."

Mark looked at both of them. "He meant to do me harm—he has bad intent. We should just stay away from him as much as possible. Fighting never solved many things anyway."

Mark rose and crawled into his bunk. "Tomorrow is Friday—payday. Tomorrow I'll be with my wife at home."

He turned his back to the men and shut his eyes, fading off to sleep. Ivar had a sad look on his face. "I wish I had a wife and a home."

Doug held a stick in his hand, messing with the fire and said in a low voice, "I wish I had Victoria."

$$\ast \qquad \ast \qquad \ast \qquad \ast$$

Spring and summer came and went. Victoria looked out at the fruit trees. The leaves were dropping, forming a multi-colored carpet at their feet. The fruit was ripe, and Victoria's baby would soon be born. Her time passed quickly, the morning sickness ended months ago and her stomach was now large and round. Victoria was happy thinking about the baby she would soon have. Mark was busy making a cradle for the little one. He would be leaving the next day for another week at Camp One.

"The baby will be here soon, I'm worried that it will arrive when I'm in camp," he said.

Victoria took this opportunity to broach the subject of Rose staying with her. Rose had made the offer weeks ago. But knowing how Mark felt about her Indian friend, she had been too afraid to mention it to him.

"I've been thinking about that," she said. "Rose has said that she will stay with me while you're away, it would be safer. Please Mark, in case the baby comes quickly."

"Hmm, you know I don't like that old woman, but it seems that she is the only person that would be able to help," he said.

Mark and Victoria talked about having a little boy. Mark, because a son would carry on the family name and Victoria because she knew that it would make Mark happy. Victoria also thought about having a little girl, but kept it to herself. Mostly she just wanted a healthy baby no matter the sex.

As her time approached, Mark hoped that he would be home when the child was born. He knew that Victoria was healthy and chances were that all would be well, but he wanted to be with her when they brought this new life into the world. Victoria's mother had not prepared her for what was to happen. In fact birthing babies had never been discussed. "It's good that you won't be alone Victoria," Mark conceded.

Rose and another Indian woman attended to her. It was Friday morning and Mark was working up in Camp One. Her labor was fast and hard. It began gently, her stomach tightening rhythmically. Soon the pain was radiating throughout her body.

"Rose, please help me, the pain is unbearable, there most be something wrong," she cried.

Rose chuckled quietly to herself. "There is nothing wrong Victoria, it is as it should be. Soon your baby will be born and the pain will pass."

Several hours later Victoria delivered a healthy baby girl. Rose wrapped the child in a clean blanket and laid her in Victoria's arms. Victoria pulled her tiny face close to her breast. The baby began to feed immediately. Looking down at her child, she searched her mind for a name. "I shall call you Rachel Rose," she said with a smile. And for the first time since she left Scotland Victoria felt content.

The child was named after her sister and her new American friend. The name sounded smooth on Victoria's lips as she said it over and over. Rachel had a dark head of hair, and her eyes were as dark. Victoria continued to hold her close, cherishing her little girl. Word was sent with one of the train engineers to the company office. Mark had become a father. He couldn't contain his excitement when he heard the news. Hammer stood watching him, shaking his head. "You can dance for now, but that will soon end."

"This is a great thing Hammer, can I leave now? I need to see how Victoria is," Mark said.

"Yeah, you can take off. It's not something that happens every day. But don't tell anyone I let you go early. I don't want them to think I'm getting soft."

Mark grabbed his things and took off for home.

Rain began to fall as he made his way off the mountain. Walking the tracks out he knew it would take him a while before he made it to town. He thought if he took a short cut off the mountain he would get home faster. He left the tracks and headed through the tall timber where the limbs kept the rain from falling on him. The branches would catch each drop and appear to swallow the rain before it reached the ground.

It was dark under the canopy of tall trees. Light was shut out, making it hard for Mark to find his way. He kept telling himself to go down hill, just keep going down hill.

There was a slight breeze in the trees as Mark walked along, thinking of the things that Victoria had told him about her talks with Rose. He listened closely but heard no names being whispered. Then wondered why he even gave any attention to such fables. Continuing his trek down the mountain, he heard someone talking to him.

"You lost? Your camp is back up the hill aways."

Mark jumped, startled with fear.

"Well, are you lost or what?"

Mark looked around and couldn't see anyone. "Who's there?"

Caleb stepped out from behind a giant hemlock tree and looked at Mark. "I know you. You run that new machine. The one that's going to cause problems."

Mark felt relieved that it was Caleb. "Do you get pleasure out of scaring people?"

"Did I scare you? I didn't mean to. Not much to be afraid of up here—maybe a few bears or a mountain lion, or maybe *Wawa Tyee,* but nothing else to be scared of."

"What's *Wawa Tyee?*"

"A bad spirit that the Indians believe dwells up here. Strange belief they have, but sometimes strange things do happen, and sometimes things just don't make much sense."

"You sound just like my wife's Indian friend—talking about spirits, believing in myths, talking nonsense."

"Maybe to you, but I know what I've heard and seen. Is everything you don't understand nonsense to you?"

Mark grumbled a bit and shook his head. McMaster was right, this boy was a fool. He said good-bye and started back on his way. He took a few steps as Caleb watched him. "Where are you going?"

"To town!"

"Which town?" Caleb asked.

"Are you dumb? To Clear Lake, that's where I'm going."

"Oh, well, you're not going the right way. If you keep going that way you'll end up in Big Lake. It's a town, but not the one you're looking for."

Mark stopped, turning back toward Caleb. "What do you mean? I'm heading down this mountain. The camp is up and Clear Lake is down."

Caleb smiled. "You're right, but you're in a hidden valley in the mountain. You need to go up that hill over there and back down—then you'll be in Clear Lake. You follow this valley and it will turn south on you and lead you the wrong way."

Mark looked at Caleb then back down the valley. "Are you sure?"

"As sure as it's raining. Follow me, I'll show you the way."

Caleb took off running through the trees. Mark had to hustle to keep pace with him. He had never seen a man climb a steep hill as fast as Caleb did. Mark was breathing hard when he finally crested the hill and saw a glimmer of light coming from the mill. Caleb seemed proud of himself for being right. He pointed his finger at the light of the mill. "There it is."

"Thank you, you were right, I would've ended up in a place far from home. What were you doing out here anyway?"

"Something told me you needed help."

"What? You're telling me…"

Mark looked back to face Caleb as he talked to him, and Caleb was nowhere to be found. It gave him the chills, and he took off for town at a brisk pace.

The rain showed no signs of slowing as Mark made his way into town. He walked through town, and arrived at his house and heard the sound of crying inside. He rushed into the house and went right to Victoria. Taking Rachel into his arms, he held her close.

"What shall we name her?"

"Rachel, Rachel Rose. Rachel after my sister and Rose after my friend."

Mark's face turned sour. "We aren't naming her after an Indian. People would laugh at us."

"But Mark, please."

"No Victoria, I won't have it, think of something else. Hell, you can name her after your mother or my mother, but an Indian, not a chance. I'm telling you Victoria I won't stand for it. Victoria knew that he wouldn't change his mind. "All right Mark," she said.

"Actually, I've decided," Mark said. "We will call her Rachel Leigh after my mother and your sister. The decision is made Victoria."

Mark walked out of the room leaving Victoria crying. She closed her eyes, feeling her tears weeping out through her long lashes.

Her heart hurt as she sat up in bed. She felt as though she had cried enough tears to fill the sea she had crossed to come with Mark to this land. She closed her eyes and thought of Scotland as she drifted off to sleep.

CHAPTER 10

▼

BETRAYAL

Victoria happily spent her days caring for her family. Being a good mother came naturally to her and Rachel thrived on the attention. Mark continued to work long hours in the woods, and was always exhausted when he returned to his family. On his arrival he wanted to relax, but couldn't find time with his growing responsibilities. It was important to him to be a good father and wished that he had more time to spend with Rachel. The changes in her from one week to the next astounded him. Mark was filled with pride about his child.

Victoria eventually grew accustomed to Mark being gone. There were things she liked about it and things she found difficult. She could visit with Rose and Jezzy, and a new lady who moved into town named Olivia, who arrived in early June. She and Victoria quickly become good friends. This pleased Mark because she was not an Indian or a prostitute. Olivia just happened to gossip more than anyone in the county, but Mark could live with that.

The town grew at a steady rate with people arriving every month. The talk around town was that a new partnership was about to take place. The mill would be updated and expanded which would mean more jobs, and more opportunities for people to make money and a better life. For the latest news most people would hunt down Olivia.

More jobs meant more men. Jezzy told Victoria her plans of opening another house for young ladies. She would always joke with Victoria. "If you get lonely for male companionship, come work for me. You can have some fun and make some money."

Victoria would always hold up her hand and shake her head. "Now, a proper lady would never have such a thought!"

Olivia would feel left out. "What about me? Would I make a good dove?"

"Hell no, you would talk too much and bore the men to death," Jezzy said.

Then they would all laugh. Victoria would laugh, but inside she felt sad, knowing that for some girls this was the only choice they had. She knew that she would never resort to that kind of work, yet she never spoke a word of condemnation toward those that did.

*   *   *   *

Another year came and went. The summer was a mild one with the sun hidden behind clouds most of the time; the forest never had a chance to dry out. The longest stretch of sunshine was eight days. Logging was good. Each month the team of Mark, Doug, and Ivar would either match or out-produce the other teams. Mark fully mastered the steam donkey, and there wasn't a part on it he couldn't fix, or a jam he couldn't work out of. He had the respect of other men in camp and the respect of McMaster.

Mark ran the levers, pulling in a turn of logs always aware of the things around him. Danger was everywhere in the forest—you never knew what would jump out and bite you. As Mark worked he saw Ivar running up the skid road. He ran up to Mark and began speaking but was out of breath. "Doug has been hurt."

Mark turned a valve draining off the steam of the donkey and took off running, following Ivar. They found Doug lying on the ground next to a tree. He was unconscious, and Mark dropped to his knees next to Doug, and lifted Doug's head into his lap. Doug opened his eyes and tried to focus on Mark.

"Are you all right?" Mark asked.

Doug responded with a nod, as he tried to focus on Mark. "He took a blow from a falling branch," Ivar said pointing at a large branch lying next to Doug.

"That widow maker almost got you," Mark said.

"I'm not married, so how could it have been a widow maker? It was just a damn heavy branch," Doug mumbled as he tried to stand up.

"We need to get him help right now," Mark said.

Ivar and Mark helped Doug to his feet. Then Ivar started to shake his head back and forth. "If we take him to town, we'll all get fired. I need this job so I think we should just wait, or McMaster will fire us for sure."

"He needs help now. Help me get him to the connects, at least we can get him back to camp."

Mark and Ivar walked Doug back toward camp. Hammer happened upon them as they were almost into camp. He let out a line of obscenities that could have been heard all the way to Seattle. "What in the hell are you men doing away from your logging site? You better have a good answer, or you'll all be sent packing with your brindles."

"Doug was hurt—a widow maker almost got him."

Anger had never found a better host than Hammer. His face was as red as it could get. His ears were glowing so much that had it been dark, they could have supplied the whole camp with light. "Didn't I tell you when we used oxen and horses that you could stop work to care for them if they were injured because animals cost us money? But men are free, they cost us nothing—if one dies or gets hurt, he can be replaced without any cost to the company. There's always someone waiting for a job, so you three better get back to work now, damn it!"

Doug faded in and out of consciousness, and Mark knew he was in no condition to work. "Mr. Hammer, let us take Doug to the bunkhouse and Ivar and I'll get back to work."

Hammer looked at Doug seeing that he wasn't in good shape. "Well, hurry up! You've already cost this company money by slacking off."

They helped Doug into the bunkhouse and left to return to work. As they were walking back to the site they both thought about Hammer and Doug. "When work is over tonight I'll take Doug into town on the last train," Mark said.

"Yeah, that will be a good thing."

"Hammer is a real bastard—what if he were down? Would he just want men to keep working or take care of him?"

"I'd let him die," Ivar said.

"I'd help him—show him how men should be treated."

"I wish you were our boss. Anything would be better than him."

Later that night Mark arrived in town with Doug. The nearest doctor was in Mount Vernon. They would send for him in the morning. Doug was able to walk and talk, but his vision was blurred. Mark didn't want to leave him alone, but knew he had to get back to camp or risk losing his job. Mark decided to take Doug to his house and have Victoria care for him. It was the best thing he could do for his friend.

*   *   *   *

Victoria's days were filled with work of every kind. Caring for Rachel and Doug took up most of her time, though Doug spent most of his time sleeping. Doc Meadows showed up at the house and checked Doug over. Victoria watched. "Is he going to be okay?"

"He will recover fully in about two weeks. He has taken a hard blow to his head and suffered a concussion."

"Will his sight return to normal?"

"Yes, he sure is lucky that the blow didn't kill him."

The doctor gave some medicine to Victoria to administer to Doug twice a day. "If he gets worse send for me."

"I will, thanks for your time Dr. Meadows."

Rose stopped by every day to help Victoria. She would take Rachel out for walks, and show her the wonderful things found in nature. She would sing Rachel songs of the legends handed down to her from her grandparents. Stories of how things came to be, of her people, and of things to come. It was a blessing for Victoria to have some help.

Rose would make medicine from plants that she took out of the forest and try to get Doug to eat it. He refused and threw the medicine on the floor. Victoria knelt down and picked up the mess. "She makes a good strong medicine."

"If that's the case then why are so many of them dead?"

Rose shook her head. "Some things can never be healed. Your head may be better in time, but I doubt if your heart will rid itself of the sickness that dwells there."

*   *   *   *

Sometimes Victoria wondered if she would make it to thirty years of age. The work it took to keep a fire going in the winter and all the work to put food on the table drained every ounce of strength out of her. Some nights she would fall into a deep sound sleep, and not even Rachel's crying could wake her. She would look into the mirror that Mark had bought, see her face and think that she looked old, older than her nineteen years. But this was the life she was destined to live, and she would make the best of it for Mark, for Rachel, and for herself.

Doug began to feel better and spent more time awake. He would get up and bring in wood for Victoria in the mornings. During the day he would ask if there was anything that he could do to help her out. He followed her around all day, reaching for every opportunity to have a conversation with her. He thought if he could talk to her, she would see that he was the man she should be with instead of Mark.

He was consumed with thoughts of holding Victoria in his arms, with thoughts of kissing her, with thoughts of making love to her. He worked hard to make eye contact, anticipating her moves to make sure that her eyes would meet his. As they were talking one morning, Rose walked into the house. Victoria was happy to see her because Doug's presence was making her increasingly nervous. Doug wasn't happy to see Rose, because he knew that with Rose there he wouldn't have Victoria's undivided attention.

Rose walked into the kitchen as Victoria followed. She turned and faced Victoria. "That man doesn't have good intentions with your soul."

Victoria thought about how helpful Doug was being.

"Oh, Rose, he's just lonely, and I've cared for him, so he feels for me."

"No, I can see his heart and it's not good. The robin told me to come here because someone was trying to steal your affection. When I walked in the house, I could feel his badness—like the fox he is sly and cunning."

"If you were alone, wouldn't you want to feel loved? It's that way with Doug, I think his intentions are not all bad."

Rose sighed. "Your compassion lacks understanding—it distorts your view of what is real sometimes. Please watch yourself and guard your heart, that's all I ask."

"I will."

Rose left out the back door as Doug walked into the kitchen. He stopped and leaned up against the table. "What did that old squaw want?"

His voice was condescending—not only to Victoria, but his tone indicated that he was superior to Rose. Victoria responded quickly, defending her friend. "She's not an old squaw, she's my friend, and she was just checking to see if I need any help."

Doug laughed at her. "One thing that I do agree with your husband about is that you should stop visiting with all these Indians. It's not a good thing."

Victoria slammed a cup down on the counter. "Why? Why is that not a good thing? Because they're different? Because they're brown? Or is it because you don't understand them, you fear them, or maybe you think you're better than they are? You have a lot to learn, Doug. I think you're well enough to go back to work now."

Doug put his head down and didn't respond. This isn't what he desired. He made a mistake and he shouldn't have said anything bad about her fiends. Instead of drawing her closer, he had pushed her away. He didn't know what to say to make things right. As she started to leave, he reached out and touched her arm.

She stopped, turning toward Doug as he pulled her close and started to kiss her. She let the kiss linger for a moment, becoming lost in the rush of excitement. His kiss was more passionate than Mark's. Momentarily she found herself lost in his strong embrace. Her feelings surprised her. She didn't even like this man yet she allowed him to kiss her. She pulled back trying to break free. She knew that this wasn't the love she was seeking. "Doug, I can't be with you, I belong to Mark. I owe my loyalty to Mark."

She took a step back from Doug as he moved toward her again. Doug pulled Victoria close as she resisted. His hands were strong as was his voice of reason. "If Mark loves you he has a strange way of showing it, he's totally oblivious of your needs, he can't even see when someone is in pursuit of you. I know what you need Victoria, give me the chance to show you how I can make you happy. Doug held her tightly and kissed her again. She turned her face to the side. Doug grabbed it and turned her back to face him. "Be with me Victoria, be with me," Doug pleaded. "I could love you more than Mark does."

Victoria longed for more love in her life. She remembered the things she discussed with her younger sister before she came to America. How they both talked about falling in love, and to have their days filled with romance. Then her mother's words flooded her mind. "Romance was a story with no factual base, a myth."

As Victoria thought about the people she knew, she saw no romance. She knew that Doug was trying to appear romantic, but she could see right through him. What he wanted had nothing to do with love.

"You don't know me, you don't know me at all. You think beauty is my whole being. My outside will grow old like Rose's and what's inside, you will never know. Doug, you and I are further apart than Mark and I will ever be."

He forced her backward as she struggled to fight free. "You will never have me, I have no desire to be with you."

He lifted her hands above her head pinning her to the wall "You do want me Victoria, I have seen the signs."

Doug looked at her with fire in his eyes. Within seconds she realized that Doug meant to take her against her will. "Dear God, don't do this to me Doug, I'm begging you."

He was strong, much stronger than Mark. He pulled at the buttons on her dress till they opened and then ripped it from her body. Looking down at her creamy skin he pushed her to the cold hard floor. Victoria was paralyzed with fear.

As he forced himself into her she screamed in horror. "You bastard! You bastard, I hate you!"

It didn't take long for him to finish. He hadn't said a word through the whole event. He moved off her body, leaving her sobbing quietly on the floor. She couldn't believe that it had actually happened. She curled up on the floor feeling dead inside. Rose appeared as Doug left the house. "Better watch yourself old squaw," he said.

"I saw *Cultas maah* so I returned. You are like him-taking things that don't belong to you. It's one thing to steal food-to steal tools—*Tyee* will take his wrath out on a man that steals the soul."

"Shut-up with your fables old woman, you'll soon be dead like the rest of you kind. Then I won't have to listen to this drivel."

"You are a bad man, soon *Tyee* will demand your soul, you will be dead long before I will."

She entered the house to find Victoria curled up on the floor. "What brought you back Rose?" she asked through her tears.

"I saw the bad *Cultas maah*. I returned as quickly as I could. It saddens me that I couldn't save you from that wretched man."

"What is *Cultas maah*?" Victoria asked Rose.

"The whites call him the camp robber-the bird who takes what doesn't belong to him. He steals in plain sight-not like the weasel that hides his deeds. You can be sure Victoria, justice will be visited on that man."

"I am so glad that you are here Rose, I am fearful that he may return."

"I will watch over you-you are safe now. Go and fetch Rachel, I hear her crying."

Victoria pulled a small rug over her nakedness and went to the bedroom to get Rachel. She lifted her from the crib, looking at her in wonder. She held her close and prayed that nothing hurtful would happen to her. "As God is my judge. I swear that no man will ever do that to me again."

On Friday evening Mark returned home from camp. Victoria had spent the afternoon preparing a nice dinner for him. Mark sat down at the table and started to eat. "I asked Doug to come for dinner this evening and he declined my invitation."

"Oh, really," she said.

"Yes, actually I was troubled by it, not so much that he said he wasn't able to come but he seemed edgy," Mark replied.

"Did something happen between you two Victoria? I know that you don't like him that much. I'm sure that it wasn't easy for you having him here."

"It was difficult as times," she replied, trying to keep her voice normal.

"Well you know how much having Doug as a friend means to me. I thank you for looking after him while he was ill."

Mark gobbled up his food and retired to his favorite chair. Victoria came over and sat down on the floor next to him. She reached her hand up and put it on his knee. "Mark, Doug makes me feel really uncomfortable. I don't want him here."

"Why is that Victoria?"

"It's a feeling I get, please Mark just don't allow him here when you aren't home."

"That's ridiculous, Doug's a good man, he will always be welcome in my home, he is like my brother."

She felt betrayed by his words. Mark often said that he didn't like her going into town by herself, or wandering in the woods alone. Yet he was blind to the fact that the greatest danger to her was in having Doug in their home.

On Saturday morning Mark worked chopping wood when Doug came walking up. Mark nodded at him as Doug walked past. "Hi Mark, I'll be right back. I'm going inside to thank Victoria for taking care of me."

Mark nodded to him as Doug headed toward the house. Victoria was busy bathing Rachel and didn't notice Doug's arrival. He walked up behind her and put his hand on her shoulders. She thought it was Mark and let out a soft sigh. "Nice to know that you miss my touch Victoria."

Startled, she turned around facing Doug. "Don't come near me, don't you ever come near me again!"

She wrapped Rachel in a towel and walked to the door. "Mark, can you come help me please? I need some more water."

"Ask Doug to help you, I'm busy," he yelled back.

Doug smiled when he heard what Mark said. "See, he has complete trust in me. I can have you at the same time he does."

Victoria wanted to slap the smirk off Doug's face. He made her sick, but she couldn't make a scene with Mark around. She couldn't tell Mark what happened. She needed to do something to stop Doug's advances. "Doug, you are leaving me no choice but to tell Mark what you did to me. If he leaves me, so be it. But one thing is certain. I will never be with you. I hate you with every part of my heart and soul! You disgust me!"

Her words cut into him deeply, and he realized that she meant them. He left by the back door walking slowly into the woods. He wondered why Victoria couldn't see that he loved her. He felt as though he couldn't live without her in his life. Doug thought about many things as he walked, some good, some bad, and some plain evil. Above all he wanted Victoria and knew that he would never have her. He walked into camp and went to his bunk with evil rooted deep in his soul.

$$*\qquad*\qquad*\qquad*$$

Mark showed up in camp on Monday morning with all the other men. In the cookhouse he sat next to Hammer to talk about a new skid road. Doug kept his distance from Mark fearing that Victoria had told him. He was sure she had, because every morning Mark had sat next to him, and this morning Mark sat next to Hammer.

After breakfast Doug made his way out into the timber, some of the biggest timber he had ever been in. The trees were over two hundred feet tall and averaging nine to fourteen feet at the butt. There were Douglas fir, Western Red Cedar, and Western Hemlocks. The trees were solid to the heart and so big that they were more work than one man could handle. So this day Ivar was on the other end of the cross-cut saw.

McMaster had cruised through this timber and ordered new crosscut saws fifteen feet long. This would speed up the time it took to fall these huge trees. Doug and Ivar worked along at a good pace as they chopped away on a big fir. They fell two monstrous cedars in less than three hours. They handled the double-bladed axes with precision, with each swing being exact. Chips were flying everywhere, and as Doug and Ivar swung their axes, they talked of life, of love, of their dreams, and of their desires.

"Something wrong Doug?" Ivar asked.

"Just don't feel good about things."

"I think you should take some more rest."

"Rest won't make this right."

Wrongful emotions ate away at Doug's heart as he watched his ax eat away at the heartwood of this giant tree. His desire to have Victoria was strong. He wanted her at any cost.

Ivar and Doug finished the undercut. Doug put his ax down and climbed inside. He stretched out under the lip and smiled at Ivar. Ivar looked at Doug and shook his head. "You're crazy! What if a strong wind came along and blew the top of the tree? You'd be crushed!"

"Well, sometimes that isn't a bad thought," Doug said, laughing.

Ivar looked at him motioning him to get out of the undercut. "It still isn't a smart thing to do—you could get hurt."

"I should have my photo taken lying in this undercut. Someday all the big trees will be cut down, and no one will believe that there were trees this big. Climb in here Ivar, there's enough room for three men in here."

Ivar shook his head again. "No thanks, I like being out here. I think you're still suffering from being hit in the head. Now get out of there so we can finish our work and fall this tree."

Doug climbed out of the undercut and stepped down off the springboards. He picked up the cross-cut saw and climbed up to the undercut. He and Ivar started the back cut, pushing and pulling with all their strength.

They were almost finished with the back cut when Doug saw Mark walking toward him. Fear struck his heart as he saw that Mark was carrying a gun. He thought that Victoria had told Mark what had happened. He knew for sure that Mark would kill him. He knew that he would never have Victoria. He knew his life was over.

He didn't say anything to Ivar but started pulling faster on the saw. The tree started to cry as the last of the heartwood holding it tall started to give way. The tree moved toward the undercut and seemed to stop. Ivar jumped off his springboard, running for safety. Doug was usually the first one to run, but this time Ivar was in front. Ivar turned to check to see if Doug was behind him, fearing that he had tripped or fallen. He saw Doug standing on the springboard staring at the undercut.

"Doug! Jump or you'll get killed!"

Mark heard Ivar screaming at Doug and started running towards the tree. He saw that Doug wasn't moving away from the tree. "Doug! Move! Jump!" Mark screamed.

Doug lowered his head and slid right into the undercut of the tree. The tree fell with a long whining cry as the heartwood fought to hold on. The bite crushed Doug as the tree fell hitting the earth. Boom! It sounded as if Mark had shot the rifle. Ivar and Mark waited for the dust to settle and then looked in horror at their friend's body flattened and tore to shreds.

Tears filled Mark's eyes as he looked at Ivar. "What in the hell did he do that for? Was his mind totally lost?"

Ivar shook his head, and cussed Doug for being so stupid. He looked at Mark with disbelief. Mark searched for words to say. He looked up at the stump that was covered in blood and flesh. "I was coming up here to warn you two that there's an aggressive bear running around. He attacked a faller over on the other side of the hill. Hammer brought me this rifle in case we saw it—then I had to see Doug kill himself. Why?"

They walked over to see what was left of Doug. They couldn't tell it was a man. There was only a pile of flesh and blood as his body was crushed. There wasn't much left to carry out.

"We'd better go get Hammer," Mark said.

They left for camp to tell Hammer what had happened to Doug. "Doug must have lost his mind when he was hit by that branch. Why else would he kill himself?" Mark said.

"It doesn't make any sense to me. He crawled into the undercut before we started on the back cut, and I told him to get out of there or he could get hurt. I knew he'd lost his mind."

Hammer saw Ivar and Mark walking into camp and came running out of the office screaming obscenities. Mark looked at him. "Shut up, you old bastard!"

This stopped Hammer cold. He had never been told to shut up by one of his workers before. As quick as he stopped, he started up again. "What is it now? Did the bear scare you away? That's what I brought the gun out to you for. So you wouldn't be scared and run back to camp. Wait! Where's that other guy, Doug? Did the bear get him, or is he still resting up from being hit in the head? I thought I saw him back in camp this morning."

"Doug's dead, crushed by a tree."

Hammer thought for a moment, shaking his head. "Damn, he was the best faller I've ever seen. It'll take some time to get another one like him."

Hammer stood silent for a moment. "I know he was a friend of you two, so when the day's over you can take him to town to prepare for a proper burial. Until then get back to work and watch out for that wild bear. I don't want to have to report two deaths today. It's not the kind of image we want to project."

Mark and Ivar walked back to the site, as they crested the hill they saw the bear Hammer had been warning them about eating the remains of Doug's body. Mark raised the rifle, aimed, and squeezed off a shot that killed the bear.

"Damn thing, had no respect for the dead."

They made their way down to the bear and the remains of Doug. Ivar rolled the bear over checking it out. "Biggest bear I've ever seen. Grizzly bear, huge!"

"I haven't seen many bears, let alone shoot one. Looks like he made more of a mess of Doug. There really isn't much we can carry out. I think we should bury him up here on the mountain. He loved the woods, and as far as I know he has no family."

Ivar looked around. "We can bury him right over there under the cleft of that rock outcropping. I'll go down to the steam donkey and get some tools to dig a hole."

Mark watched Ivar walk off into the forest. He sat down and started talking to Doug. "When I first came to work, no one said a thing to me. You stuck out your hand and welcomed me. That meant a lot to me. You watched out for me—made sure I was safe and kept Hammer off my back. You were like a brother to me—I'll miss you. I just don't understand why you did what you did—it makes no sense to me."

He wiped the tears from his eyes as he finished his words. He sat looking at what was left of Doug, and waited until Ivar returned with a peevee bar and a shovel. When Ivar came back they dug a deep hole below the rock out cropping and buried his remains. They placed a large granite stone on his grave and walked away. "This coming Sunday I'll make a head marker for Doug and bring it up here."

"Yeah, good idea. I'll come with you, but for now we should get back to work before Hammer fires us," Ivar said.

As they were talking, Caleb came walking out of the trees. He looked at Mark and Ivar and then at the bear. "Why the sad faces? Something bad happen?" Caleb asked.

"Our friend died," Ivar said.

"Sorry to hear about your friend," Caleb said, as he looked around.

Caleb walked over to the bear. "Was it that bear that got him?"

"No, he was killed by a falling tree."

"Sorry to hear that. Sometimes bad things happen up here and for no reason at all. Sometimes there's nothing but trouble. You know the Indians believe that—yep, always said this was a bad, bad place."

Mark was devastated by Doug's death, and listening to Caleb was upsetting him even more. "Will you shut up about trouble, or I'll give you some trouble."

Caleb stood shaking his head at Mark. "Nature has an order, and when you disturb that order, trouble happens. It's the way things work. You should know that—but then again, many men never come to know that."

"Shut up and leave us alone!"

Caleb shook his head. "I was only being friendly."

"We don't need your friendship," Mark said.

"Watch out for yourselves, death is in this place and a second life it will want. Maybe not today but sometime someone close will be gone."

Caleb left and vanished into the forest as fast as he had appeared.

The rest of the week went slow. Two new men were assigned to work with Ivar and Mark. Ivar taught them well and by the time Saturday came, they had all of the big trees out of the site where Doug had died.

*   *   *   *

Victoria smiled as she saw Mark walking up the trail to the house. She stepped outside to meet him and saw that he had a long, sad face. She moved to comfort him. "What's wrong, Mark?"

"Doug was killed by a falling tree at the beginning of the week."

He walked on past Victoria into the house. She stood outside and started to cry. There were tears of relief, and there were tears of sorrow. She would never have to tell Mark what happened between her and Doug, yet she wished things had been different and that history could be changed. He would have made a good friend if he didn't have wrong desires, she thought. She walked back into the house and sat next to Mark. She took his hand. "How did it happen?"

"I think he killed himself—he must have still been suffering from that blow to his head. He jumped into the undercut of a tree as it was falling—it just doesn't make any sense. He was like a brother to me. I would trust that man with my life."

Victoria didn't say another word. She held Mark's hand in silence, hoping that he would never find out what Doug had done to her. She sat with Mark for a while, and then she went and made dinner. After dinner as they were getting ready for bed, Victoria drew close to Mark hugging him. "Mark, make love to me."

"Sorry, but I don't feel like it."

"It'll make you forget the bad things—so come, be close to me."

"I told you, not tonight! I really don't feel like it—so leave me alone."

Anger covered his face as he turned his back to her and fell off to sleep. Victoria thought she could understand how Mark felt. She fell asleep dreaming of the day when things would return to normal.

CHAPTER 11

▼

LOSS

Mark felt depressed about Doug's death, and camp wasn't the same without him around. Mark and Ivar would eat together, play cards, talk some, but the atmosphere was different. For three straight weeks Mark came home from camp and slept almost the entire weekend. He wouldn't approach Victoria. It was as though she wasn't even there. She tried to talk to him but received no reply. She became desperate in her attempts to get Mark to make love to her. She was experiencing morning sickness and feared she was pregnant. Not that being pregnant was bad, but she feared that the father was Doug, and not Mark.

The next week Rose stopped in for a visit. She sat down with a cup of tea. She looked at Victoria as silence filled the room. After some time she looked into Victoria's eyes. "I can feel your heavy heart. Tell me why it's this way."

"The man that forced himself on me—I am with his child," she said crying.

"I told you that he didn't have good intent toward you in his eyes. Are you sure it's his? Have you laid with Mark since?"

"Mark won't come near me."

"The *spee-yow*, the fox is watching your house—seeing what you will do?"

Victoria hung her head. "I don't know what to do. I don't want Mark to know what happened, and since Doug died, Mark hasn't wanted to be with me."

"The man passed—the evil one took him—I heard the trees whisper."

"I think I heard them also—but didn't know what they said. I don't know what to do Rose."

"It's a hard thing, but we can fix it. Tomorrow I'll go deep in the forest and get for you snowberry. This you will eat—it will make you sick—it will cause the child to be lost."

"Will it hurt? I don't want to hurt."

"It will hurt, I cannot lie, but I'll be with you the whole time—I'll keep you safe."

Victoria wrestled with what Rose said. It scared her about aborting a child, yet she knew that somehow Mark would find out the truth if she carried through with the pregnancy. What if the child was born with the same color hair as Doug and not Mark? What if the child looked the same as Doug? Mark and Doug's features were totally opposite from each other.

The only choice she thought she had was to eat the snowberry and abort the child. "I fear what may become of me if I have this child—I could lose everything. I could hurt Mark beyond measure. Please help me—help me make this right."

"I can see that this will ease the pain in your heart, but remember that in coming times your sorrow will be greater than what you feel now."

"What do you mean?"

"When you disturb the natural way of life—sometimes it will correct itself. If you eat the snowberry you may never conceive again. A life taken must be given somewhere else. *Tyee* will demand this of you."

Victoria pondered what Rose meant. She could remember the words her father would often repeat. "You reap what you sow." It didn't make much sense to her—she was just correcting something that should have never been in the first place.

"I need to do this, Rose," she pleaded.

"Tomorrow I'll help you, my friend."

*   *   *   *

Victoria had never been so sick. She vomited over and over even when there was nothing left to vomit. After a few hours she started to bleed, and she felt great pain as her body gave up the child. She slept on her bed sweating with a fever while Rose sat in a chair chanting in her native tongue. She dipped a cloth into cold water and sponged Victoria's face.

After some time had passed Rose took Victoria's hand. "It has passed. I prayed that all would be well with you. I asked the Great Spirit *Tyee* to have mercy on you because of the choice you made. Rest now and in a few days things will return to as they were."

∗   ∗   ∗   ∗

Mark stopped to have lunch. He turned off the steam donkey and sat on a large stump close to his work site. The wind moved through the trees as Mark looked to the sky. There wasn't a cloud in sight, which brought a smile to his face. The wind moved stronger through the trees and they spoke. "A child."

Mark looked around as he had before. "Who's there? If it's you Caleb you're not scaring me."

Mark stood up and looked around trying to see any movement. The only thing moving were the branches of the trees dancing in the wind. He sat back down thinking of the things Rose had said about the trees to Victoria. "Trees can't talk—if they could they would tell me of Doug."

Mark returned home on Friday night. He took his seat at the table and listened to Victoria talk of different things. Mark noticed that she moved slower than normal. "Is anything wrong?" he asked.

"No, just a bit tired, that's all."

Mark grunted as he shook his head. "Strange thing happened a couple of days ago."

Victoria turned her whole attention to Mark. "What's that?"

"As I ate lunch the wind moved through the trees and I swear it made a sound as though they spoke the words 'a child.'"

Victoria reached deep to catch her breath.

"Funny how a mind can work when you miss someone," Mark said.

Victoria nodded in agreement and thought if he only knew.

∗   ∗   ∗   ∗

Mark found it difficult getting over Doug's death. He and Ivar spent many hours together after work. Ivar always wanted to go to the river and fish. Mark found this pleasurable, and Victoria enjoyed the salmon. Rose taught her how to cure and smoke it.

A new partner bought into the mill. It was renamed Waite and McMaster. They added a new band-saw and ten new shake bolt splitters. They shortened the work week to four days while they completed the work on the mill.

Mark and Ivar made use of their time off fishing in the river.

While they were sitting down by the river watching an eagle fish on the other side, they saw a body floating in the water. Ivar focused his eyes on it. "It's a dead Indian."

Mark nodded his head in agreement. "Yep, just a dead Indian."

As they sat there, two more bodies came floating by. Over the next twenty minutes another ten bodies came floating by. They looked upriver and saw about thirty other bloated bodies floating down the current. Mark brought his line in and picked up his things. "This is no good—let's get out of here—the whole river is full of dead Indians."

They made their way back into town and stopped to tell a few people at the store what they'd seen. Mr. Beddall overheard. "There's a smallpox epidemic upriver, and it's starting to affect the local Indians. I just found this out today— so everyone should be careful."

Panic overcame the valley. The epidemic again attacked the Natives with four out of five Indians dying. The Indians who survived, fearing for their own lives, threw most of the bodies in the river, knowing they would be washed out to sea.

The disease quickly spread throughout the valley, showing mercy only to mature whites. Mark came home to find Victoria crying. "Rachel has the spots."

Fear, anger, and pain struck at Mark's heart. "No! No! No! It can't be, maybe she touched something that gave her the spots. It just can't be."

"She hasn't been outside—she's sick, Mark."

"It's your damn Indian friends—they're the ones who made her sick! I told you—yes, I told you not to keep visiting with them—they're nothing but trouble. It's your fault she's sick!"

Mark fell on his knees and started crying. It was the most emotion he had displayed in front of Victoria. Her heart went out to comfort him, but he just pushed her away. "It's your fault—you let them in our house—you let them hold my daughter!"

She wept. Victoria's heart was being crushed by Mark's words.

Later that evening, Rachel Rose passed away. The next day they took her little body and laid it to rest in the new cemetery on the north end of the lake. The ladies' society purchased the ground from the Isaacsons, and made a place where people of white origin could have a place of rest. A few friends attended the funeral. Ivar, McMaster, and Jezzy were in attendance. Mark told Victoria that Rose wasn't allowed to attend. "She could be a witch. She might have been the one to bring this to my daughter."

Victoria's eyes strained to hold back the tears as she wondered who was the one believing in fairy tales now. There seemed to be no time when her eyes were dry. Maybe God had taken Rachel because of the sin she had committed. She took a life, so maybe this was her punishment. It was nature correcting a wrong.

Mark wouldn't speak to her. He would look at her and shake his head in disgust. To him Rachel's death was all her fault. How she wanted at this time to reach out to him and tell him all of what she had done. She wanted to confess her wrongs. She wanted to feel clean and honorable in his sight, but she knew that would only break his heart more, and she wanted to spare him. She had brought enough pain to Mark already.

Victoria sat in her house and looked out at the apple trees. One of the main branches had died and lost all its leaves. A lone robin sat on the dead branch singing. She swore it was the same song she used to sing to Rachel. A smile crossed her face as she walked to the door. The robin turned its head and looked at Victoria.

"You're free Rachel. I will always remember you," Victoria said quietly.

The robin raised its wings and flew away.

$$*\qquad*\qquad*\qquad*$$

Rose hadn't been infected by the smallpox epidemic. She lived through one epidemic, and she vowed to live through this one. She again had to watch as her tribe shrank. She cried over each member that passed on, as she remembered a great tribe with a thousand people that had been reduced to less than thirty.

As she walked through their encampment overlooking the Nookachamps Creek, she came across a young man holding his infant daughter. They both cried as the baby reached for her dead mother lying on the ground before them. Rose spoke in her native tongue. "You need to leave this place, run far from this sickness. Take your child and go or there may be none left of our people."

"How do I care for a child that still needs her mother's breast? She needs the milk that flows from a woman's breast, but all our young mothers have died, and there is none to be found."

"Maybe this is the way of our life. I fear that she might pass, not because of sickness but because of the death of others. Why have we been forsaken by our Great Spirit *Tyee*?"

Days passed and Victoria didn't see any of her Indian friends. Not even Rose had visited. Maybe the disease had overcome Rose. America wasn't the dream she had thought it would be. Maybe it was all a big mistake to come here, she thought.

Being worried about Rose, she set out to find her. She went over the hill toward the Indian camp on the slope overlooking the Nookachamps. As she drew near, she could smell death. The smell of rotting flesh hung in the air along with the smoke from a lone fire. As she entered the camp, she saw Rose sitting next to the fire with four men and one other woman. In one man's arms was a girl, softly crying. Victoria wondered if these were all that were left of Rose's people.

Rose didn't show any emotion when she saw Victoria, though she motioned for her to sit down. Victoria drew close to her. "I've been worried about you, Rose."

Rose had tears in her eyes as she took Victoria's arm. "I'll live, but my brothers and sisters won't. When I was young we would live and die on our land. We all lived long lives unless the Salts came and killed us or accidents happened. Before my grandfather, all Indian people lived in peace together. Then one day two chiefs started to fight. One chief was stronger than the other, so the weaker chief had to flee. He fled up this river valley and called it the *Skagit*, meaning sanctuary, a place of safety. The Indians that stayed on the shore called us the Sticks, and we called them the Salts. We became strong in our sanctuary and believed we would be safe forever.

We only wanted to live in peace, but the Salts would never accept our peace, yet the Salts could never completely destroy us. Sometimes we would battle with them and win.

Then the whites came and said they would trade with us. We freely gave up our land for nothing, and they told us we could live in peace. It was fine, for they gave us work picking hops and provided places for us to trade salmon or items we made.

We didn't know they would bring something that would kill most of us. They didn't war with us, but killed us in their peace. Was that their desire? To bring sickness so that we be no more? Why don't the whites die like we do? Is their God more powerful then the great *Tyee*? Here is one of the last children of our people, yet she will die, for she has no mother to feed her the milk that she needs."

Sorrow showed in the eyes of every person there.

"Rose, Rachel got the sickness and passed away last week. Though my loss is not as great as yours, I can feel what you feel. I'm so sorry that we've brought this sickness to your people. I wish I could heal your heart—help your people."

Rose reached out and put her hand on Victoria's thigh and squeezed it "You can help my people by doing something for me."

"I will."

"Take this child home with you. Feed her milk, raise her in your ways, and teach her the things I taught you. Tell her about her people so that she will remember us, lest we be forgotten and remembered no more."

*   *   *   *

Mark arrived home on Saturday and heard the sound of crying coming from the house. He quickly walked inside, wondering why he heard the sound of a crying infant. He saw Victoria sitting in her chair, rocking back and forth trying to get the child to take a bottle. As soon as the child took the bottle the crying stopped.

Victoria had a beaming smile on her face, and she didn't notice Mark walking into the room. He watched her looking at the child and holding the child close as she sang to it. He could see that she was happy to have a baby in her arms. He came close to her and she looked up at him. "Where did that child come from?"

"Her mother died, and there's no one left to take care of her. So they asked me to care for her. I decided to bring her home, or she'd die."

"Maybe that would be best."

Victoria's turned her head away and then back at Mark. "What did you say? Maybe best? Mark, I can't believe you'd say something like that. This is a child who has nothing left. I must care for her—we must care for her."

"What do you think people are going to say? Whites raising an Indian—what's she going to say when she grows up? How are you going to tell her that she's lesser?"

"She won't be, she'll be better. She hasn't taken down with small pox, so I believe she's special."

"Well, if it makes you feel better, keep her, but realize that I won't treat her as my daughter. She's not from me."

Tears filled Victoria's eyes. She turned her head away so Mark couldn't see them. She would be a great mother to this child. She named her Nomi, just as Rose had asked. Her name meant the last one.

*   *   *   *

The county authorities called a meeting to deal with the smallpox epidemic. The meeting was held in the city of Mount Vernon. There was much anxiety among the residents of the valley fearing the spread of the disease. Some purposed this and others that, but it was McMaster's idea that won the crowd. McMaster headed the meeting. "I insist that all remaining Indian villages east of the Swimn-omish Channel be burned to the ground. That all remaining Indians be sent to the reservation."

Mark was in attendance and agreed with McMaster that the villages should be burnt. He, like the rest of the people, feared that if this were not done, that the disease would likely spread to the whites. He hoped the action would end Victoria's friendship with Poor Lo.

The men set out from Mount Vernon that night, and the first place they stopped was the Indian camp by the Nookachamps. The dead bodies were piled in the long house. Mark took his torch, threw it on the roof and watched the fire grow. The structures were made from cedar, and the fire grabbed quickly. A couple of the Indians who were there made their way out of the area. They were sent to the reservation to live with the Salts. The men burned anything that would ignite. What were once a proud people had returned to the earth from whence they came.

Rose watched from a distance as her camp burned. She sang a prayer, and her voice could be heard for miles in the stillness of the air. In her native tongue, she sang. "Where is the bear? Where is the wolf? Where are my people who cannot be found? For seasons we lived, we died, we birthed new life again. We've been here as long as the big trees. The whites cut the trees and leave only the stumps to remind us of what used to be. The sickness the whites brought has eaten our flesh, and only our bones are left. Like the big trees that every day fall, my people have fallen, never to rise again. Oh, that we may never be forgotten."

Her voice filled the valley as the men left working their way up the Skagit River to burn the rest of the infected villages. Any bodies they came across, they threw into the river. By the end of the night, the river was full of bodies floating out to the Puget Sound.

People came to the river to watch the bodies float by. In Mount Vernon it was said that a person could walk across the river on the dead Indians It should have been a sad time for all, yet, there were no tears, and not much was said as the white people watched. The Nookachamps tribe and the other upper Skagit tribes were no more.

Caleb had seen some of his friends die from the epidemic. He knew natives from around Clear Lake to the farthest reaches up river. He worked inside his stump house making dinner when he heard a knock on the door. He climbed down the ladder and opening the door, he saw Rose. "It's late, what are you doing here?"

"My people are no more, my village is no more, and I've no place left."

"Well, you're welcome to stay here. You're my friend, and you were a friend of my grandfather. You'll always be welcome here."

"I won't be a burden to you. I'll keep my own and much more."

Caleb smiled as she walked into the house. She could stay downstairs and he would make a place for her so she could have a private area. He thought it would be nice having another person around because sometimes on a long winter night loneliness felt as sharp as the cold north wind.

CHAPTER 12

▼

THE FIRES

The years passed by quickly. Victoria pruned her apple trees so they would bear more fruit. They were no longer just twigs in the ground, but growing into producing trees. Mark was always busy in the forest and didn't have much time to fall all the trees he had planned on his property. Victoria walked Nomi through the forest showing her all the wonderful plants. Their property became the sanctuary as she had dreamt. The sounds, the smells, and the different lives of each tree held a special place in her heart. Magic drifted through the trees floating on the filtered sunlight. Dust floated off the forest floor and danced outlining spirits as the light reflected them. Music played as the wind moved through the leaves of the trees and plants. "This is a wonderful place—we will always be here," Victoria said.

As had been rumored, Waite and McMaster sold the mill and their logging rights. The new owners were a group of men interested in acquiring great wealth from the big trees. They changed the name from Waite and McMaster to the Clear Lake Lumber Company. Hammer was appointed president to oversee the entire operation.

The men at Camp One saw it as the lesser of two evils. It was nice to have Hammer off the hill and out of the camp, but to have him boss over everything was a scary thought. Hammer could do the job, but he was a hard taskmaster that would always demand more from the men.

As the new owners increased the size of the mill the town grew in population. The mill had plans to add a more modern steam turbine engine to create more electricity to run the operations, and maybe enough to meet the electric needs of the town.

Expansion was completed in 1902. The mill doubled in size, and the logging operations followed to keep up with demand. A second camp opened out toward Mundt Creek.

Mundt Creek started on the top of Cultas Mountain from various small streams. They all joined together and flowed into the Nookachamps at the base of the mountain near the town of Clear Lake. To the south of Mundt Creek lay the property that belonged to Caleb Cultas. There were no property lines, only landmarks: Mundt Creek to the north, the top of Cultas Mountain to the east, the bottom of the mountain to the west, and the east fork of the Nookachamps Creek to the south. Some of the tallest trees in the valley grew inside the bounds of these landmarks.

✳   ✳   ✳   ✳

Hammer promoted Mark and Ivar to new positions in the company. Mark was in charge of building new railroads into the timber, and Ivar was his assistant. Hammer could see that Mark had a good mind for engineering, and Hammer would put it to use to profit the company.

The first task assigned to Mark and Ivar was to build a high trestle across Mundt Creek. This wouldn't be easy because the canyon was two hundred feet deep and as wide. They punched out a road through the timber to the edge of Mundt Creek and brought out a steam donkey converted to act as a crane. They would use the crane to set all the support logs to begin the trestle.

In early April, Mark set up the first piling. Caleb had been keeping a close watch on the activities of the loggers and road builders. He didn't think they would actually cross the creek to start logging on his land. He wandered over to the creek and sat on a large old fir that had fallen years before. He chewed on some jerky that he had cured early in the fall.

Mark saw him and wondered what the crazy boy was up to. He had grown accustomed to dealing with Caleb and his strange thoughts. Mark saw Caleb wave at him, and he waved back. Caleb rose and started across the gully on a tree that had fallen and rested across the chasm. Mark watched in amazement, figuring that at any time the tree would break in half under Caleb's weight.

The tree was stout near its trunk but was less than a foot through at the end. He thought for sure that if Caleb fell, it would be his death. No man could fall two hundred feet and live. It looked as if Caleb were walking on air near the end of the log. He showed no sign of fear as he stepped off the end of the log onto the ground. He walked over to Mark. "What are you doing?" Caleb asked.

He chewed on his jerky, smiling, looking at Mark, waiting for him to respond. "What does it look like we're doing?"

Caleb stopped chewing, and looked around then back at the gully. "Looks like you're making a mess. When nature makes a mess, it cleans itself up, but when men make a mess, they don't clean it up. Nature has to do it for them. Did you know that?"

Mark shook his head. "I didn't know that, but we're not making a mess, we're building a trestle across the creek, do you understand that?"

"Well, that's nice of you people, because that log someday is going to rot, and I would hate to saw down a tree just to get over the creek."

"You just don't get it—do you? We're building a bridge so we can get to the other side to log all that land."

Caleb looked back over his shoulder toward his property then back at Mark. "You can't do that. Those trees don't belong to you."

He took another bite of his jerky. "I don't own the trees, but the mill does, so we'll be cutting them in less than two weeks."

"I don't think so," Caleb said calmly. "That land was my grandfather's, and since he has passed on, I guess that means it's mine—and I like all those tall trees. Do you know someday there won't be many of those trees left? It looks to me like you're trying to cut them all down. You got to leave some. Taking everything isn't good."

Mark started to laugh as he walked away. "There are so many trees here that men will never see the end of them—never."

"Yes, and the Indians never thought that something unseen could put an end to them," Caleb shouted back as Mark disappeared behind the donkey engine.

As the day wore on, Mark couldn't get what Caleb had said out of his mind. He would mumble the words over and over. He didn't think Caleb was as dumb as others said. He maybe didn't have the social skills that others had, but how could he, being raised on a mountain by a wild man and an old Indian woman? He had always been nice when Mark had seen him. He didn't seem like he was a troublemaker. Yet Mark realized that Caleb didn't like the idea of the mill taking trees that he thought belonged to him.

That night back at camp, Mark had the camp foreman send a letter down to company headquarters.

Mr. Hammer,

Caleb Cultas has made the claim that the land and the trees south of Mundt Creek belong to him. Are there any such records of who owns said property? And if so, may I see a copy to satisfy Mr. Cultas and myself? I believe it would be in the best interests of the Company to treat Caleb Cultas as respect to a property owner.

Herman Lannier
Camp Two foreman

When Hammer received the letter he became enraged. As far as the records showed Isaiah Cultas had never filed for a homestead. Hammer knew that Isaiah had lived on that land since the mid-seventies, but that didn't stop him from making the decision to have it logged. Caleb would have to be dealt with if he caused any problems, and Hammer knew just the right man for that job.

Glen Preston was called down to the main office in town. Hammer gave him orders to go and have a nice talk with Caleb Cultas. Glen knew what he meant and smiled, knowing that this job would fit him just fine.

The next morning Glen arrived at the end of the road where the trestle was being built. He walked up to Mark as he looked over towards Caleb's property. "Have you seen Caleb Cultas?"

"I saw him walking toward town this morning. What do you want with him?"

"That's none of your business," he said as he started back down the tracks.

Glen had passed Caleb and didn't even know it. He had seen a man walking toward town. He hurried back down the tracks with one of his sidekicks, the only friend Glen had, a man just as disgusting and evil as himself. They made quite a pair. If ever one of them lacked evil, the other would be able to pick up the slack. Next to Hammer, they were two of the most miserable men in the woods.

They caught up with Caleb near the log flume on the east hill above the lake. Glen walked up to him, and Caleb could see the bad intent in his eyes. Glen stopped about three feet from Caleb and looked him up and down. "We're looking for a Caleb Cultas. Could you be him?"

Caleb smiled at Glen. "I know the man. What do you want him for?"

Glen was confused. He didn't know what Caleb looked like; he hadn't bothered to ask. "We just want to have a few words with him about some land."

"As far as I know, I don't think his land is for sale."

"We aren't looking to buy it, the company is just going to take it, and that's why we need to have a talk with him."

Caleb leaned back against the flume as if he didn't have a care in the world. "Now that wouldn't be a nice thing for the mill to do. I don't think Caleb would like it. You see, his grandfather taught him it's not right to steal, and I'm sure he wouldn't like anyone stealing from him. How would you like it if someone stole from you?"

"Listen, we're not here to get a *Bible* lesson. Have you seen this Caleb or not?"

Caleb smiled. "You're looking at him."

Glen moved toward him, trying to grab him. "You som'bitch."

Caleb jumped up on the flume and balanced himself on the edge out of Glen's reach. George, Glen's sidekick, started to climb up the beams that were holding the flume. Caleb stepped over to where he was climbing and stood on his fingers. It caused him to fall back on the ground. Glen screamed out a few obscenities as he picked up sticks to throw at Caleb. Coming down the flume was a log pushing the water over the edge as it lumbered down the mountain. Caleb stepped onto the log and waved good-bye to his new friends as the log started picking up speed on the steeper slope.

The ride was pleasant for a time. The log was moving at a manageable pace, but as it neared the last descent into the lake it picked up speed to almost ninety miles an hour. As the log crested the last flat spot before the final descent Caleb could see a group of people standing near the platform next to the flume at the lake.

He let out a scream as the log plummeted like thunder toward the lake. The people heard the scream and all eyes turned up to see Caleb riding a log into the lake. It was a sight to see. Hammer was leading a group of visitors and locals, showing them all the highlights of the new company. He wasn't planning on showing them the flume, but the visitors all wanted to see the logs that made the thunder.

As he watched the show, he figured that no man could survive the force of hitting the water at that speed. All eyes watched as the log crashed into the water with a terrific bang. It sent spray high into the sky, making rainbows and showering them all with water as it plunged into the lake. They watched the water and waited to see if the man would surface. The log disappeared under the water and then rose up, breaking the surface and quietly coming to rest. They saw no sign of the log rider.

Hammer figured his body would float to the surface in time. People gasped as all their eyes were focused on the water. Near the shore where they were standing, a figure could be seen moving toward the surface. Caleb stuck his head up out of the water, letting out a loud howl. "Cold water!"

He stepped up onto shore, soaking wet, as the people began to applaud. He smiled. "I hope I didn't upset your get-together. I just had to get to town faster than normal."

He shook himself off like a wet dog and started walking to town as though he did this everyday. Hammer recognized him and wished that he had died He knew that with Caleb alive there would be trouble logging the land south of Mundt Creek.

Caleb knew that things did not look good for him. He needed to find some help in making sure that he could keep his land. He stopped at Mr. Cheasty's office and inquired about his property to see what he had to do to legally protect it.

Mr. Cheasty didn't give Caleb much time. "You have to go to Seattle to register it, record how long your grandfather lived on the property and lay claim to it. We have no such records here."

Caleb had never been to Seattle—he had never been out of the county. He had been all over the mountains, the hills, through the valley, but never out of it. "How do I get to Seattle?"

"You can go by train or leave from Mount Vernon by boat."

"The boat might sink, the train might crash. I think I'll walk."

Cheasty started to laugh. "It's over sixty miles, it'll take you three or more days."

"Nope, only two days."

Caleb left returning home. He would get a good sleep and make sure Rose was taken care of before heading off to Seattle in the morning.

$$* \qquad * \qquad * \qquad *$$

Nomi grew as fast as the apple trees. Victoria loved Nomi and enjoyed that she was able to talk. She put her whole effort and being into raising Nomi. Mark, after some time, started warming up to the little girl. Victoria even saw him smile at Nomi at the dinner table.

Rose came and visited only when she knew Mark wouldn't be home. Rose didn't have bad feelings for Mark. She understood that many whites viewed Natives as lesser. Victoria smiled each time she saw Rose walking up to the house. It was always a pleasure having her around to talk with and to help with Nomi. Rose would hold Nomi and sing to her the traditions of her people. She always ended by saying, "Nomi, the last of our father's seed."

Jezzy visited sometimes in the late morning. She would tell Victoria about all the men that patronized her establishment. They sat and giggled, carrying on. One morning during a visit Jezzy got a serious look on her face. She reached out and took Victoria's arm. "Mark was in last week. He watched the dancers, then left."

Victoria's eyes turned down. "Yes, he was later than he usually is the other night."

"Is there something wrong between you two?" Jezzy asked.

"No, he just hurts over Rachel's death, and he blames me for having Indian friends. I don't know if he'll forgive me."

Jezzy took her into her arms and hugged her. "He'll forgive you some day, dear. Remember and know that you have friends here, so don't make yourself scarce. People talk around town about you—about you raising the Indian girl. They talk about your choice of friends, but they don't know your heart. Hell, all those women who're talking—well—I've seen most of their husbands in my hall at one time or another. I've never said a thing to them about it because they aren't my friends. But you're my friend, and that's why I mentioned that Mark was in the other night."

"I understand. I don't worry about Mark being at your place, watching girls dance. The thing I fear is his unwillingness to share with me his deepest thoughts. Real intimacy is what we lack, and that's what makes me sad. Sometimes I even wonder if there is such a thing as real love."

"Real love—ha—dear, I don't even know if real love exists myself. I see lonely men, lonely married men. I see sex-starved men—I see men who only want sex—I see it all. Yet I've never seen real love."

"I thought I saw it before—thought I saw it in people's eyes when they looked at each other. I saw it in my mom's eyes when she looked at my father. I see it in Rose's eyes when she looks at Nomi. So if there is such a thing as real love, I know that some day real love will be mine."

"Go ahead and dream, dear. Dream and dream some more—I do hope your dreams come true."

*   *   *   *

Caleb prepared to leave for Seattle in the morning. He had a brindle, a few items of food and some gold to purchase a place to stay. Cheasty had told Hammer of Caleb's intent to get the title to his property. As Cheasty watched Caleb walk out of town, Hammer was already on his way to Seattle, by train, to lay formal claim to it.

It took two days, just as Caleb figured, to arrive in Seattle. He asked around and found the government office of land management. He laid out his papers on the counter and asked for a title to his land, but the man behind the counter looked confused. "Funny thing is that just yesterday another man was in here saying he owned this said land and I issued him the deed. I'm sorry, but there's nothing I can do for you."

Caleb left the office shaking his head. He knew that the mill owners were the ones who had laid claim to his property. He started to think of ways he could fight and win his land back. He was too angry to sleep, and in the darkness of night he left, walking back to Clear Lake.

*   *   *   *

Mark worked building the trestle across Mundt Creek, and it was going faster than he thought, which made Hammer happy. All the pilings were in place and the final cross braces were being fastened into position. It was a bright, sunny day with no clouds in sight. On the mountain the snow melted filling the creeks with water. "It's so peaceful," Mark said to Ivar as he listened to the rushing water. "This is a wonderful work of art we have designed and completed."

Ivar looked over the trestle. "Yes, it is."

"We have conquered nature, and it is a first in a series of conquests that we will complete."

Mark and Ivar walked across the trestle inspecting the structure with each step. Mark saw Rose watching them from the other side. He continued across the trestle to where she stood. "I bet your people never built anything as wonderful as this."

It wasn't a question, just a statement of superior intellect. She looked at him and felt his hatred of her. "In your lifetime this will not stand, it will rot and die, and you yourself will be forgotten. Like my people, it will fall, and like the trees that fall, you will fall some day, and I believe the whole mill will fall."

"You make no sense—this trestle is well built. It'll stand for a lifetime, and the mill will be here forever."

"What is a lifetime? For some it's a hundred years, but for others, it's an hour. I fear that you don't know much about life."

"I know more about things than you'll ever know. Soon, old squaw, you will be no more. You'll go the way of the rest of your people, but everything we build will exist until the end of time."

Rose sat down on an old log next to the gully and started to pray in her native tongue. Mark looked at her shaking his head. "What the hell are you saying?"

Rose looked up at him. "What I speak you will know when it happens."

Mark glared at her and then walked into the timber with Ivar. Mark and Ivar surveyed some of the tall trees on Caleb's land. After an hour they walked back across the trestle. Half away across they heard a tremendous roar coming from up the canyon. It sounded as if the whole mountain were falling down. Mark looked up stream to see logs and water and ice moving like a solid wall, destroying everything in its path. Mark took off running toward Caleb's land with Ivar close on his heels. Mark made it safely to the bank and stood next to Rose and watched in horror as the wall of debris brought destruction to his trestle. The trestle snapped as though the logs were nothing but twigs. The center section collapsed first, pulling the sides along with it as the wall continued down the canyon.

Mark didn't say anything to Rose as his heart was shaken, and he couldn't believe his eyes. He couldn't believe that what Rose had spoken happened as though she had made it. Maybe she was a witch. He couldn't help but think about how Caleb had said the mountain was bad. This idea went against his whole reasoning.

As Rose started to walk back to Caleb's place she looked at Mark. "*Cultas naw,* sometimes good comes out of bad."

The men who'd been working on the trestle took off running for camp. Some of them had heard the legends that the Indians spoke of and fear took a hold of their souls. Mark wasn't looking forward to reporting to Hammer about the destruction. He knew this would slow down the mill from meeting its projected production goals.

*   *   *   *

Caleb arrived back in Clear Lake without being noticed. It was dark as he walked through town making his way up to his property. Rose met him at the door of his house and told him about the events of the previous day. A huge smile came upon his face as he heard her account. "The mill now holds the deed to my land," Caleb said.

"Why is it that some of your people are only content with taking what belongs to others?"

"I don't know Rose—but I will not let them take my land without a fight."

*   *   *   *

Hammer sent men out to find out why the mudslide had come roaring down the canyon. They found their answer near the headwaters of Mundt Creek where there were a series of beaver dams. Because of the unusually heavy snow pack and the warm weather, the dams couldn't hold the volume of water created from the melt off.

Hammer was satisfied to know that the incident could be explained. He sent word to the workers. "The slide on Mundt creek was caused by excessive melting snow. Any relation or thoughts of the foolish Indian fables will not be allowed to continue in camp."

Hammer walked with Mark as they viewed the damage to the trestle. "It would be best to abandon the idea of a new trestle until the ground becomes stable. Lest we spend all kinds of time and money just to lose another one to the same fate."

"What about the trees?" Mark asked.

"We'll log that property some other time. We will work north from this point at the present time."

The loggers started a clear cut at the edge of Mundt Creek heading north. They took everything standing. It was some of the best timber they had seen. Each day they would run close to twenty-four connects off the hill with one and two log loads. The lake was full of logs, and running out of room for more. The mill could not keep up with the timber crews. Both flumes were operating and both camps were at full capacity, limited only by the lack of equipment and the shortage of men.

*   *   *   *

The summer winds were unusually warm and strong blowing in from the south. Rain hadn't fallen on the hills above Clear Lake for over a month. It was nice weather to work in, Mark thought.

The heat would cause pleasant smells to rise from the forest floor. It also created dry conditions in the forest, which allowed production to increase. The timber crews set new records every day. There was no mud to deal with, and the men were in good spirits because of the weather. Some of the loggers would sleep outside under the stars for a change from the stagnant confines of the bunkhouse.

The mill grew in strength. Trains ran up and down the mountain, and steam donkeys yarded in the logs. Smoke from the donkeys could be seen all the way down in town.

Just south of Camp Two, toward Mundt Creek, a firebox tender threw in another chunk of wood to keep the fire going, and a spark flew out of the stack. It floated through the air and landed on a small pile of slash.

It smoldered going unnoticed until smoke was pouring from the slash. A few moments later flames leaped into the air. The donkey operator grabbed a bucket of water, used to fill the water tank on the engine, and threw it on the burning pile, but this didn't slow the fire down. The fire gained in size bringing fear to the loggers working in the area. The workers started running for camp. They looked back at the fire and in just a few short minutes it seemed as though the whole hill was ablaze.

Caleb saw the smoke from his upper story window. He could see that it was too much smoke for a campfire, and knew it was something bad. He hurried down the ladder and ran outside where he found Rose busy weaving a basket out of bark. "Rose, head to the creek, there's a fire in the woods."

She grabbed a couple of things and headed to the sandbar down at the creek. Caleb took off running toward the fire. He crossed the creek making his way to the smoke. He could see the column growing larger as the fire consumed all the fallen logs, standing trees, and brush in its path.

He felt the wind at his back as the fire pulled in its needed air supply. Caleb stopped to view the fire heading toward him. It looked as if the whole earth was burning. He took off running back toward the creek, crossed it and ran to his house where he grabbed a bucket full of wood shavings and some flint. He ran back across the creek and quickly gathered together some branches, making a pile. Caleb put the shavings down, and took his flint and started striking the stones together. A small fire started to grow. Caleb ran back across the creek and watched as the fire he made gained in size.

The wind that was being created by the first fire acted as a vacuum for Caleb's fire. The first one needing more oxygen drew Caleb's fire in to itself. He watched his fire as it spread north being pulled and pushed by the wind. He knew he had saved his timber for the time being. Caleb's fire raced the half-mile to meet the other fire. The fire on the south side of the mountain died out, but the fire to the east and north continued to burn.

Caleb ran and caught up with Rose near where Mundt Creek enters into the east fork of the Nookachamps. She smiled when she saw him. "I worry about you sometimes—you need to learn fear. Smart animals run from the fire, not toward it."

"I needed to see—see what it was—it was probably the machine they use to drag out logs. I warned them about that—nothing but trouble."

"Fire purifies the earth. It will make all this logged off land new again."

"Yes, but it'll look mighty ugly for a long time."

"Ugly in your eyes, but maybe beautiful in another's eyes."

Caleb understood what she was saying. Come next spring, the blackness would be washed away and new growth would be rising everywhere in splashes of green. He knelt down next to the creek and lapped up some water. Looking back at Rose he motioned her to drink. "I'll go home and get some blankets and food—tonight we'll sleep near the water in case the fire spreads."

Down in Clear Lake, Victoria looked up to the sky to see why the sun had suddenly been blotted out. She saw the large column of smoke. It was more than she had ever seen. Other people in town gathered in the streets, watching the hill, seeing the smoke column double in size within minutes. Women and children cried as fear gripped the men in town. It looked as though fire covered the whole mountain. Victoria cried, afraid that Mark might not make it off the mountain. The wives, sons, and daughters of the loggers started walking toward the log dump. They knew that the men that made it off the hill would come the fastest way.

As they waited they heard the engine coming down the grade. It was a joyous sound to Mrs. Warner, the engineer's wife. Men were piled on top of the logs that were loaded on the connects. Joe Siddle, Camp One foreman, jumped down and shouted. "All the men from Camp One are accounted for, but I haven't heard anything from Camp Two, where I think the fire started."

Camp Two consisted of two bunkhouses, a cookhouse, the camp office, the dining hall, five outhouses, and a large water tank next to the tracks. Mark was in the office when the fire started. One of the cooks ran into the office shouting. "There's a fire!"

They rushed outside and stared in horror. The acrid smell stung Marks nostrils, as the fire rapidly approached. The awful part was the deafening roar. It was something Mark had never heard before. It was the sound of a giant monster feeding on everything in its path. It brought fear to his soul.

The train had just returned from one of its many trips to the log dump. The camp foreman, in a panic, started running down the tracks to town.

Mark looked at the terror on every man's face. "Everyone on the train! Let's get this thing moving!"

The men who were working the donkey engine that started the fire came running into camp. Blistered skin hung from their faces. Two of them burned beyond recognition.

The train started down the tracks with men running and jumping on it as it moved away. Mark moved through camp to make sure no one was left behind. He figured he could run fast enough to catch the train.

As he made his way around the last bunkhouse, he realized he could no longer hear the train. He ran down the tracks searching through the dense smoke for the train. He ran out of breath, and he knew he couldn't catch the train, and he could see fire was starting to appear in the trees next to the camp. He stopped and looked for the fastest way to escape.

Fire seemed to be all around him. He ran back toward camp, only to find the buildings starting to catch fire. The heat was unbearable; he could feel himself starting to cook. The only structure that wasn't on fire was the dock in the camp pond. Mark ran over to the dock and looked down into the water. The smoke was so thick he couldn't see how deep the water was.

As he lowered himself into the water he was overcome with fear. He couldn't swim, as he had never learned. He put his hands on the edge of the dock with his fingers in a death grip to hold himself up.

He could feel the deck of the dock becoming hot. He held on with one hand and with the other started splashing water over the edge up on to the dock. This kept the dock cool until he became tired. Every few seconds he would switch hands. He noticed that the skin on his hands blistered from the heat. Being in shock he didn't feel the pain of the burns, but fear ran through him as he knew that time was running out.

The fire swirled in a circular motion as it burned everything in its path. He dipped his head into the water to keep it from burning. He figured his hair would be long gone if he lived. His strength was failing.

Finally he couldn't hang on with just one hand. To keep from falling into the pond he put both hands on the edge and grimaced as the heat burned the skin off his hands.

*   *   *   *

The train from Camp Two pulled in at the log dump repeating the same scene that happened when the train from Camp One had arrived minutes before. Victoria's eyes searched for Mark but didn't see him. Other wives and children ran to meet their men, while Victoria stood alone, holding Nomi.

Herman Lannier, Camp Two foreman, had run ahead of the train and was picked up. He was the first off the train. He looked at all the people gathered at the log dump. "I think most men are accounted for."

He looked at Victoria shaking his head. "Mark and two fallers are the only ones not on board."

Tears came to her eyes as the crowd started to disperse. The smoke rolled down the hill, blackening the sky. People ran for their homes, some screaming, some crying, and others showing no expression at all.

The trains pulled onto the newly completed pier that ran out in the middle of the lake so they wouldn't burn. Steam powered pumps were spraying water on the pier to keep it wet. Sparks from the fire fell all over the mill and holding yards. The fire hoses in the mill were turned on to water down the whole area to keep the sparks from becoming fires.

Victoria made her way through the darkness taking Nomi back to the house She felt alone, and afraid of what might have become of Mark. The thought that the fire might spread and destroy their home terrified her.

Once inside she paced back and forth, praying for Mark's return. She looked out toward the mountain but could only see thick smoke. It was mid-day and it looked as though a long winter night had set in.

*   *   *   *

The fire raced north along Cultas Mountain, devouring Camp One, destroying a few scattered cabins and burning over the ridge toward the river. The winds created by the fire helped push it eastward, away from the town of Clear Lake. Other fires were burning all along the western slopes of the Cascades adding to the smoke filled skies. The smoke from the fire became so thick that a man couldn't see his hand in front of his face.

Caleb lit a lantern, hoping to make things bright, but the smoke drowned out what light the lamp offered. Rose coughed and hacked from breathing the thick air, and Caleb knew that he should get her to someplace inside. "Come with me Rose," he said as he helped her up.

She stood and put her hand on his belt loop, and he led her down the creek toward town. "Where are we going?" Rose asked.

"I need to get you to a safe place. My house may be burnt so I'll take you to your friend's place. The lady you visit with all the time."

They arrived at Victoria's house and Caleb knocked on the door. The walk had taken an hour longer than normal because of the heavy smoke. Victoria's face looked worn when she opened the door. "Rose, are you all right?"

"Yes. Caleb thinks I need to be inside, out of this smoke."

Victoria ushered them in. "Why the worn face?" Rose asked.

"I think Mark might have been caught in the fire—I'm afraid."

"This might be the fire I saw when I was a young girl. It will make everything new. I feel that Mark is alive," Rose said as she took a seat.

"I am so worried about him—he's out there somewhere."

Caleb heard her words and saw the concern on her face. "I'll go find him."

$$*\qquad*\qquad*\qquad*$$

Hot embers fell from the sky, causing spot fires all around as Caleb walked through town. It wasn't until they gained in size that they were noticed, and then it was too late for anything to be done. They burned themselves out in a short time running out of fuel.

Caleb put a handkerchief over his mouth so he could breathe easier. As he walked to the edge of town he heard a woman screaming for help. Running toward the screams found a woman holding her husband. He had been shot, and was dead. She was crying. "Don't hurt me," she said as she saw Caleb.

"I'm won't hurt you ma'am. Who did this?"

"Two men came—they robbed us and killed my husband!"

"I'll get you help."

Caleb ran to the closest house only to find that they had been robbed also, but no one had been shot there. He told them about their neighbor being shot. Caleb shook his head. "Bad things breed other bad things. That's the way life is sometimes. You should go help your neighbor."

*　　　*　　　*　　　*

Mark held on to the dock with all his strength. He couldn't feel his hands and knew they were burned to the bone. He wondered if this was his end. His body was no longer cold from being in the water as the burning wood kept him warm. He could still hear the fire raging through the forest and the sound of trees exploding as the fire swept through them. He looked at the water in the pond and saw tiny bubbles rising to the surface. The water seemed to boil as the bubbles rose faster. Mark knew it was the end for him. What a way to die, he thought. It was like being a chicken boiled for dinner.

Mark, exhausted from holding onto the edge of the dock lost all track of time. He wondered if it was it minutes, or hours? His fingers were burned to the point that they lost most of their feeling. He couldn't hold on any longer. He let go of the dock slipping into the water as he took his last breath letting his body sink down, and closed his eyes hoping for a quick end.

*　　　*　　　*　　　*

Caleb kept to the tracks knowing that it was the safest place to be. Fires were still burning in the fallen timber, and the heat was intense. The fire contorted the iron rails, burned the ties, and melted the spikes. He was sure that no one could have lived through such heat, yet he'd still search for Mark knowing how much that would mean to Victoria.

*　　　*　　　*　　　*

As Mark hit the bottom of the pond he found his head above water. He let out a laugh as he thought he could have been standing in the pond all along. He splashed water on his head, as the heat was unbearable. After sometime his mind started to come and go and his thoughts weren't clear. Mark was stunned as he tried to make sense of where he was. His thoughts turned to Victoria. "God, I'm not ready to die—help me!"

When he looked up toward the sky all he saw were thick dark clouds of smoke rolling by. He could still hear the roar caused by the intensity of the fire, but it sounded like it was moving away. He climbed back on to the dock and rested his tired arms by lying on his stomach on the burnt wood. Because of the smoke, he couldn't see much but glowing embers burning in the place where buildings once stood in Camp Two.

He managed to get onto his feet and walked into the ash and smoke. He knew it wasn't Heaven and thought maybe this is what Hell looked like. He thought how fitting it was that he should die because of fire and then be sent to Hell. Steam rose off his clothes as he started his journey.

There was nothing nice here just black trees, black ground, black skies, black souls, and the embers that he'd heard the preacher talk about when he was young were all around him. Two crisp bodies lying next to the tracks looked as if they were demons coming to get him. The wind made an evil howling as it raced by him adding fuel to the fire ahead. It pulled smoke from distant fires down south. He walked with the wind, thinking it would take him to the center of hell.

He saw a figure walking toward him through the dense smoke. Caleb pulled a scarf over his head to keep the falling ashes off his hair. The scarf had two points sticking up, which looked like horns. Mark stopped then looked at Caleb. "Damn you, Satan, damn you to Hell. I haven't yet begun to live and you take me now. Damn you!"

"Are you all right?" Caleb asked as he reached out to steady Mark.

"Mark looked at him closely. "I knew it! I knew you were in bed with the devil."

"You've been hurt—you're not thinking right. Come with me and I'll take you home."

Mark didn't fight, but took hold of Caleb's arm, and they started back toward town. It was evening and the sun had set, but Caleb couldn't tell what time it was, for the sky had remained dark all day. It took them most of the night to find their way to Mark's house. When they finally arrived, Victoria ran out and hugged Mark. She cried with joy to know he was alive. For the first time she was beginning to feel love for him. It was nice. It was the way it should be. Love grew in her heart as her parents said it would.

When morning came, so did the rain, a welcome sight for everyone. The rain washed the air clean, and the fires were put to a stop.

Caleb ventured back up to the land he loved, fearing that all was lost. The sky was filled with misty clouds, and the smell of burning wood hung in the air as steam and smoke rose from the hot ground. He made his way past Nookachamps Creek, up Mundt Creek, and to his amazement, the trees to the south of Mundt Creek were still standing fresh and green. He ran with excitement to his house. He stopped and viewed the large tree of life that was his home. Happiness beamed from his soul.

Fires consumed timber all the way from Northern California, along the west coast up into British Columbia. Around the mountains of Clear Lake the fires destroyed so much timber and equipment that Hammer knew it would be some time before the mill would be running again. The summer of 1902 went down as the year of the great fires.

In the falling rain he walked the tracks up to Camp Two. He found the two missing fallers lying a few feet from the rails. He knew that many more could have been lost, but men were expendable. There were other men waiting to take their place in the forest. He walked through the remains of Camp Two seeing what could be salvaged. "We'll have to rebuild this damn place," he said kicking the dirt.

He saw green trees to the south and started walking towards Caleb's land. He came to the edge of Mundt creek and started cursing upon seeing that Caleb's trees weren't burnt. "Damn fool doesn't know what he has."

"Oh yes I do."

Hammer turned around to find Caleb smiling at him. "You're going to get yourself shot one of these days sneaking up on people like this!"

"Wasn't sneaking—men like you just don't pay attention to things around them."

Hammer shook his head as he looked again at Caleb's trees. "Can you tell me why those trees are not burnt and mine are? It seems strange to me—don't you think?"

"No, this mountain has its own mind most of the time—I don't understand it and you surely won't."

"I'll log those trees someday and there will be no misunderstanding about that."

"Greed sometimes will kill the greedy. I saw some beavers that had taken every tree around their pond. They couldn't raise the water level any higher to get to new trees. So they would leave the safety of the water to get more trees and as they wandered away from their pond the fox and coyotes got them."

"What does that have to do with me?"

"You're the beaver—greed will get you sometime."

"No, you're the animal—try living in civilization sometime. It might help, and forget all these fables you believe in."

"We just see the world in different ways."

"Yes, and if you don't come to see it like me, you will be the one that vanishes."

CHAPTER 13

▼

HATE

Mark recovered from his burns and before long he was back to work. The mill started to log some of the burned timber. Most of the timber on the east side of Cultas Mountain was left untouched. Caleb's timber to the south was tempting, but Hammer knew that the mill couldn't wait for timber, and a long drawn out fight with Caleb could drive the mill and company under. Times were tough and every penny would make a difference. Caleb's words stuck in Mark's mind as he drew out new maps.

New tracks were laid north to the river, and then upriver east to Day Creek. Billions of board feet, as far as the eye could see, lay in the basin and surrounding hills. The fire had passed over this area. This valley cleft in the mountains was protected from storms by Cultas Mountain to the west, Haystack Mountain to the east, and Deer Peak to the south. The trees grew straight and tall, some of the cleanest wood Hammer had ever laid eyes on.

Mark became head engineer over all road building for the company. Hammer planned on building many new roads to hopefully entice others to make an investment in the company. New money was needed to keep the operation going. With all this new timber it wouldn't take long to double the cut and mill production.

*   *   *   *

Victoria worked in her kitchen preparing dinner when she heard the door open. Tom Bearskin, an Indian from the upper Skagit, stood in her house. In his arms was his girl Shasa, crying from hunger. Tom and his wife were two of a handful of Indians from the Upper Skagit tribe that hadn't been taken by small pox. He stood in the kitchen holding the child out to Victoria. "Me kill him. Me kill him."

He ran to the door and looked out the window. He couldn't stand still. His eyes darted back and forth, looking for someone or something that might get him. He kept walking over and looking out the windows down the path. Victoria looked at him trying to reason with him. "It's not right to kill someone. That's something you should never do. Life is a gift and it shouldn't be taken."

"No! Me kill him."

"Oh my! When did you do this?" Victoria said, realizing that he had already committed the act. "Who? Who did you kill?"

"Me kill him. He hurt wife—me kill him."

"You need to go, Tom, and you need to get far from here. They'll come after you, kill you and they may even kill your daughter. So you'd better go as far from here as you can."

"Me no place—no place for Shasa—you keep her."

He handed Shasa to Victoria and left heading north toward Woolley.

Victoria took the girl and put her in clean clothes. She smiled as she thought about how life changes. She had lost one girl and now had two. This was a blessing to her as life was a gift and she believed that God had given her another chance to prove herself. She pondered what she was going to tell Mark when he arrived home. She would deal with that then.

The next morning Victoria heard a knock at her door. She went to answer it and found Rose and two other Indians on her front porch. "Did Tom stop here last night?" Rose asked.

"Yes, why do you ask?"

"These men are looking for him. They're brothers of the man that Tom killed."

"Tom left heading north…"

As Victoria talked, the men left, running north. Rose began to weep. "There will be no one left. The invisible has killed most, and spirits will kill some, and those left will kill each other. They won't even spare his daughter."

"What happened? Do you know? Why did Tom kill that man?"

"We were at summer potlatch with the Swimnomish when the chief's son of the Samish tribe made advances toward Tom's wife. She rejected them and he became upset and forced himself on her. Tom was drunk that night and didn't know what had happened. The next day the man again tried to force himself on Tom's wife. There was a skirmish between Tom and the man. Tom defeated him and everything seemed back to normal, but later that night the man gave Tom's wife Indian Hell Borne plant. He forced it down her, and she died.

Tom grieved, and then left. He waited on the path leading back to the Samish village, and when the man was on his way back, Tom attacked him and killed him. He cut him into a hundred pieces and threw the pieces in a pile and then placed the head on top of the pile in the middle of the trail."

"That's horrible" Victoria said.

"Now these men will hunt Tom down and kill him. But Tom has no one left to avenge his death."

"Don't they understand why Tom did it?"

"Yes, but it has been this way from the beginning. One man kills another, and then the relatives of the dead hunt down and kill the man who killed. This goes back and forth, sometimes for years. Our wars have been mostly over just the killing of one man and the revenge taken for that life. It's our way."

Victoria leaned close to Rose. "Rose, I have Tom's daughter. He left her here in my care. I don't want anyone to know, so you must help me keep it a secret."

Rose's eyes turned down. "How do you keep it a secret? Do you keep her away from the sun?"

"I can hide the child."

"If they find out, they'll come for her. Tell no one about it, but I don't know how that will be, because all the whites will know that you have another child, and then those who want her will come for her."

"I won't let them take her—I won't!"

Later that day word came to Victoria from Rose that Tom had been killed in the same method that he had killed. They had found him just upriver from Sedro-Woolley. Rose stood on Victoria's porch. "They're looking for his daughter. They'll come here soon—they know you have her. Please keep her safe."

Mark came home late Friday night. He entered the house and found a large meal waiting for him. Meat from Mr. McDonald, the local butcher, steamed potatoes, and fresh greens were all set on the table begging to be consumed. Victoria had put Shasa to bed for the night, and Nomi was up playing. Mark heard a faint cry coming from Nomi's bedroom. "What's that crying I hear?"

Victoria walked into the room and came back out carrying Shasa. Mark looked at Victoria. "What's that?"

"It's Shasa, a baby girl."

"Where did that Indian come from? Are you the dumping ground for all unwanted Indian children?" He asked.

"She has no mother or father, and if she were to go with what Indians are left, some might kill her. So here, she is safe with us, and I'll raise her to be a nice young lady. And besides Nomi needs a sister, and I seem to be barren, or we don't make love enough."

Mark became angry at the words he heard. "I work long hours—I give you more than most would be able. Maybe God knows you can't take care of your own and that's why he chooses not to give you another—don't blame your barrenness on me!"

Her choices in life weighed heavy on her heart. Mark was right, as it wasn't his fault. She had no words to respond. "This is it. No more of these Indian kids. We should be having our own—I just don't understand why you can't become with child," Mark said.

He turned away, sat down at the table and started eating. Nomi looked at him. "You like the new baby, Daddy?"

He smiled and patted her on the head. "Yes."

Victoria smiled also. She knew that in time Mark would come to love them as his own.

The next morning Mark was awakened by the sound of his door opening. He rose out of bed, and walked into the next room. He came face to face with three Indians standing in his house. "What do you want?"

"We come for the child. We know she is here."

Victoria heard the voices. She rose and walked into the room and became frightened. She knew what they were after. "You cannot have the girl!"

"She was given as a gift to my wife," Mark interjected, "and our customs say that gifts cannot be given back."

The men pressed toward them and Mark pushed Victoria behind him.

"This is my house, now leave!"

"You have what belongs to us—we will leave in peace if you give us what we want."

Mark touched Victoria on the shoulder. "Get them the child."

"No!"

"Get the child—they may do us harm if we don't."

"No! They'll take her and kill her."

Mark looked at the three men, fearing that they might become violent, wondering why they would want the child. It was beyond his thinking that they could hurt a baby. "What do you intend to do with the child?"

"Take her to her father."

Mark turned back to Victoria. "I thought her father was dead."

"He is—and they're the ones who did it."

The men came closer to them. "Did you kill her father?" Mark asked.

"We kill him. Now we take her."

The door opened and Rose and Caleb were standing on the porch. Rose spoke to the men in their native tongue, and the men backed away from Mark and Victoria. Caleb walked into the house and stared at the three Indian men. Rose again spoke to them in her tongue and they turned and ran away. Mark and Victoria were relieved. Victoria hugged Rose. "How did you know to come here and help us? And what did you say to them to make them run away so fast?"

Rose laughed. "I saw the Raven and he warned me that things were not good here. I brought Caleb, because those men all knew his grandfather, and I told them that if they tried to hurt the girl, Caleb would use the same magic that his grandfather did. I told them Caleb would cause the terrible darkness to fall upon them, and that he had the power to make them sick. I told them to never come here or they would die—they won't be around again."

Mark didn't have much to say. He shook his head and went to get fully dressed. He was relieved that things turned out all right. Rose and Caleb left, heading back to the hills, and Victoria smiled that she was being looked after by something greater than she could explain.

*   *   *   *

The mill was again running at full speed. A hundred more men were hired to work in the woods, the mill, and on the trains. There were so many logs coming off the mountains that the mill couldn't keep up. Clear Lake was one large holding pond. The logs were packed so tight that men could walk across the lake without touching the water.

Lake pigs were the name given to the men who moved the logs through the lake to the conveyer chain. The chain had hooks on it to grab the logs and pull them out of the lake into the mill. Hammer surveyed the logs in the lake. "We'll add another shift to the mill. Run that damn thing twenty-four hours a day. Make thousands of dollars."

In the spring of 1906 the mill added a second shift and production was doubled again.

The town continued to grow. New houses were being built, with new businesses following. A few people were making plans to incorporate the town. A meeting was called, and the important men in town were invited. After the meeting was called to order Hammer stood up and spoke. "I propose that we rename the town."

Everyone's attention turned to Hammer. "I think it should be Hammerville."

"Are you serious?" one man asked.

"Sure am. I've been here since the start."

"I don't know if the rest of the long timers in town will like that," Mark said.

A few men laughed and mocked Hammer for having such high thoughts of himself. "You'd be lucky to have a street named after you," one of the mill owners said.

"Things will be different around here soon. Sooner than most of you think," Hammer said as he left the meeting.

At the meeting the prominent men from the mill organized and formed the Skagit Club. The purpose of the club was to encourage and promote the growth of the mill and the town of Clear Lake. Members had to be in good standing in the mill and in the community. No man of questionable character, no thieves, liars, or the like could belong.

Mark was asked to join and felt honored at the invitation. His dreams of being successful in America were becoming reality.

The mill installed two new steam turbans to produce electricity, which supplied enough power to run the mill, and provided enough power to light up the town. Lines were hung and they soon ran to the houses throughout the down town area. A great party was held on the night when all the wiring was completed. Hammer and the owners of the mill were in attendance. As the sunset, Hammer pulled the switch, and lights went on all over town. It was a sight to see. "Clear Lake has all the modern conveniences of a large city and we're one of the first towns in Skagit County to supply both water and electricity to its citizens. The mill is great."

People clapped and cheered for most of them felt the same as Hammer.

From the third floor of Caleb's house he could see the lights sparkling in town. Things were changing fast from the times he remembered as a boy. He knew that the mill would at some time, come after his trees. Even with the lights shining in town, he knew that the dark hearts of those who wanted to do him harm would not be illuminated.

As the night wore on the lights went off one by one. Caleb watched until only the lights from the mill were left. Smoke rose from the burner standing out against the clear sky like a large evil dragon. The lights ran out to the side buildings and into the storage area made the dragon look as if it had legs and wings. This was Caleb's monster, a powerful beast that was never full, but always consuming more to meets its insatiable need for timber. It devoured not only the forest but also the men that fed it. This was one beast that bit the hand that fed it. This was the war that Caleb knew he had to win. He had to defeat the beast or be consumed.

Caleb awoke in the morning and met Rose for breakfast. She looked at his face. "Why the long look? You look as though *cultas* is weighing on your heart."

"Yes, something bad is on my heart. It's the mill. You know they're going to come and take my trees soon, and I don't know how to defeat them."

"You have to become as the *putch chub*, the silent moving cougar. Be as fast as *dere*, the deer that runs fast. You, Caleb, have to be as *whay-kwah dee tyee*, the thunderbird that brings fear to the hearts of those that hear him. You need the help of *kub-kah-date-suh*, the giant monster that eats men."

"Those are powerful men that run the mill—men with money—they're giant men."

"No man is taller than the trees. They may think they're big, they saw down the giants in the forest—they move giant mountains, but they are not giant men. I thought my father was a giant but the sickness took him and he is no more. It takes many swings of the ax and much pulling of the saw to bring down a giant tree. Hundreds, maybe thousands, but with one swing of the ax a man can be brought down."

"I wish it were that easy."

"Caleb, stand strong and brave, stand taller than the trees—then you will appear as a giant to them. Be firm like the big rock that we honor—a mountain of stone is hard to tear down. Violence will not help you—killing will not do you any good. There will always be more behind them. Let peace rule your heart. Root yourself in doing right—that will win over everything."

"If I sit and do nothing they will take everything."

"When all is done men sleep. That's how nature works—after the storm things are at peace—they will destroy themselves."

"I hope they do before they destroy me."

Caleb knew that he would have a hard fight ahead of him no matter if he sat or took action. He wished he had help, but he knew he would be hard pressed to find someone in this town who would stand with him.

*   *   *   *

Victoria worked with the girls picking apples off the trees. They were getting huge and producing abundant fruit. The girls were growing fast. They were not welcome in the white school and Victoria took the time to teach them as if they were in school. They learned fast and could speak good English, do math, and write well.

They had all the apples picked and were making cider with the bruised ones. Nomi lifted a bruised apple and looked at it close. "Mother, why does dad say we're bruised? I don't understand what he means."

Victoria picked up a bruised apple and pointed at the bruise. "When an apple is bruised it turns brown where the bruise is."

"Dad says those apples are no good."

"What he says isn't true—if they were no good we would throw them out, but we take them and make something better. Sometimes the sweetest cider is made from bruised apples. So I believe it is with you and your sister—you will grow up to be strong, wonderful, loving women, and leave your mark in this valley."

Nomi smiled and threw the apple into the press.

When Mark came home on the weekends, he would spend his time cutting, splitting, and stacking firewood. He didn't like the idea of Victoria being cold with out heat. The girls would help him stack it, and not much was said between Mark and the girls.

*   *   *   *

Thirty miles from Clear Lake up the Skagit River a few men were scavenging the remnants of gold from Ruby Creek. The rush had taken place quickly and only the diehards stayed for a few years hoping to strike it rich. Caleb himself had panned for gold in many of the streams throughout the North Cascades. He had found a few flakes here and there, but never enough to make him wealthy. Yet, it was always enough to purchase a couple of nice things from the local stores.

In his travels he met a man by the name of Jimmy Washington. Jimmy was a black man who came to the Washington territory because it had the same name as him. He arrived in 1885, heard of the gold rush in the Cascades and headed up to stake his claim. He worked his claim with some success and stayed on for twenty years. In that time he met Caleb and the two became good friends. Caleb was one of the few white men who would take the time to be friends with Jimbo the gold mole, as he was called. The name came because of the extent of the mineshafts and tunnels that laced his claim.

In the winter the snow in the upper part of the valley would reach twenty to thirty feet. Jim would make a trip to visit and stay with Caleb for a month or more. It was a nice break not having to fight all the deep snow, and being able to have human company. In the early spring he would return to Ruby Creek. It was here that he was truly a free man. The upper Skagit was his sanctuary. It was his place of escape.

The rain fell hard outside as Caleb worked inside. He heard a knock on his door. A warm fire glowed in his firebox and Rose sat next to it weaving a basket. Caleb opened the door and smiled. "Come on in Jim."

Jim had a couple of bags of gold with him and some clothes. "Make yourself at home and fill me in on any news," Caleb said.

Caleb knew he would be staying for a while. Caleb didn't mind, for he was always fond of having company.

Rose hadn't seen many black people. She had seen Jim once previously at Caleb's place, but other than that, all she knew about black people was what she heard from the first whites she had met.

Now Jim didn't fit the description that Rose was given. She had been told that blacks were just slaves to the whites at one time and not smart. She knew about slaves, for her people were pressed into slavery when they were taken into captivity by other warring tribes. She figured that Jim must have some magic to keep him free, because he never did anything for white men, and that's all there were up in the gold fields. He was the lone man that wasn't white. Rose called him *hassla moha* meaning the free black bear.

When he entered the house Rose looked at him. "Don't work your magic on me," she said with a smile.

Caleb laughed as he poured a hot cup of tea for Jim. The drink was made from the plant called "Trappers Tea" which grew in the mountains. Caleb and Rose would collect and dry the leaves, so they'd have enough for the winter. Rose held up her cup. "It's good medicine."

They sat around and talked into the late hours of the night. Sharing stories, dreams, and desires of what they wanted in life. "Having good friends warm my soul," Caleb said, as he headed off to bed.

*   *   *   *

Mark stayed busy with his crews laying out new roads into the hills. All variables were taken into consideration to gauge the chance of success in logging a particular site. If enough board feet of lumber stood in a site, they would build a road, a few bridges, lay tracks, and turn a handsome profit. The timber cruisers would come back with their results on the number of board feet in any given area, and Mark would send his crews to clear the way for the logs to be hauled out.

In the winter the town of Clear Lake would see rain more days than sun. Snow would fall once in a while, but most of the time it didn't amount to much. Things were different in the mountains. At an elevation of two thousand feet or more, snow could fall and accumulate to several feet. This would bring a great burden to all those who had to work in it.

In December it started to snow in the whole valley. It snowed three days accumulating to a depth of three feet. The mill was paralyzed with logging coming to a halt. Rose was at Victoria's house when the snow started and never had a chance to make it home. She watched the snow fall from inside the house "This isn't good."

"Why not? I like seeing the snow making everything white."

"A long time ago when my people were many there came a big snow. It killed a few of us. My father, the chief asked the medicine man to make the snow go away. He went to his home and came out the next day and as he walked out of his home the winds started."

"What winds?"

"Chinook winds—warm winds that melt the snow. The snow melted fast covering the whole valley under water."

"What happened then?"

"It killed many and destroyed our home."

Fear showed in Victoria's eyes.

"Tyee is like that—sometimes you ask for one thing not seeing what that will bring. Life is like that—you never know what the thing you desire will bring—good or bad."

Just as soon as the snow stopped the winds came. A temperature change of over thirty degrees made it feel like spring in the middle of December. Victoria watched the creek slowly start to rise and then overflow as the snow melted. In town men that had been in the valley a while knew what was coming.

Farmers, living near the river and in the flats, were busy moving their cattle and horses to higher ground. The floods came fast and some were caught unaware. Whole houses and barns were under water. Two men and a woman with her children drowned when their small boat capsized in the swift current of the Skagit.

It was over a week until the flood receded. Logs, stumps, and other debris were left in fields and against houses and barns. The clean up would take months, Mark thought as he looked over the mess. A few slides had covered the tracks up the south side of the Skagit. It would set the mill behind another month or more. No matter what progress the mill made, nature still ruled.

Ivar had experienced colder weather back in the mid-west and in the old country. He could live with the rainy, cold northwest weather. The cold winds didn't bite here, and the snow didn't last long. The other men did nothing but complain. Wet snow, wet rain, the air loaded with moisture, all amounted to wet cold bodies for those who were working outside.

Few men were fortunate enough to have inside jobs with the company. Most of the men wished for a job in the mill during the winter. A man like Ivar would endure the cold weather in the winter so he could be outside in the summer, for in the summer working in the mill was a hot and tiresome job. The noise, the sawdust, the heat, and smoke from the burner would all seem to bear down on a man's body and mind.

In the summer the air in the mountains felt clean and refreshing. The sights were beautiful, and what more could a man ask for?

Down by the mill Hammer built a company bunkhouse for the men who worked in the mill but didn't live close to the town. At the same time he had another house built a couple of blocks away from the bunkhouse. This house was the company brothel, known by most, denied by many.

He built a new store that was owned and operated by the company. He figured the men could spend their money there as well as anywhere else. He opened a company bank called the Clear Lake Lumber Bank. The town needed a full time doctor, so the company hired Dr. Meadows from Mount Vernon. He had treated many men who had injuries from forest accidents, and the company paid him well. He was immediately asked to join the Skagit Club, but declined. "I have better things to tend to than men trying to feel important."

Hammer carried out all the orders from the board of men that owned the company. The company believed it was good to provide the men with the best possible working conditions and all the services they needed. The company store gave the men credit and took their payment out of the wages owed them. The men kept their money in the company bank and received loans if needed. The company doctor met all their health needs. The best part of it was that the money stayed within the company. Even when men visited the brothel, the money would come back to the company. "We'll own everything and everyone before long," Hammer said to the owners.

∗   ∗   ∗   ∗

Christmas was three weeks away. Caleb came into town to get some supplies and a few gifts. He brought Jim with him. Jim planned on buying a couple of gifts for Caleb and Rose. "There seems to be new buildings every time I come here," Caleb said as they walked into town.

He walked into Beddall's store and pulled a few things from the shelf when he heard Mr. Beddall mumbling to a woman. "That new company store is hurting my business and I'm thinking of selling."

The woman paid for her things and left with out responding. Caleb walked up to the counter to pay for his things. Caleb watched as Mr. Beddall put his items in a bag. "Why is your business hurting?" Caleb asked.

Mr. Beddall was happy to have someone to complain to. "The company isn't only doing the business of logging and milling, but they're putting their hands in everything else, too. They want to own the town and everything in it."

Caleb sighed a breath of agreement as Mr. Beddall went on. "They have a bank, a doctor, and that new store."

He leaned close to Caleb and said in a low voice, "Even that new brothel is owned by the mill, and that doesn't set right with Jezzy."

"Why's that?" Caleb responded.

"Her business is down also. They have younger ladies at the company house. Oh, but I guess you have no idea what those ladies do—since you've never been with a woman before—or have you?"

Caleb thought for a moment. "This isn't good. It's almost like being slaves to the pharaoh. You're correct about what you say, I do understand what's going on. My grandfather told me about relations and all that stuff. Told me not lay with just anyone—so I listened."

"I understand what you're saying son."

"So I know what they do, but it's not for me."

"You will find a nice woman one of these days," Beddall said.

"A nice woman isn't my concern at the moment—it's the same as yours. The mill is becoming a monster."

"Not much we can do about it. Especially you."

Caleb smiled as Mr. Beddall added up his bill. He paid and headed out the door. Across the street in front of the Skagit Club he saw a few men gathering, shouting, and pushing each other. He wandered over to see what was going on and saw Jim in the middle of them. He was on the ground and some men were kicking him. "Kill him! Kill the animal!"

Caleb put his things down and ran into the center of the men and shielded Jim. "Stop! Leave him alone—what has he ever done to you?"

A big man stepped up to Caleb. "There are a few things that have been stolen from the mill. It just happens that nothing ever has been missing from the mill until this man showed up in the area this last week."

"You have over a hundred men working there. Jim hasn't been near the mill, and besides, he doesn't need to steal. So let him be."

"Don't you understand? He's black, he's a thief, and he might even take advantage of our women."

"He has never hurt anyone!"

A man pushed Caleb down from behind, as the men started kicking Jim again. Caleb fought to get free and managed to throw two men off him, but four more jumped him and he was taken down. A few others grabbed Jim and tied him to a nearby tree. They tied Caleb to another tree about thirty feet away. One of the men picked up a freshly cut branch of an alder tree. They cut Jim's shirt off and started beating him on the back.

All Caleb could do was watch as different men took turns beating on Jim. When his back was all bloody, they cut him lose and then cut Caleb lose. Three men came up to Caleb. "You'd better watch whom you keep as friends—who knows? Maybe you even helped him."

Caleb didn't respond. He got up and ran over to help Jim to his feet. As they walked out of town, the men yelled, "We better not see you around here again, or you might not make it out alive."

Mark returned home from the Skagit Club and sat down at the table. Victoria could see that he had a troubled look on his face. She walked over and rubbed his back. "Tell me what's wrong?"

"Things aren't right at the club."

She continued rubbing his back and arms. "What things? Tell me what's not right."

"Things down at the club, they're wrong, just wrong. I may not like that Caleb Cultas, but they don't have to treat him like they do."

"What happened to him?"

"Nothing, nothing that you should know about."

She knew not to press him more for the answers. He was done talking. She finished cleaning up the table and dishes and put the girls to bed. Mark went and stretched out on the bed in their room when Victoria entered. She crawled in next to him and gently kissed his cheek. She put her arms around him. "Make love to me, Mark."

He rolled over, turning his back to her. She drew closer and whispered in a soft voice, "Tell me why you won't make love to me."

There was silence. The silence seemed to grow and tears started to flow from Victoria's eyes. Mark turned onto his back. "Don't you understand—I work long hours. I'm tired and besides, we've tried for another child, and you're barren. It's all you want every time I come home."

"I only want to feel close to you. I want to have you next to me, inside of me. I need to know you love me, Mark, I need to feel it."

Again there was silence as Victoria watched Mark. Mark stared into the darkness of night. Sleep overcame him as Victoria wondered what she was doing wrong. Her heart hurt and she didn't know how to make it well. Her thoughts moved to her sister wondering how she was and what she was doing.

C H A P T E R 14

▼

DEATH

Mark walked through the forest searching for the best route to build a new road. He wanted to avoid canyons and ravines, because building trestles took too much time and money. The week dragged on as if it would never end. The wind moved through the big trees bringing the smell of snow. Mark looked up and saw the first flake falling through the canopy of the trees. A bad feeling overcame him as he walked. He heard his name called in the trees. "Just nonsense," he said as he headed back to camp.

Mark arrived back in camp and felt better being around all the men. Working and walking alone in the forest gave many men a feeling of doom. It was nothing uncommon, Mark thought.

Mark walked toward the train. He was finished for the day and wanted to get home. It was Friday and if he didn't catch the last train he would be stuck up in camp until next week unless he walked home. Over a foot of snow had fallen in Camp Three, and it was still snowing as men jumped on the train. Steam poured from the stack on the engine as it waited for the last few men to climb onto the loaded connects. A slight wind moved through the trees like they were whispering to each other and to the men if they would listen.

It was a cold ride as there was only cover for the engineer and the brakeman. The fireman stood on the open rack, between the engine and fuel car, putting wood into the firebox. The rest of the men sat close to each other on the connects for the fifteen-mile ride into town.

When Mark jumped on the train the engineer invited him into the engine cab. Mark always wanted to run an engine and was fascinated watching the engineer manipulate the levers to make the engine move.

The snow fell and the wind grew stronger as the train pulled out of camp. The engineer felt sorry for the men riding on top of the connects. He traveled faster than he usually did trying to shorten the time it took to get to town. The fireman worked hard adding fuel to the box to keep up with the engine's demand for heat. Steam and smoke poured out of the stack as the train barrelled down the tracks.

The train came around one of the many bends on the railroad, and the brakeman went to apply the brake, but nothing happened. The brakeman applied the brakes a second time and still nothing. He looked at the engineer. "Better throttle down or we'll lose it."

The engineer throttled down on the engine, but it was now being pushed by the twelve connects. The brakeman looked over the edge seeing snow packed between the wheels and the brake pads. He pointed to the brake pads as he looked at the engineer. "Ice and snow are packed in there."

The engineer nodded to the brakeman then looked at Mark. "You'd better hang on—it's going to be a rough one."

Mark grabbed a handle inside the cab as the train sped around the bend. Men feared for their lives as they clutched the chains that held the logs in place. The train made the curve and headed down a steep grade toward a trestle. It was one of the biggest trestles in the northwest. "We're not going to make it over that trestle going this fast!" the engineer said.

The men on the connects knew that the train might crash, and fearing for their lives, started jumping off.

Most of the men jumped off the connects before the engine started across the trestle. The engineer prayed that he would make it safely across, and then it would be just a straight stretch the rest of the way into town. As the train started across, the trestle began to sway back and forth. The train's weight and speed put stress on the cross members.

In the rush to get to the best timber Mark had built this trestle lightly, knowing it would be abandoned after the timber was cut. The engineers knew this and would normally slow down to make the crossing, but this train was being driven by another force that was out of their control.

As the train crossed the middle section, the trestle began to collapse, starting at the far end and moving toward the engine. A few of the men who had jumped off were standing on the edge of the gully, watching in horror.

As the engine moved forward toward the collapsing supports its nose pointed downward and fell crashing 150 feet to the bottom of the gully.

The fireman jumped just before the engine fell and started running toward the edge, but the trestle collapsed too fast. He fell face down and held onto one of the timbers, hoping to ride out the fall. The brakeman jumped, falling to the bottom of the gully to his death.

The engineer and Mark held onto whatever they could grab inside the cab. On impact the engineer was killed instantly. Mark was thrown out of the train only to have the boiler land on him, pinning his legs under the metal. A puncture on the side of the boiler started to leak steam. Mark tried to move away from the heat as it burned his body, but he was unable to escape. The steam gained in intensity, as did Marks screams of pain.

Men worked their way down the steep ravine to the engine to see if anyone was alive. They found the fireman hanging onto the timber he rode down with the trestle. He was wide-eyed and scared, but alive. He couldn't speak, being still filled with terror. They continued to the engine, and found Mark screaming in pain as he was being burned. Two men grabbed some broken timbers and slipped them under the boiler. They pried the boiler up only gaining an inch. Two other men pulled on Mark's body to no avail, burning them in the process. Mark's screaming could be heard for miles. Men up on the ridge could hear his cries of pain. Then, there was silence.

Men started toward town on foot without speaking. There was nothing they could do. Some were limping, and others were holding their arms, and other parts of their bodies that were injured. Those that could walk helped others who couldn't walk on their own. The snowstorm intensified making the trip wearisome.

As the snow landed on Mark's dead body it would melt. As the minutes passed into hours the snow no longer melted but slowly covered his body. Nature laid him to rest.

Darkness surrounded the men as they dragged themselves into town. Word spread fast about the wreck of engine number two. Ivar was one of those who had made the jump before the train went down. When he arrived he went straight for the company office. Hammer wasn't there so Ivar set off for Hammer's house. Hammer ran for the office and met Ivar half way. "What the hell happened?"

"The train crashed. Three people are dead and Mark is one of them."

"Is anyone left up there injured?"

"No, everyone that's alive is here in town."

Hammer went into his office and sat down. This accident would put them behind for the whole winter. He thought about how he was going to get the engine out of the gully. He wrote up a company memo and had it sent out to all three camps. The memo to Camp Three would have to be delivered by horseback.

"No men will have Saturday off. They will show up at the wreck and help with salvage until it is all removed."

Victoria sat in her house waiting for Mark to come home when she heard a knock at her door. It was Jezzy, standing on the porch with a worried look on her face. Victoria opened the door and invited her in. "Did someone hurt you, Jezzy?"

"No," she responded, dreading the news she had to tell her friend.

"Then tell me what's wrong—are you leaving?"

"Victoria, there was a train accident—I wish I didn't have to tell you this, but Mark was killed."

Victoria started to shake and fell to her knees, sobbing, crying. Jezzy bent down and put her arms around Victoria. Nomi and Shasa came running out of their room to see what was wrong. When they saw their mother's grief, they started to cry. Jezzy put her arms around them all and gave what comfort she could.

Rose heard the trees whisper Mark's name and left to see Victoria. She arrived at Victoria's house shortly after Jezzy. She walked in the room, finding them all on the floor weeping. She knelt next to them. "The greater the loss the greater the hurt—it's always that way with life and death. There is no comfort in knowing that the one you love is lost forever, so mourn, and mourn until your hurt is washed away."

There was silence for a time. Rose waved her hands in the air. "Hurts are like rocks in a river. A rock falls in the river and is washed clean. All the dirt is washed off, but the rock stays in the river. Over time the water washes at the rock, breaking it, making it into smaller rocks. The water runs over those rocks, turning them into sand. Then the river washes the sand away to the great waters. The bigger the rock, the longer it takes—it's the same with hurt. The bigger the hurt, the longer it takes to heal. So let your heart mourn and weep, let yourself feel it all."

Rose wept with them. They stayed there all night weeping, caring, and comforting each other. In the morning Victoria left the girls with Rose as she and Jezzy made their way up to the wreck. She wanted to see the place where Mark had died. Not much was said as they walked through town.

They started up the hill traveling on the tracks. Company engine number three had left the mill a few minutes ahead of Victoria and Jezzy. Hammer had ordered more supplies to the scene. The train cleared the tracks of snow making it easy for Jezzy and Victoria to walk since another foot of snow had fallen over night.

It was afternoon when they arrived. Men stood all around the wrecked engine. Cables were strung around the boiler and water tank. Hammer was directing the operation. They raised the metal off Mark's body. Victoria began to cry as she saw him being brought up out of the gully. The men laid him next to the engineer and the brakeman.

Caleb had heard about the accident and was sitting up on a rock, watching the recovery operation. Hammer saw him. "Go get me that worthless fool."

A couple of men walked up to get Caleb.

"I wonder what he's doing up here watching?" Hammer said to Ivar.

The men walked up to Caleb. "Our boss would like a few words with you."

Caleb jumped off the rock made his way over to Hammer with the men beside him.

"What are you doing here?" Hammer asked with an accusing voice.

"Watching."

"I can see that, but what for? Did this accident happen because of you? Did you damage the trestle? Maybe your nigger friend did?"

"Nope, none of those."

Caleb didn't fear Hammer or his wrong reasoning.

Hammer's anger showed. His attempts to get a rise out of Caleb had not succeeded. "It just seems strange to me that the trestle by your property went down, and this trestle just happened to go down. Can you tell me why that is?"

"Some things just happen. Can you tell me why those good men are dead, and you're alive?"

"You bastard! I know you had something to do with this—and when I prove you did it, you'll hang!"

Caleb looked over at Victoria and Jezzy then back at Hammer. "You're upset that your train crashed, maybe you should be upset that men have died. You say things that aren't true to hide from others that you're the one to blame. You push and push for more logs, cut faster, build trails faster, you push, push, and push. Then when things go wrong, you blame this or that, when it's you that should stop pushing! You may overcome nature for a while, but nature always fights back. And when it does, it does with fury."

Caleb disappeared into the forest as Hammer's anger burned. Victoria and Jezzy had overheard the whole conversation. Hammer turned around looking at them. "What are you doing up here? Get back to town! Women don't belong up here. If these are your husbands, they'll be brought down this afternoon on the train. Now be gone with the both of you!"

Jezzy stepped toward Hammer. "You should have compassion for her—she lost her husband."

"I don't have time to baby-sit. Now leave!"

Victoria looked at Jezzy. "Let's go. I've no more to see here."

Hammer had the men take out the engine piece by piece. They worked all day on Saturday and Sunday. He needed that engine back and running to keep the mill supplied with logs.

They buried Mark on Monday. None of the workers were in attendance. Ivar asked Hammer for the day off, but he was told he could have the day only if he wanted to find a new job. The minister said a prayer over Mark and when he finished, he left Victoria with her friends.

"Jezzy, Rose, I'd like to be alone for a while—could you take the girls and go to the house?"

"We can do that for you," Jezzy responded.

As they walked away, Victoria searched for words to say. Standing at the foot of Mark's grave, she stared at the temporary marker. Victoria wept. "Mark, I grew to love you. I'm thankful for what you gave me. I'll miss you greatly—miss the love you gave—miss the love you would have given in the future. We could have grown so close—if only there'd been time."

Tears streamed down her face as she paused to catch her breath. A cold wind blew out of the north, and mist fell from the sky. A lone eagle cried as it circled the trees. It landed on a limb high in a cedar tree and watched Victoria. She lifted her head as she heard the eagle cry again. She watched it and smiled as she thought the eagle was Mark, and he was finally free.

She started back home, thinking of how she was going to let Mark's parents know of his fate. It was a letter she wished she didn't have to write.

The girls ran to meet her as she walked up the path to the house. Under the apple trees the girls gave Victoria hugs. The snow made a canopy in the limbs of the trees. Victoria looked at the trees remembering the day they were planted. "Fifteen years and it's gone in a flash."

"What did you say mother?" Nomi asked.

"Thinking about your dad."

Jezzy and Rose watched from the front steps as Victoria and the girls made their way into the house. Not much was said among them. After some time, Victoria let out a long sigh. "What am I going to do? How am I going to feed my girls?"

"You can go cook in the camps or come work for me," Jezzy said.

"I need a way to make money. I need to be able to keep this place."

Rose listened to Victoria and Jezzy talk back and forth. "There is no sense in worry—I've never worried about tomorrow, and you don't need to worry about tomorrow. Things will take care of themselves. You can sow, you can harvest, the salmon swim up the river, and their offspring swim down the river. Winter does not last forever and spring brings forth new growth. You will survive and overcome," Rose said.

✳   ✳   ✳   ✳

A businessman from Minnesota heard of the logging opportunities in the Northwest. He came with his son to view the operations and the holdings of land. He fell in love with the Skagit Valley and desperately wanted to have a piece of it. They were big men in the logging industry back in Minnesota who were looking to buy an existing company and improve upon it. His name was Lee Lowland.

They bought a small logging company just northeast of the Clear Lake Lumber Company. Talks soon began between the Clear Lake Lumber Company and Lee Lowland. Soon Lowland bought into the Clear Lake Lumber Company and became the principal owner. He set up his main office on Fourth Avenue in Seattle from where he could oversee the operations in Clear Lake.

Hammer was put in charge of company sales. He could sell anything, and Lowland wanted to keep him around to watch over his sons. His sons were in their early twenties and were just learning the timber business.

Lee Lowland had many things he wanted to do to improve the working conditions in the woods and in the camps. Lowland desired to be seen as a good employer, but his desire for profit instilled in him greed of every kind.

The trestle was rebuilt and connects loaded with logs were again flowing to the mill from Camp Three. The engine was rebuilt and ran on the same line that it had crashed on. Another crew and camp were added to the backside of Cultas Mountain.

The new Camp Four was to be the biggest camp yet with four full bunkhouses, and a cookhouse to feed three hundred men at once. The camp was built on portable flats so they could be moved with ease when the timber ran out. And to the surprise of many, a new building was added to the row of small houses—a reading and card room for the men. No longer did the men have to sit in the bunkhouse to enjoy after dinner activities.

Lowland added a steam boiler in each camp, not only for the kitchen, but also for the men to have hot running water. Company brindles were handed out to each new employee. A speeder was built to run back and forth to town a couple of times a day to bring mail and to transport those who needed to get to town for any reason during their off hours. No man was to do personal things on company time. They could ride inside where it was warm, instead of out in the weather. Some things didn't change—if someone were hurt, they were to wait until the end of the day to be taken to the doctor in town.

Spirits were high, and there wasn't a lumberman around that didn't want to have the chance to work for the Clear Lake Lumber Company.

CHAPTER 15

▼

THE LOGGERS

Summer came and went. There were no fires as it was a wet summer with few days of sunshine. Victoria and her girls planted a vegetable garden, and raised a few chickens to lay eggs. Money was in short supply, but they made do with what they had.

Rose stopped by often to lend a hand with the girls. She would take them for walks, teaching them of the things in the woods. The girls loved playing in the creeks and running through the meadows. They were becoming beautiful young women.

They often had visitors stopping by, mostly men desiring to court Victoria. She always turned them down politely, as most of them didn't interest her. She needed more than what these men could offer. It wasn't material things, but something that could be given from the heart.

Whenever Victoria took the girls into town, other ladies would talk behind their backs. She could hear their voices, and the feel the scorn of their eyes on her as she walked down the streets and shopped. The talk was always nasty as they mocked her daughters and assumed that Victoria kept men at night because she was a friend of Jezzy.

Yet, even with the things that had happened in her life, time had done her well. She was as beautiful as the day she arrived in America, and people knew that one so beautiful couldn't be alone for long.

As the winter drew near, Victoria knew she needed to find work to keep her girls fed and clothed. She went down to the company office and applied to become a server in one of the company camps. She went into talk with Lee Lowland when he was in town. He fell in love with Victoria at first sight. "Have a seat Mrs. Victoria," he said with his eyes covering her.

She took the seat in front of his desk. She could sense that he was interested in her.

"What kind of work are you looking for?" he asked.

"Something that would keep me close to my girls. I'm not afraid to ride the train to and from the camps each day. I just don't want to stay there because my girls need me."

"Well, things can always be worked out. I heard that Mark was a faithful worker for this company," he said with a grin across his face while leaning toward her.

"I need the work, Mr. Lowland, please."

"You can start this coming Monday in Camp Two. You'll begin by waiting tables and cleaning. If there's anything else I can do for you, just let me know."

The lecherous grin on his face made her feel uncomfortable, however she was too relived with his offer to give it much thought. "Thank you Mr. Lowland, I'll do a good job for you."

*   *   *   *

The work was long and hard. At every meal Victoria was hounded and harassed by the men. She would almost be brought to tears by the end of the day. She would arrive home late and spend what time she could with her girls. Rose came over every day and helped with things around the house. Rose watched the girls and told them the legends of their people. Victoria worked herself to the verge of exhaustion. At times she thought she'd die if she kept going at this pace.

As she waited tables, she would listen to the stories the men talked about. Some were great storytellers and others would just listen. Few men, if any, talked about the death of a co-worker. Some men came to camp, went to work and died without anyone knowing their name. They had no friends, no family, and they had their memories buried with them. Victoria felt sorry for such men.

At dinner the men told stories about the biggest trees, or the strongest logger, or their last love, or the soiled dove they knew the last time they were in town. Some would talk about their wife or their mother, and others would talk about their children. They would share their dreams, desires, and hopes. These were the loggers. These were the men.

"Your tales are as tall as the trees you log everyday," she would tell them.

As she placed bowls on the table filled with hot potato soup she searched the faces of men looking for signs of life. Their toil showed in the creases and lines around their eyes. When the men saw that she looked into their eyes that's when a flicker of life would appear. A simple touch would last these men for days. After some time, she became accustomed to the advances made by certain men. She soon learned to laugh it off and let the men have their dream.

As the weeks went by the men began to confide in her about many things. They told her of their loves, their hopes, and their fears. She listened attentively and encouraged them, all the while rejecting any offers to be courted.

Lee Lowland stopped by to visit Camp Two often, always looking for Victoria. He would hardly venture into the forest where the loggers were doing their work. He liked the comfort of a warm place and to gaze at a beautiful face. He would sit at a table in the large dining room and have Victoria bring him coffee.

Victoria kept herself busy trying to avoid him. She cleaned off a table near where Lowland sat. "Come over here," he said.

Victoria came over and stood in front of him.

"I would like to court you," he said looking her up and down.

"Thank you Mr. Lowland, but I'm not ready for that."

"It's been some time since your husband passed."

"The hurt still lingers sir."

He took another drink of his coffee. "I could make life much easier for you Victoria. If you court me, you can have everything you desire."

She looked at him shaking her head. "You don't know what I desire."

"I am sure you desire what everyone desires. A big house, nice things, an easy life, pretty dresses, and things like that. These things I can give you."

"True, those things are nice, but what I desire are things that cannot be bought. I was bought once, and never again will I be bought. I refuse to be owned! I'll someday have the things I desire—things that have no price, but are given. And no one can ever purchase the things of the heart."

He laughed as she spoke, not believing what she said. He had learned from an early age that everything could be bought. If he worked hard, and made smart choices, he would have the money to buy the things he desired. The feelings that overwhelmed him when he bought the mill proved his thoughts. "Money can buy you anything you want—if it can't be bought, it ain't worth having," he said.

"Guess I'm not worth having."

"You'll be with me sometime soon. I have everything you want," Lowland said.

She smiled at him and continued working. He became frustrated with her rejecting his advances. He got up to leave. "How would you like to be one of the cooks in the kitchen? We're adding two more units this next week and we're going to have another three hundred men to feed."

Her countenance lifted. "Yes, I would love to be a cook."

"There's a pay increase in it for you."

He nodded his head giving her a wink as he left. She watched him leave and looked forward to telling her girls that she would be in the kitchen cooking, and not waiting tables.

*   *   *   *

The big trees fell fast, and mill production grew each day. The mountain they were logging became a massive hillside of stumps and small broken trees. Switchbacks were being built so the trains could climb higher onto the mountain.

On average a man a day died in the woods. They would be brought to town at the end of the day when the last train came in. There the undertaker would meet the train and take the man to be prepared for burial. Every day the women and children would fear that maybe this day their father or husband wouldn't be coming off the mountain alive. Yet, just as Hammer had said, "There were men always ready to take the place of the fallen." The draw of good money made the men unable to resist putting themselves in such danger.

*   *   *   *

Being a cook was better than waiting tables. Men were lonely, and when a young lady was in their midst, it didn't matter whether she was pretty or not. She received the unwanted attention from almost every loved-starved man in camp. As one logger put it, "she was ugly on the first day of camp—not so bad on the third day, and she was downright beautiful by the fifth day."

A lonely heart has a way of doing that to a man.

Victoria started cooking long before the men arrived at the dining room. The loggers would eat as much as they could, and as quickly as they could. They would savor the dessert with coffee and head off to the bunkhouses.

Young boys gathered up the dishes and did the washing. Some of these young boys worked for themselves, and others worked because their families were large and needed the extra support. Others worked because their fathers had been injured or killed in the woods and they were the sole providers for their families. Victoria became like a mother to the boys in the camp. She watched out for them and made sure they were fed right, and if it were in her power, she also made sure they were treated right.

Once a day she would take the time to teach the boys the basics of education. It was her chance to be the teacher she longed to be. There wasn't any complaining from the boys, as they were all eager to learn and sit in the company of Victoria.

*   *   *   *

The mill continually expanded its properties, reaching further back into the mountains. They always kept their eye on Caleb's land desiring to log it someday. It was the only stand of pure timber on the west-facing slope that hadn't been burned. It was close to the mill and loaded with large trees.

Caleb would often climb up to the top of Cultas Mountain and look over the areas that had been logged. His grandfather had told him of the destruction that happened to the land during the Civil War, and seeing the clear cuts, the broken logs, the snapped off trees, and the thousands of stumps, he imagined that this wasn't much different.

He thought of his property, how he wanted to keep it for others to see what the land was like before the loggers came. It would be a sanctuary, a natural park, and a place where time would stand still. He thought of a time in the future when grandparents could bring their grandchildren, and show them the way the land used to be. They would be able to feel the moss that was over a foot deep, lay on it and feel as if they were floating on clouds, and smell the musk of the forest floor as the mist rose up through the trees, dancing on the sunlight that filtered through. He wished for all of this wonderful beauty to be preserved for generations to come. It would be a wonderful thing.

A far-away explosion and the wailing of men interrupted his daydream. He ran toward the sound and arrived shortly after to see what remained of a donkey engine. The pressure became too great and it blew apart. The engineer's lifeless body was thrown thirty-feet from the remains of the donkey. Two other workers were badly injured and Caleb began to care for them. He put them in a safe place and started running down the tracks. He needed to find one of the trains to get the men into Clear Lake to see Dr. Meadows. He ran for about two miles down hill and caught up to the train on a lower switchback as it headed to the mill.

Upon convincing the engineer to back up and get the injured men, he set out for town on foot. Arriving in town, he sat near the depot and waited for the train to bring in the injured men. Hammer sat in his office when he noticed engine four running on the main track full of logs. It should have turned off to the middle log dump. He came running from his office to find out why the train wasn't dumping the logs. "A big waste of time and money," he said as he approached the train.

Caleb helped the injured men off the connects and into Dr. Meadows' office. Hammer was busy screaming obscenities at the engineer for wasting company time. "They could have waited until the last train out!" he screamed.

His ranting angered Caleb. "A man who shows no value for life has no life himself. He is among the dead."

Hammer turned his aggression on Caleb. "You're a moron, an uneducated ass. You mingle with Indians and live in a tree and barely have a pot to pee in. You tell me I've no life? I'll take what you do have and make it mine!"

Caleb looked at him with a puzzled expression. "Stealing isn't right, and I won't stand by and let you have your way."

"How could you do that? You don't even know how to fight or to defend yourself. You're the weakest man around these parts."

Caleb smiled at him and shook his head, knowing that Hammer wouldn't understand. "Strength isn't found in how loud a man is, but in what he does. You can yell and puff yourself up, but you don't scare me because I see through your words, and I know, that inside you're a little man."

Hammer drew back his arm to strike Caleb, but Caleb turned and walked away. People gathered around looking at Hammer. He shook his head and returned to his office. Lee Lowland had watched the fight from his office. He smiled at Hammer as he walked in. "It would be best to get rid of that man."

"We've tried before, but this time we'll get that som-o-bitch."

Sitting at his desk, Hammer, wrote up a company memo to be sent to the Camp Two foreman.

Begin at once to reconstruct the trestle over Mundt Creek. The property south of Mundt Creek belongs to Clear Lake Lumber. Caleb Cultas is squatting on said property and shall be removed if not voluntarily, then by force.

Company Sales President, O. Hammer.

Victoria worked preparing the evening dinner for the logging crews. The food for the camp was in short supply. Victoria would make use of whatever she could find; she would get bran from the cattle feed sometimes early in the morning before work. Lula Mac was the other cook. She was from North Carolina and thought nothing of shooting squirrels and using the meat to make stew. If the men knew where the bran and meat came from they would have lost their meals at the tables. It was something that both Victoria and Lula kept between themselves.

The men would tell the ladies how good the food was and make remarks, wishing they had that kind of cooking all the time. Victoria would smile at Lula and remind her never to tell them where some of the food came from. Yet, most of these men would eat anything set before them.

As the second crew came in for dinner Victoria saw Lowland coming into the cookhouse. She went over to inquire about getting some supplies for the men. Upon seeing her he motioned for her to come sit. "Are you ready to court me yet?"

"No—Mr. Lowland. I work for you and it wouldn't be proper for you to court me. People would talk."

"I can change that," he said as an evil grin came across his face. "I can make it so you have to be with me."

"Are you saying that you'll fire me if I don't let you court me? Is that what you're like?"

"Don't put it in those words. Court me and all your troubles will be gone. You can be out of this hell hole—away from all these lowly men, and be with such a man as I."

"Do you think your money will buy my heart? If you do—you're deceiving yourself."

"Yes, why not? All women want the good life. Look at you—you work twelve-hour days—six days a week, and you're growing old fast. You work around dirty men that pester you all the time. Then you go home and have to take care of those Indian girls—who, when you come be with me, will be sent off to the reservation to be with their own. If only you would see all I've to offer— you could have a real fine life if you'd just come be with me."

Victoria took a long look at Lowland and spoke in a tone that Lowland wasn't used to hearing. "My friend Rose has nothing, and she's full of life. I have my girls and they're full of life, and I would never let them go. I have work, a home, my family and friends—I have a good life!"

"Oh, you do, so you tell me. Well, let's test what you believe. This is your last day. Lula can become head cook, and you can decide what you desire to do with this wonderful life of yours."

Victoria put down her apron and walked out of the cookhouse. She started down the tracks and headed toward home.

Lowland watched her walking away. "You can ride the train if you want—it would be much faster. Fine looking ladies shouldn't be walking in the forest alone—never know what might come after you."

Victoria said nothing, but kept walking toward town. She didn't want to give him the satisfaction of needing him for anything.

A couple of men that heard him mocking her laughed. Lowland turned around and motioned them to follow her. "You two go scare her. Let her get down the tracks a ways, then go jump her. Don't hurt her, but just give her a good scare. She'll come running back to me."

The men nodded their heads and took off through the forest to meet up with Victoria. They ran ahead of her for about a mile and waited. "I don't care what the boss said, I'm going to have my way with her."

"He said not to hurt her."

"Hell, I won't hurt her—goin' to give her some lovin' I have always found Victoria to be a beautiful woman."

"I don't know if Lowland wants you to do that."

"He just said don't hurt her—that's it."

They both laughed. Then they heard a voice from behind them. "I don't want you to do anything to that fine lady."

Both men jumped out of their skin as they turned their heads to see who spoke. Caleb stood behind them shaking his head. "Now why would you think of scaring a nice lady like her? Hasn't she been doing your cooking for a long while?"

The men didn't respond but took off running. "Weird things happen when that guy shows up to places," one of the men said as they ran.

Caleb had scared them more than they could have ever scared another.

Victoria saw the men running out from the trees on to the tracks. They ran right past her heading back to camp. Then she saw Caleb walking out on to the tracks. He smiled at her. "Hi."

She was happy to see Caleb. "What are you doing out here with those men? You weren't going to hurt them were you?"

"Oh no, I just stumbled across them—you know those men sometimes out in the woods doing strange things."

"I wouldn't know much about that," she said.

"What are you doing walking out here alone?"

"I don't have a job anymore with the company—I've been let go."

"That isn't any good—nice person like you—I bet all the men are going to be sad now."

"Why do you say that?"

"They all look at you with desire—I see it, even hear them talk about the wonderful woman who cooks."

She smiled as he walked up to her. "You wouldn't mind if I walked with you into town?"

"No, not at all—I would enjoy the company."

As they walked Caleb talked about his life. "I've never had a job before—I really don't understand it. I go out and get things out of the forest and trade it for money and other things."

"What things do you get?"

"Gold in the streams, cascara bark off the trees, mushrooms, and other things that grow in the forest. People want them."

"Yes I can see that."

"I live with the forest, but the mill fights and destroys it. I hope the destruction ends sometime before all is lost."

Victoria listened to him understanding his point of view. "I feel that things are not right with everything the mill does. Too much money makes men do things that are not good sometimes."

"Men can choose to do right or wrong—nature never has to make that choice."

"What do you mean by that?"

"Whatever our choices, we're always at the mercy of nature—sometimes it sets things right."

"I understand now."

"Good, I believe that you will be provided for. Pursue what you desire—do what you know you can do and things will work out fine."

"Thanks, I'll do that—it's not easy sometimes."

They talked all the way to the log dump. "Thanks for the walk. Take care now."

"You're welcome, and take care Caleb."

When she arrived in town she was cold and wanting to warm up. She stopped at Jezzy's house. Jezzy was in the kitchen brewing her magic tea to relax the men when they started arriving in the evening. It was made from mushrooms that

Caleb would sell to her. Victoria sat next to Jezzy and started to cry. "I've lost my job because I won't court Lowland."

Jezzy put her arm around Victoria. "That's men for you—thinking they can buy whatever they want. Think about it Victoria, I'm really no different than the women who are married in this town. All their men have to pay for it one way or another."

Victoria looked surprised at what Jezzy said. "Oh, but there's a difference. You don't love the men you're with, and married women do."

"Did you love Mark the way you should? Didn't he buy you?"

Tears welled up in Victoria's eyes. "I'm sorry—I was just trying to prove a point. I'm sure you loved Mark as you should," Jezzy said.

"I was young and had much to learn about love—I think I still have a lot to learn about love."

Jezzy smiled as she shook her head. "I may never know this love you're seeking, but by no means do I want to make you cry—I only want to see you happy."

"I'm not crying because of you—I'm crying because I know I didn't love Mark as I should. I was bought, and I know it. I wanted to love him, but I just didn't know how. I'm sure he loved me, but he didn't know how to show it. Life is sad because I don't know if I'll ever be deeply in love. I don't know if love equals happiness."

Jezzy sat down at the table, poured some magic tea into a cup and handed it to Victoria. "Deep love doesn't exist. It's a myth—something to keep a woman's heart in bondage and a man's heart forever searching. That's why I have such a great business—they all come looking for this thing called love. Men don't know it, but you can't find love inside a vagina, and most men think the road to their heart is through their penis. I'm afraid too many women think that way also."

"For you it's the road to their money purse," Victoria said.

They laughed. "Yep, they come looking for love, they do their thing, put it in and out—yet never find love. The more I think about it, the more I understand how they look in the wrong place on the body. Never has a man tried to search my heart or my mind. They're always just waiting for me, or one of my doves to open our legs or to show them our breasts. I don't know if men will ever search anywhere else. They search for gold, search for bigger trees, and those things they find, but why don't they dig for the gold of a woman's heart? Why would they not see if a woman's heart is as pure as the heart wood of a giant tree?"

"Men only search for what they can see," Victoria said.

"They just don't know. Maybe someday a man will find a way to a woman's heart and not try to travel through her legs."

Victoria pondered the things Jezzy said. "You offered me a job once. Does that offer still stand?"

"Do you really want to do what I do? You won't find love here."

"Well, if there is no real love—then why not? I know I'll do well—I have what men want. I have a nice body and a nice face."

Jezzy smiled. "Oh, yes you do dear, and you can start tomorrow night if you're serious."

"I am serious, and besides, I need the money."

"Good, now run home and take care of those beautiful girls of yours."

CHAPTER 16

▼

GREED

Caleb watched the men building the new trestle across Mundt Creek. He crossed the creek and made his way up toward the foreman. "Whatcha' doing?" he asked.

"Building a trestle so we can log that property over there."

"You guys did that once—failed, you did."

"We won't fail this time—and the first tree we're going to cut down is the one you live in. You're living on company land."

"Nope, that's my property, and I'll fight to keep it."

He walked back over the creek to his home. He sat in his room trying to figure out what he could do. The company had the title to the property, so he would need to find people to help him protect his land. He went outside and walked through his property touching the big trees, trying to think of any way to keep them from being logged. Saving the trees was the only thing on his mind as he finished walking his land. He knew he had to go and confront the company face to face. He hoped that they would listen to reason.

His grandfather had always told him, "Keep your friends close and your enemies closer."

"I will ask them to make a park out of this property, that would be in the best interest of everyone." To convince them of the idea he would appeal to their egos.

The next morning he showed up at the Clear Lake Company head office. Lowland and Hammer were having their morning coffee when Caleb came walking in. Their contempt for him could be seen in their eyes. He approached them.

"I'd like to talk about where I live—I have an offer for you that could benefit all concerned."

Hammer looked at Lowland with surprise and then back at Caleb. "Sit down and tell us."

Caleb was pleased that they were going to listen to him. "The way I see things—is that with all the logging happening not only in this valley, but in the Northwest, there will come a time when there will be no big trees left. I know that you love the forest in your own way, and you profit from all that nature has to offer. Just think of what you could do for your names and for all those that come after us if you were to save some land with the big trees and make a wonderful park."

Hammer and Lowland laughed as Caleb spoke. "There will always be big trees to fall—don't you understand that the cut will never run out? There's no need for a park with big trees—who would want to visit that place anyway? A park is a place that man has created for himself out of nature—it's not what nature is. You sound like those people down in Northern California fighting to save the giant Redwoods, radicals bent on destroying the American dream."

"We could put your name on it," Caleb said.

Lowland looked into Caleb's eyes. "We'll log that property and there's nothing that you can do about it, so my best advice to you is that you'd better find a new place to live. If you like, you could stay in one of the company bunkhouses until you find a new place. We start logging tomorrow, and we wouldn't want you to get hurt."

Caleb sat silent. Tears formed in his eyes as he thought about the land he loved being logged. He knew that if he fought, he might die, but he had no choice. He would fight the mill, and would overcome them somehow.

Seeing Caleb in this state gave Hammer and Lowland great satisfaction. Hammer got up and walked over to Caleb. "Your way of life is coming to an end. You, like others, will have to conform to the new advances of machinery, the advances of mankind—maybe even live in a real house and not some tree. You do know that it's not too late for you to become educated."

These words brought anger to Caleb. "I was educated by my grandfather and Rose. Nature has taught me more than I could learn at school. You see value in the trees you fall—in the things you make. I see a different value, one not measured in dollars, but measured in the feelings and the joy it can bring to others. You can try to log my land—ultimately I may have no choice. You lied and cheated me by stealing the deed to my land. I believe that the wrong you've done will visit you. There's something more powerful than men at work here, and it's not a friend of yours."

He walked out, heading home to get his things. When he arrived at his house it was lying smashed on the ground. While he visited with Hammer and Lowland, they had sent some men to fall his home. He searched through the split wood and found a few of his things. Some were destroyed, others broken, and some in good shape. He was amazed that they didn't steal his things. He gathered what he could carry and headed east toward a place called Charlie's cabin. It was about three miles away on the south side of Cultas Mountain. It would be years before they logged that section of the mountain, he thought.

It was a long walk over some rough land. He had to pass through the far end of his property that he called the Garden of Rocks. It was created where a slide had occurred over a thousand years before. It left huge boulders the size of buildings all covered in moss and licorice ferns. There were pools created where water ran through the moss. With each drop of water there would be sound, which became music if one listened. Twin Flower, Bunchberry Dogwood, and Trillium dressed the moss-covered rocks in the spring, making them come alive.

Caleb knew that he had to save this section of land before it was logged. It was a natural rock garden. It was a garden made by God. It was a place that if known many people would visit.

Caleb sat on a high rock enjoying the view of the garden. Sadness came over him as he thought of the days he had spent with his grandfather walking the mountain. Things were changing fast in the valley, and he would have to make the proper adjustments to survive.

Caleb knew he had to take action, and he went to find Rose's friend Victoria. Caleb could read, but his writing was poor. He knocked on her door and she answered and invited him in. She smiled at him as she showed him to a seat. "Would you like some tea?"

"I sure would."

"What brings you here today?"

He sighed. "Rose tells me that you write well. I need to send a letter to some people down in California. It needs to be a proper letter, and I was wondering if you could write it for me."

Victoria smiled. "Yes, I'd enjoy writing for you. When we finish our tea we'll sit down and write it and have it sent out tomorrow."

The letter made a plea to the people involved in saving the giant Redwoods in Northern California. "I would appreciate any advice, guidance, or any help that you can send our way…"

Caleb mailed the letter and waited for the reply. The response came soon after, and it was favorable. In a few weeks a man would come to help set up an environmental group to raise money and fight for the trees.

A representative showed up from Northern California and met with Caleb. It was hard for Caleb to find any others to meet with the man. Caleb's hope for this to make a difference soon faded. Almost every person in town depended upon the timber being cut; saving trees seemed like a stupid idea. After a short visit the representative became discouraged. "In order for there to be success you need a lot more support than what I see here. This is a losing battle."

Caleb eyes dropped to the ground then back at the man. "You may think it's a losing battle, but I've heard of giants falling before—I'll never give up."

The man stood up. "I've a train to catch. I will send what information I can afford. I do hope you find more support, but I doubt it."

*   *   *   *

With the growth of the mill, Clear Lake was becoming a large town. Another brothel opened doors for business, but Jezzy wasn't worried because she had the woman that most men wanted to spend their money and time on—Victoria Southerland.

Victoria could pretend. She had pretended for so long that she found it easy to make men feel loved and wanted by her. The touch of her hand, the feel of her lips, and the sound of her voice all made each man she was with feel as if he were the only man in the world.

Men would come in and sit for hours waiting for their turn to be with her. Yet, when the night was over, and she'd had her fill of men, she'd walk home feeling just as empty as she'd always been. Maybe Jezzy was right. Maybe there was no such thing as true love. It was just romanticism or a fantasy that would never come to reality.

Every night was the same. She would tell lies. She would tell every man he was the best or the biggest or the greatest she had ever been with. Marriage proposals would flow like the waters of many rivers along with promises of fame, fortune, security and all the other things that men said hoping to have her in their bed every night. She would turn them down, saying that they would be better off with a woman who hadn't been with so many men.

On her way home, she would cry out her grief so she could have all her tears gone before she reached her house. There, Rose would be waiting up to meet her and help her get the girls up before she went to sleep. The girls thought that she worked in the main kitchen for the mill. It's what she wanted the girls to believe—she knew they would be heartbroken if they knew their mother was soiling herself to provide for them. She prayed that her girls would never find out what she did, or that they would have to do the same to make a living.

One evening Jezzy came up to the room where Victoria prepared for the night. "There's a man asking to be with you tonight that I've refused to send up. I think you should meet him and decide for yourself whether you entertain him or not. He says he's willing to pay more money than any man here to be with you."

"Why? Who is he?"

"Come see for yourself."

She left the room, walked downstairs and saw Lowland sitting on the waiting couch. He rose when she approached him and took off his hat. She looked surprised to see him. "Hi, I never thought I'd see you in here."

"I never thought I would be here either, but when I heard that you were here, I thought I'd come see for myself. And I see it's true."

"Yes, it's true. I was fired from my last job, and I do have children to feed."

"What I don't understand is why you turned down my offer of a good life—a life where all your needs would be met and you'd want for nothing."

She almost walked away but felt as if she had to answer. His words brought anger up from within her soul. "Because Mr. Lowland you disgust me. You and your high and mighty attitude thinking that you can have anything you want because you have money.

In truth sir—I prefer to be with the lonely souls that don't hold their power over me."

"Ha! I have everything you need."

"Needs and wants and the things that I lack are things that cannot be bought. I've told you that before. Tell me, Mr. Lowland, what's the difference between other men paying to have my body and you paying to have my body? Is the only difference that we would be married, and that my payment would be having all the things you think I desire? A big new house, horses, jewelry, and other such things? Would you die for me, Mr. Lowland? Would you die for my girls? Can you meet the needs of my soul, my heart, and my mind? I think not. You're not the man for me."

Sweat ran off his forehead as he wiped it with his handkerchief and stumbled for words to answer her. "When you're tired of this life, you'll be knocking on my door. Until then I'd like to have my time with you."

She stepped back and turned toward the stairs. "You could pay me a thousand dollars tonight and I still wouldn't give my body to you. Not now, not in the future—not ever!"

Jezzy stood close, listening to the conversation and silently cheering Victoria on. As Victoria walked away, Lowland looked at Jezzy. "You own this place—order her to be with me! I'm a paying customer, and I will pay you well."

She laughed at him. "I don't run my business that way Mr. Lowland. My ladies only sell to whom they desire. Now, there are some other nice young ladies who I'm sure would spend their time with you."

"No, I want Victoria and if you were smart you would do as I say. I can make it difficult for you to keep doing business in this town."

"Oh, I'm sure that you could, Mr. Lowland, but how would you like the new papers in Seattle to know that you visited a house of ill repute? I can play that game also. So my best advice is for you to leave and never come back."

Not another word was said as he put his hat on and headed out the door.

∗   ∗   ∗   ∗

The logging started on Caleb's land and things went wrong from the beginning. The first day a log rolled on one of the buckers, killing him. The second day a faller lost his footing and slipped and was crushed by the tree he was falling. Three days later a cable snapped on a turn of logs and decapitated two men.

Up on the second logging site, one of the donkey engineers, named Bryson, was getting proficient at running the donkey engine and bringing in the turns of logs. He could make a turn of logs faster than anyone in the whole company, and the company had over twenty donkeys running in the forest. Others in the company would come and watch him to learn how to run their donkey engines better. Bryson was a great teacher. He always pushed the machine to the limits of speed and downplayed the rumors and Indian legends to the men on his site. "It was all hogwash," he'd tell his co-workers. Bryson was a man who didn't fear death.

On this particular day as the logs were being yarded in, they became hung up on an old snag. The cable tightened on the drum, and Bryson immediately slacked the line. The logs rolled off the snag and he started to yard them in again. As he pulled the lever to pick up speed, the cable jumped up off the drum and grabbed his coat sleeve, pulling him right into the drum and wrapping him around it as if he were the cable.

The fireman put another stick of wood in the firebox and looked up to see his engineer pinned to the drum. He ran over to pull the lever to stop the donkey. The drum came to a stop. He looked at Bryson. "You alright?"

Bryson could barely breath and cold only speak in broken words. "Do I look alright?"

The fireman became frightened and confused. "I'll run to get help."

He took off running for some choker riggers who were working down the skid road. He saw the men in the distance. "I need your help! Now!"

They took off after the man following him to the donkey engine. They came to a stop upon seeing Bryson spun on the drum. Ivar heard all the yelling while he was crossing the ridge searching for a new trestle crossing. He came running to the site.

The men talked to Bryson, trying to figure out how to get him off the drum. The cable was tightly wrapped around his body in almost every area, but there was no visible sign of blood loss. The men thought it would be safe to take him off. Besides, it was all he could do to breath and talk.

Ivar jumped on the donkey and slowly put the drum in reverse. The cable became slack as the men pulled it out of the way. Other men waited to catch Bryson once the cable was all the way off him. When he fell into the men's waiting arms, he looked up at them and screamed out his last words. "Damn this work!"

The men put him next to the tracks and returned to their work. It was just another day in the woods, a man dying along with the big trees. It was the way of life and death. Ivar looked at the fireman. "I guess you're the engineer now—be careful or you'll end up like Bryson. I'll feed the fire for the rest of the day, so we can get these logs out before quitting time."

Later that night up at Camp Two, the loggers sat in the bunkhouse and talked about Caleb and his beliefs and his relationship with the Indians. They talked about the stories they'd heard of his grandfather and how he could move like a ghost all over the mountain. They talked about the Indian legend of the bad mountain *Cultas*.

It wasn't long before men were asking to work at other camps because they feared that they would be the next to die. They all started to believe that Caleb's land should be left alone. Some of the men who believed strongly in superstition left and headed off to work for other logging companies in the valley.

During the second week of logging near the rock garden, a turn of logs undercut a huge rock that rolled down the hill and came to rest on top of four men, killing them all. The rock, the size of a small house, became a natural headstone for the four men with the words rest in peace inscribed on it.

Finally, the camp foreman ordered all logging stopped near Caleb's land. He sent a memo to the company office. "I am asking for a review of logging practices. My loss of men on the site, and the injuries to others has lowered morale. It's only right to make the work safe for the men."

He received a reply from the main office. "Men are expendable, time is short, and there will be no time off to review anything. Just get the logs out!"

The following day two more men were killed in two separate accidents and the rest of the men walked off the job. The foreman sent another memo to the office.

> *"The men have refused to work on the site. I would prefer that you send me new men from Seattle who will have no regard for the fables and fairy tales that the local men have. Only then will we be able to resume work and get the logs out."*

There was no reply from the office and the foreman decided to go to town and make a plea to Lowland and Hammer in person. Things were different in camp. Men were afraid to venture beyond the periphery of the camp. They swore that at night they heard voices in the trees calling their names.

Fear gripped their hearts and the religious began to pray. Their fears only became stronger when the camp foreman didn't return. Maybe the voices in the trees had consumed him, they thought. Four days after the foreman left, Hammer showed up with another man. Calling all the men to the cookhouse for a meeting. "I'm sorry to say that the camp foreman has died. Mr. Boyd will be the new foreman of Camp Two, and if any of you decide not to work tomorrow you can grab your brindle and head for some other place—you won't have a job."

The men grumbled and murmured, but no one left to get their brindle. There were questions unanswered that they wanted to know. "How was the foreman killed?" A man asked.

"He was murdered. If anyone sees Caleb Cultas, we would like to question him. He's the man we suspect of carrying out this awful deed," Hammer responded.

"Now think about work and forget the fables—I'll be back early next week to check on things."

Hammer arrived back at the office and sat down across from Lowland. "Do you think people will believe that Caleb killed the foreman?"

"I don't know, but I hope so," Lowland said.

"I don't see how they can't think it's him. He surely has motive."

"If Caleb is found guilty it will help the men in camp to see there is nothing behind all these Indian fairy tales. They will be able to resume their work without any further interruptions. We need to make money."

Work resumed, and men continued to die. Caleb would sit unnoticed on a high rock that overlooked his property and watch the trees fall every day. What was once nature's garden was now becoming a wasteland of slash and stumps. Someday it would grow back, he thought, but not in his lifetime. And when it did grow back, it would be logged again, and after that again. Just like a farm growing corn. The only difference was that it would be a century between crops.

Caleb walked into town a week after the death of the Camp Two foreman. He was surprised to find himself as the lead suspect. A few men tried to convince the townspeople that Caleb was the killer, but the people who knew him, knew he wouldn't hurt anyone.

The county sheriff found Caleb in the post office. "I would like a few words with you Caleb."

"Sure, what would you like to know?"

The sheriff and Caleb walked down the street through town. "Certain men are saying you are responsible for Herman's death."

"I wouldn't kill anyone."

"I know that, but I am being pressured to question you."

"If I were you, I would question the men that sent you to me."

"I'm watching them. You just be careful."

"I will—I'm watched after by things greater than them—thanks."

After questioning Caleb the Sheriff went to the mill to talk with Hammer. Hammer saw the sheriff and ran out to meet him. "Did you find that bastard yet?"

"Yes, I did."

"Arrest him?"

"No, I have no reason to do that yet."

"He's an evil man."

"Caleb has every reason in the world to want to destroy your company, but no reason at all to kill the camp foreman. The foreman was killed—of this there's no doubt, but it wasn't at the hands of Caleb Cultas. I fear that his killers might be standing in this place. Think about it, Mr. Hammer. I'll be keeping an eye on things in this town. The mill has hired its own policeman, but it's still in the County of Skagit, and in this county—I am the law."

Hammer knew when to back down. Clear Lake wasn't incorporated and the mill had its own police force consisting of two men, but the county sheriff had more authority. To anger the Sheriff might shed light on things they didn't want lit up.

*   *   *   *

It wasn't long before a third crew was added to the mill's operations. Trains ran daily from Seattle to Clear Lake bringing men back and forth. The mill employed almost two thousand men. It was said that Clear Lake Lumber always had a crew going, a crew coming and one working. Seattle was seventy miles away, but it was the only city that had enough men to supply the mill with workers. At the end of the train before the caboose was a car the men called the dead car where bodies were placed of those that died while working in the woods. This was the place where they took their last train ride to be buried in their hometown of Seattle.

Clear Lake Lumber Company became one of the biggest sawmills in the world. Lee Lowland was worth over ten million dollars. There seemed to be no end to the wealth that the land could produce.

The Clear Lake logging road was extended up the valley on the south side of the river all the way to Finny Creek. The timber seemed to go on forever "Truly, the cut would never end," Lowland said.

He was proud of the company that he helped build. He had become an important man. He would sit in his office down in Seattle and boast of his greatness to anyone who would listen.

The Secretary of the Interior of the United States was sent out by the President to view the holdings of the Clear Lake Lumber Company. It was considered the most efficient mill in the world. Upon his arrival, the thing that stood out most in the mind of the secretary was the arrogance of Lowland. Lowland showed him the town and the mill. "If God Almighty were to come to earth to make His home, He would make it here in the town of Clear Lake," Lowland said.

Working conditions for the men improved somewhat because Lowland believed that if he could increase the morale of the men, he could get more production. He worked at providing as many modern amenities as were available. He ordered more and better food for the camps. He provided more boxcars that served as reading and card rooms. Workdays were shortened from twelve to ten hours and then down to eight. Pay was increased to make up for the lost hours, and just as he figured production went up. His goal in doing all of this was to keep the men from forming or joining a union. The union, he thought, would bring death to his company. He would always say, "No radicals needed here."

The International World Workers Union was pushing for all loggers and mill workers to join and fight against what they considered the evil employers. In their mind there were no fair employers in the country. Lowland was against any kind of organized labor in his company and would do anything to keep them out. His first step was to make working conditions better on his own. Then if that didn't work, he would threaten layoffs, and if that didn't work he'd use outright force.

He, of all men knew that money could buy a lot of things, including acts of violence. It could buy popular opinion. It could move people to do things for him, and yet they wouldn't even know they were doing his work.

Two men arrived in town and entered Tuffy's Saloon. They began talking to the workers and asking about working conditions and benefits and whether they would be interested in having the IWW represent them. Word quickly spread and drifted into Hammer's office. Hammer dispatched three men from the Skagit Club who went into the saloon and sat next to the union men. Avoiding eye contact, one of the club members walked over and stood next to the men. "Best for you two to head out of this place. Your type aren't wanted around here. Our men are happy, and radicals serve no purpose but to divide, so you'd better leave before the weather changes," he said.

The union representatives didn't move. "This is a free place, so we have no intention of leaving until we have a chance to talk with all the workers."

The three men walked up to the union men. "We are the workers and like we said before—your kind are not welcome here. So you'd better be getting up and heading out!"

With those words the three men laid hands on the representatives and threw them out the door. Once in the street, they proceeded to beat the union men, kicking and hitting as a crowd formed and cheered them on. The union men were badly beaten and they couldn't walk. A few men carried them to the outskirts of town and left them there.

Hammer and Lowland were happy about what took place. Their own workers had dispatched the union men, and they appeared to have no part in it. Sometimes things just seem perfect. They were sure it would be a long time before they saw another union representative in town again.

It was early the next morning when Victoria was walking home, and she heard moans coming from the side of the road. At first she became frightened, but then recognized the sounds as moans of pain and knew that someone needed her help. She found the two injured union representatives and helped them to her house.

Rose cleaned the men up and dressed their wounds, listening to them describe how they had been attacked and beaten in town. Rose agreed. "It's a horrible thing to happen to men who were only trying to help make things better for others."

Rose left later that day seeking Caleb. She figured he could help the men get back to Mount Vernon to catch a train or boat to Seattle. Even though she searched most of the day she had no luck in finding Caleb.

Before Victoria went to work, she went to town to buy some extra things that she needed to take care of the men staying at her place. Lowland saw her walking into town and approached her. She looked at him. "It's a shame what you did to those union men?"

"They got what they had coming, yet I didn't do a thing."

"Everyone knows what you're like."

"I own this town—people look after me—I never laid a hand on them," Lowland said.

"Do you get joy from having men beaten almost to the point of death? I have them at my house. It's not enough that you don't care about the men that work and die for your company, but trying to kill men that want to make things better for those that work for you is a horrible sin."

"Don't talk to me about sin, lady! You live in it every day—I believe they call it whoredom."

"That puts us in the same boat. You sold your soul a long time ago."

"I'm far better than you'll ever be, and the only way you can rise out of your mire is to be with me. Besides, I care greatly about the men that make me money. As long as they work, things are fine—it's too bad if one dies because it takes too long to break in a new man. It's just part of life in the woods—you win some and lose some."

Tears formed in her eyes as Lowland moved in close to her. Reaching, he took hold of her arm. "Let's go pay those men you've taken in a visit. Maybe they can form a union for whores. Give you better working conditions, better pay, and maybe make it a law that men should clean up before lying in your bed. Maybe they'll say you can have relations with only ten men a night instead of the twenty you do every night."

"You must keep close tabs on me to know everything I do."

"Someone has to watch out for you—you'll learn that one day. You should just come with me now."

Just as he finished his words, Caleb tapped him on the back. Startled, he turned around and saw Caleb. "You best remove your hand from her."

"And why should I do that?"

"If you don't, I'll make you, and I don't think you'll like that."

"Strike me, and I'll have you arrested."

Before another word could come out of Lee Lowland's mouth, Caleb's right hand landed on the side of Lowland's head, sending him to the ground. Caleb stood looking down at him. "You can take my land—you can accuse me of terrible things, and you can try to destroy my life, but when you mess with people that are my friends, I won't stand for it!"

Lowland rubbed his head, trying to sit up. Never had he been hit so hard in his life. Caleb held out his arm and escorted Victoria back to her house. Rose was there smiling, for she knew that the raven had told Caleb to go and find Victoria.

Rose walked up to Caleb. "I knew you would come. We need your help to get these men to Mount Vernon safely. I'm afraid if the men from the mill find them again, they'll kill them."

"I can do that. Tell me when and I'll get them to Mount Vernon."

One of the union men sat up looking at Caleb and Rose. "Get us out of here tomorrow so we can make a call for more men to come and help us bring deliverance to the oppressed workers of the Clear Lake Lumber Company."

Caleb looked at the man confused. "I don't think the workers feel repressed, and why would you want to help men that hurt you?"

"They just don't realize they need us yet—soon they will and we will be there."

"Well, tomorrow I will take you to Mount Vernon," Caleb said as he started to leave.

Victoria stood up and walked over to Caleb. "I don't feel like going to work tonight. I'd like to know if you would honor us by staying for dinner."

Caleb smiled. He wouldn't have to be asked twice. "Sure would—been a while since I had a good meal."

He stayed for dinner and enjoyed his visit with Victoria, Rose, and the men. He agreed to help them set up the union when they returned to town. Anything to make trouble for Lowland seemed like the right thing to do.

Caleb sat over his dinner plate, watching the others finish their meal. He looked at one of the union men as he ate. "Since I'm helping you—maybe you could help me."

"What kind of help do you need?"

"All the big trees are falling fast, and soon there'll be no more. I'm trying to start a movement to save some of the big trees and would like your help."

The union man sighed as he looked at his partner. "I wish we could help you, but our job is to help the workers who're falling the big trees. If we don't log the big trees, there would be no work, and no work would mean no union. I'm sorry, but it wouldn't serve our purpose to help you."

Caleb wasn't upset with their words. He took a drink of his tea and set his glass down. "I understand what you're saying—it just seems to me that your movement and mine would fit hand in hand. Someday you'll see that."

Caleb helped the men to Mount Vernon and saw them off on a train.

All over the northwest the IWW grew, setting up locals and organizing labor. In Seattle the union men drummed up support and tried to get on the train heading for Clear Lake. As they approached the gate they were stopped. The Chief of Police stood in their path. "This train is reserved for Clear Lake Lumber employees only."

"I don't see a sign stating that," one of the union men said.

Other police officers stood in line with the Chief. The union men looked at the officers and backed away. "Let's find another way to Clear Lake men. Our fight isn't here."

The men left walking down to the water front.

The two union men along with fifty other men boarded a steamer in Seattle to travel up the Sound to Everett. From there they would take the train into Mount Vernon and walk to Clear Lake. They planned on having a large demonstration to hopefully force the company to accept the union. It would be a long up hill fight as there was great opposition to the IWW, and different companies and groups formed alliances to put down the union movement.

Upon hearing of the group traveling to Clear Lake the company hired the Everett Police chief to stop the crowd. His job was to send the ship with the union men back to Seattle. "This will put an end to the radicals," Hammer said.

When the IWW workers arrived at Everett, the police chief and his officers met them at the dock. A few other men joined them to oppose the union. Most of the men on the steamer stood on the deck waiting to get off. They lowered the gangway and the police chief moved to stand in their path. "My best advice for all of you is to stay on that boat and go back to Seattle. Go back to the East with your radicalism. You're not welcome here and dire things will happen if you choose to get off."

Will Dickson, the leader of the union, stepped off the ship onto the gangway. "Sir, we have every right in this country to go where we please and to conduct a peaceful demonstration—and we will. Your scare tactics and threats will not deter us from doing what we plan."

He stepped onto the dock and the police chief raised his pistol and fired, killing Dickson. The rest of the officers and men opened fire on the other IWW workers still on the boat. Bullets flew everywhere with men screaming, crying, and dying. When the gun smoke cleared and the air became quiet, five men lay dead on the ground. Six were missing and twenty-four were wounded. The police chief looked at the dead bodies. "I warned them—yep, told them what would happen, but they didn't listen."

There was silence as each man weighed in his heart what he had done. A crowd gathered and some scoffed while others grieved at what they saw. "Could this be America?" a woman asked. "Land of the free—home of the brave? Where is the justice served?"

No one answered, for what could be said? Men lay dead in the Sound and the water was red with blood, and there was no one who could tell her why this happened. The bodies were removed and word spread quickly throughout the Northwest about the massacre in Everett. It was open season on the IWW.

Hammer and Lowland heard about the massacre. "It's a terrible shame," Lowland said with a smirk.

A few workers talked about it, but fearing that they would be considered sympathizers, they quickly put it to rest. They didn't want to fall into the same fate as the men on the steamer. It was an unspoken law in the Northwest that if you side with the IWW you might die.

Victoria heard about the massacre when she was in Beddall's store. In hushed tones, people spoke of a cleansing that was going to take place in the mill. Any man found to sympathize with the IWW would bear the shame of being tarred and feathered.

Some men left before the crowds could come and work their judgment on them. Other men waited in fear, hoping that what they heard were only rumors. Nothing happened that night. The company knew that enough fear had been put into the hearts and minds of the sympathizers. The mill passed a new law stating that any man carrying a red card, the sign of the IWW, wouldn't be allowed into the town or any of the logging sites.

*   *   *   *

Things moved along well for the company. More and more logs came out of the hills and mountains surrounding the town of Clear Lake. Production was at a peak with ten million board feet of lumber being cut annually and two million shingles being produced. Nothing seemed out of reach for the Clear Lake Lumber Company. Then came the start of World War I, and most of the men working in the camps and in the mill were called up to fight the war in Europe. Men left with no one to replace them. Production came to a halt.

Lee Lowland came up from Seattle to meet with Hammer. They discussed their options, which were few. Lowland had to keep the money flowing, and in order to do that he had to keep the logs coming. He remembered coming out West as a young man and seeing Chinese men building and working on the railroads. "Why not hire Chinese workers?" He asked, as he paced around the room.

"Naw, they're too small for this type of work." Hammer responded.

"So what if we lose more of them than we do the regular workers—at least we could keep the mill operating at full capacity. We could build them their own camp so they don't mingle with us—and then when the war is over, we can send them packing."

Hammer listened to all that Lowland said. "I don't like the idea of having Chinese people in or around town. They are different, and that don't set well with me."

"Sometimes we have to put our differences aside."

"I don't know about hiring Chinamen—what if they cause problems for the locals? What if the men left here won't work with them? It might be worse than having the union in town. Locals won't like a bunch of yellow men running around."

"I will talk to the towns people. They will do anything I ask," Lowland said.

"Hell, we've cleared the land of Indians why bring in another problem?"

"It's either the Chinese or shut the mill down."

"Then let's get some—where do we buy them?" Hammer asked.

Lowland laughed. "We'll have a couple of hundred of them up here next week. Go out and find a place to make a camp and build a fence around it so we can keep them in at night."

They laughed, thinking of the profit that could be made. They wouldn't even have to pay them as much as the other workers. This was going to be a good thing for the company.

A temporary camp was built to the south of town between Clear Lake and Beaver Lake. It was on low land that might flood if the river rose, but that didn't matter to anyone. If it flooded, they could move to higher land and wait out the waters.

In less than two weeks the camp was full of Chinese workers. They were quickly instructed on logging operations, and the next day they were put to work.

Hammer was amazed at how well they worked. Production increased and profits soared.

The people in town were divided on how they felt about and treated the new workers. Some traded with them, supplying them with eggs, meat and vegetables in exchange for services or money. Others wouldn't give them notice and gestured at them, screaming profanities and racial slurs.

The Chinese logged as well as the men before them. They fell the big trees, and they died with the big trees. The Chinese heard their names whispered in the trees. Language is no barrier in the spirit world. Nothing was different, as a life is a life. They brought their dead off the hill at the end of the day just as the men before them had. They weren't allowed to bury their dead in the Clear Lake Cemetery. It was only for whites, they were told.

In the confines of their camp, they would make a large fire and place their dead on the pile of burning wood, cedar being the choice, since it burns fast and hot. They said their prayers and some wailed and mourned. The ashes would glow into the night with the light of their souls drifting off into the sky.

CHAPTER 17

▼

RENEWAL

Victoria grew tired of men. Their lust, their vulgarities, and their abuse were too much to keep trying to make a living pleasing them. She was tired of her tears, tired of her loneliness, and tired of hiding what she did from her daughters. She was afraid that they knew, and it weighed on her heart. She was determined to find some other way to make a living.

Jezzy was surprised at her decision, but she understood how she felt. "It's never fun being alone when you wake up in the morning." she said.

"I long to be loved."

I wish you well, and don't make yourself scarce. Come visit often—as much as you can."

"Thank you for all that you have done for me—I will never forget you."

Victoria left heading for home, and for the first time in years, she felt like a new person. She looked at the apple trees that were in full bloom. They had grown into beautiful trees. Some of the bark had been scared over the years, from deer trying to reach high for the sweet fruit, and bears that climbed the trees seeking a treat. "The trees are beautiful," she said as she walked to the house.

In the years that passed working with men Victoria had held her beauty. Time had been good to her. Maybe it was all the moisture in the air, or the lack of sun on her face, or maybe that her heart felt young and she wanted more out of life. She had been here for over twenty years and knew she would never return to her home in Scotland. She never expected to see any of her family again, and those thoughts made her sad.

One afternoon while in town, she received notice that a special package was arriving on the 5 p.m. train from Seattle. She sat at the depot anxiously waiting to see what it was.

From a distance she saw the black smoke from the train as it crested the hill before town. Once the train stopped, people made their way off onto the platform. Victoria watched the boxes and packages being unloaded into the depot office, wondering which one was hers. A lady tapped her on the shoulder. "Excuse me."

She turned to see who it was. The voice sounded distantly familiar, and then her eyes began to water as she made eye contact with her sister. They stared at each other, and neither one moved. It had been over twenty years since they had seen each other. Victoria reached out and put her arms around Rachel. They held on to their embrace until the shock started to slow. Tears of joy flooded their souls as they drew back to look at each other again.

They walked to Victoria's house, talking and sharing the things that had happened over the years. They stayed up late into the evening remembering old times and talking of things to come, and then they fell asleep next to each other just as they used to do so many years ago.

*   *   *   *

The Sheriff came looking for Caleb again to question him about his assault on Lee Lowland. He found Caleb near town peeling a Cascara tree. The sheriff stood at the bottom of the tree watching Caleb work. "What did you go and hit Mr. Lowland for?"

"He needed it," Caleb said.

"I've never known you to be aggressive in any way."

"Well when men are acting uncomely to a lady sometimes things have to be done."

"I'm just doing my job—I hope you understand that."

"I do—only understand I would never do anything bad to anyone unless they started it."

"I know that Caleb."

"Good, because I don't think those men have good intent in their hearts towards anyone."

"My only advice is for you to stay away from Lowland and his property. If you don't I'll have to arrest you, and I don't want to have to do that."

"I understand, but he thinks he owns the whole mountain and everyone in town—and that isn't right."

"Just watch your step—if you have any problems—send for me. I'll try to help you. Let the law handle this."

Caleb nodded his head—he understood.

"Keep your eyes open. Things are not right here," the sheriff said as he walked away.

*   *   *   *

Things were better for Victoria with her sister around. The only thing she didn't like was that men were coming over to visit since her sister had arrived in town, for Rachel was as beautiful as Victoria.

Rachel fast became the most popular woman in Clear Lake. Even Lee Lowland had taken an interest in her. When Rachel and Lowland started getting serious, it upset Victoria. Rachel sat on the porch waiting for Lowland to arrive when Victoria sat next to her. "Rachel, Lowland doesn't have good intent in his heart."

"He seems nice to me."

"I fear that you will just end up getting hurt. His heart isn't pure."

"I'm old enough to make my own choices—I'll be careful."

"Sometimes I feel that he just wants to add more to his belt," Victoria said.

By 1921 the mill doubled in size a second time. A new dry kiln was built and two large planers were installed. Men returned from the war and the Chinese had been sent packing. Only one stayed on to work in the mill. He wanted to make a life in Clear Lake and seemed to be accepted by most.

Lee Lowland hired a writer from back east and a photographer to create a company travel log to celebrate the greatness that he had created. He had them come up from the Seattle office with a troop of other dignitaries. They viewed the town and then the company offices and the mill. From there they took a speeder up to Potts Station, a small town made up of boxcar houses. "Here, men can live with their families while working in the woods, an innovative concept to keep married men working in the woods," Lowland said.

After viewing Potts Station, they headed up Day Creek Canyon to see the pride of the Clear Lake holdings. It was the incline at Camp Four.

The incline rose twenty-five hundred feet straight up the mountain with a twenty-one percent grade. "Truly amazing," said the photographer.

Lee Lowland stood at the bottom of the incline pointing up to the top of Cultas Mountain. "It just shows that man can overcome anything in his path. It's a marvel of engineering to bring logs off the top of that mountain. Given the opportunity, I can log anything."

They rode a small flatcar up to the top of the incline. There they saw the 12x14 snubbing engine that raised and lowered the connects. At the top of the mountain they wandered through the big trees that were still standing. The photographer took pictures of men falling a huge fir tree, pictures of the steam donkeys dragging in the big logs, and pictures of untouched timber with their tops reaching into the sky.

The writer took notes and asked questions. Upon returning to Clear Lake to view the mill, Lowland stopped and pointed his finger toward town saying, "If the Almighty was to make his home on earth, I'm sure he'd choose to live in this place, the place I've created. I don't know of a better place that people would want to make their home."

The writer looked at the town. It wasn't much. It wasn't a place he would make his home. "If this is so, then why do you live in Seattle?" he asked.

It seemed like a reasonable question, one that deserved to be answered honestly. Lowland looked at him. "I live in Seattle because it's where I conduct the business of this great company. If I lived in Clear Lake, the company wouldn't be as great as it is now."

The travel log came out and depicted the Clear Lake Lumber Company as the model logging camp and mill. Working for them was like having a vacation every day. No person in their right mind would turn down a chance to be part of the company.

Some men liked working for the mill, while others didn't. The mill provided hot running water in each camp, good food, warm blankets, and a reading room for those who could read. Yet when someone was injured on the job, there was no mercy and no treatment until the end of the day. A man could still lose his job if he took time off to help someone who was hurt.

Logs, logs, and more logs were the words that were repeated over and over. Just get the logs out—fall the trees—build more roads. Go, go, go was the mindset of the mill.

Lee Lowland planned a gala event to advance his company. It would be the first annual company picnic. It would be for the employees, and for all the people of the town. Important people from Seattle and other large towns were also invited. The picnic was labelled as the biggest picnic ever. All seven train engines and all connects loaded with one set of cut timbers which would take the visiting guests on a trip up to the incline at Camp Four.

On Saturday morning the trains sat on the main tracks in town. All the connects were loaded with people. They were excited about the long ride up to Camp Four. At nine a.m. the trains pulled out of Clear Lake with a joyous yell from the people. Lowland hired a band to play music during the trip. Victoria and her girls, along with her sister, turned out for the event. Her girls had grown into beautiful young women.

Caleb heard about the picnic and decided he would show up for the event. It would be a shorter route to walk over the mountain than to ride the train to Camp Four. The poster he saw said that everyone in and around town could join the event. He figured that meant him also.

He arrived at Camp Four about the same time that the train did. Lowland had a big lunch waiting for the guests, prepared by the company cooks. The meal was far more extravagant than the meals they served to the men who worked in the woods. Even though it was said to be a normal meal fed to the workers each day. There were three different kinds of meat along with potatoes, carrots, and various breads. It was all anyone could eat, which was fine with Caleb. He was always hungry.

Lee Lowland saw Caleb eating and walked over to him. "Who invited you?"

Everyone within hearing distance looked at Lee Lowland and Caleb. Caleb smiled as he ate. "You did. I saw your poster—it said everyone welcome. I'm part of everyone."

Lee Lowland shook his head and walked away as too many people were watching and he didn't want to look like a fool.

The picnic was a great time for all. Victoria enjoyed the fine meal. Between bites she turned down the requests of different men who were asking her to join them at the dance that was to be held later that night in town. Lee Lowland pursued Rachel as he was behind her every time she turned around.

Victoria joined a group of people that were going on a tour of the steam donkeys and the tall trees that were still standing. She had heard Mark talking about what he did in the forest, but had never really understood all that he had done. Memories of him flowed through her mind.

Along the way she was being harassed by men who wouldn't take no for an answer. Caleb joined the group for entertainment purposes. He loved hearing men trying to talk about things they didn't know much about. He knew more about nature than any of them. Lee Lowland was in the group making his advances toward Rachel. Victoria was trying to talk her sister out of going to the dance with him. Lee Lowland looked at Victoria. "Unlike you, your sister has class—she hasn't spread her legs all over town."

Rachel's mouth fell open with disgust. Victoria's eyes watered up as her lip quivered, searching for something to say. Her eyes moved back and forth as no words would form. Lee Lowland looked at her with hard, cold eyes. "The truth hurts—cuts deep to your soul. Sometimes there's no forgiveness left for those whose sins reach to the start of their lives. You should have thought about what you could have, if you would've chose to be with me. Maybe your sister will be the one to have what you threw away."

Rachel looked at Lee Lowland with anger. "You're one sorry man."

She walked away and started talking to a couple of men that stood looking at a newly fallen tree.

Caleb stood within hearing distance of the conversation. He drew alongside Victoria and stood between her and Lee Lowland. "I may not have as much money as you do, or the standing that you do, but the thing you offer her is nothing near love. The words you speak are words of hate and resentment that run deep in you."

Lee Lowland turned toward Caleb and spit at him. "You have no concept of love! You've never loved a woman, nor will you ever. I doubt if you've ever even touched a woman, or did you visit this whore when she prostituted herself in town?"

A deep breath came out of Caleb, and anger showed in his face. He took another deep breath and thought of hitting Lowland again. He stepped up to Lee. "You're right, I've never touched a woman, and no, I've never been to a house to visit the doves, but I do know what love is."

"You know nothing."

"Nature teaches me about love every day. If you were to pay attention, the trees you fall could teach you a few things about love—about life. But you fall more and more trees each day—you consume them all. You rape the virgin forest, and take only what you want to use. The ones you don't mill, you burn with fire till there's nothing left. Your type of love is like that—it destroys the thing that gives you life. Love doesn't consume, it gives. And as I see things, you will fall just as the big trees have."

Now it was Lowland who didn't have words to respond. He turned and walked away, looking for Rachel. Victoria smiled at Caleb. "Thank you."

"Oh, don't think anything of it. He's a man that doesn't know the pain and hurt he causes. You ever wonder why he comes up to check on the company and his sons?"

"No, I never have."

"Well, come with me, and I'll show you how nature gives answers to how people act, live, and love."

Caleb held out his hand as Victoria reached for it. His hands were strong, yet soft as though he had taken great care of his skin. They walked away from the group into a clear cut. Everything looked dead except for various ground covers that could tolerate the hot summer sun. Caleb walked over to a large old stump that had a number of dying seedlings at its base.

He reached out and touched one of the seedlings as he looked at Victoria. "This stump is Lee Lowland, and the seedlings are his sons and the company. These seedlings are dying because the parent tree has been cut down. It's no longer here to give shade in the hot summer sun or provide cover from cold winter snows. The seedlings aren't ready to face the elements on their own. Sometimes these types of seedlings are never ready to face the elements, and when the parent tree dies, they soon die afterwards. Some people are like that—never making it on their own, but always hanging onto their parents. Some companies die when the leader is gone."

Victoria shook her head, motioning that she understood. She smiled. "Why have you never pursued a love before?"

"Never thought that I would be wanted by anyone. I've met a lot of nice ladies over the last few years, but I've never had much to offer one."

"You have much to offer—some women look for more than just material things."

"I suppose that I could offer a woman some things—build a new cabin or something like that."

They walked through the clear cut toward the big trees. They came upon a giant freshly cut Douglas fir, Caleb climbed up onto the stump. He held out his hand to Victoria and helped her up. It was about nine feet across. She thought he had pulled her up to get a better view, but he asked her to sit down as he pointed to the center of the stump. "This was its first year. It grew almost half an inch. It had many good years after that first year. You can tell by the growth rings—they're big and wide."

She traced the rings with her fingers as he continued to talk. "Then, here it looks as though the growth slowed down some. There must have been drought or too many cloudy days, and if you look close to the ring way out here—the tree went through a fire that almost killed it. But this tree was strong, so it survived. This tree is like many relationships I've watched over the years."

"How? I don't understand—explain it to me, please."

"I believe that love is like the growth rings of a tree. When people first meet, they have great growth. Everything seems to be right—plenty of rain, plenty of sunshine, and plenty of nourishment. Then as they grow older, sometimes drought sets in, and those years don't seem as good as the first. Then sometimes a relationship is tested by fire—sometimes the relationship doesn't make it through that fire, it just depends on how strong the love is."

"I have never known strong deep love," Victoria said.

"Can you love? Some people fear love. They spend their whole lives avoiding it—wishing for it, desiring it, but running from it when it's close."

Victoria was lost in his words and didn't respond to his question. "Tell me more, please—tell me more about love."

Caleb jumped off the stump, and he reached up and helped Victoria off as they walked in to the tall timber. The light dimmed as the limbs filtered the sunlight, making beams of light that shone down to the forest floor. He walked around the base of a big cedar tree that was over one hundred-seventy feet tall. Looking up at the tree he pointed to the top. "Trees grow by adding a new ring every year. In the spring new growth comes out on the end of the branches, the top reaches further into the sky, and the base widens. Every part of the tree grows, burying the center deep inside itself. If there is no new growth, the tree is dead, and so it's with love I believe.

If a person's love isn't growing each year, and if there's no new growth, love dies. There has to be new things in every relationship—encouragement, understanding, desire, and passion in order for love to survive. And as the first years of the tree are grown over and buried deep—so it's with love it grows until old hurts slowly get buried and a deeper love is added layer upon layer."

Victoria walked close behind Caleb as he talked. She touched the bark of the tree. "Have you ever been touched in a loving way by a woman?"

"No, I don't believe I have."

"Tell me more about these things," she said.

He noticed her touching the bark and put his hand next to hers. "The bark on a tree can hide what's inside. Some bark is thick and some bark is thin. Under the bark could be good wood or rotten wood. It could be wood filled with worms. Sometimes the way a tree looks can tell you about the wood inside, but sometimes the rot starts from the inside. People are like that—some have thin skin, some have thick skin. Some people are beautiful on the outside but rotten to the core, and on others the bark may be damaged, burnt, scarred, but they are truly beautiful on the inside."

There was a long pause as Victoria looked at Caleb Cultas. "Would you ever want me Caleb? I am not a virgin like this forest—I am scarred."

Caleb came close and looked in her eyes. "To Lee Lowland you're damaged, scarred, unclean—but to me you're beautiful, because I see something wonderful inside you. Just like that clear-cut, come winter when the snow falls, it'll be covered in white and not a scar will be seen, and in the spring it will be green covered in new growth. To me your heart is pure like the snow, and fresh like spring. I've heard it said that real love can cover a million wrongs."

Caleb moved closer to Victoria and put his hand over hers as she touched the bark. His eyes reached deep inside of her. He put his hand over her heart while keeping his other hand on the tree. "This bark is a foot thick, and some people have bark this thick surrounding their heart."

"Mine has been thick for so long."

"How can I begin to peel away years of scars and hurts from your heart?"

Victoria moved away from Caleb walking around the tree trailing her hand across the bark, letting it linger, hoping that Caleb would follow. "To most it's a mystery, but you're peeling the bark away from my heart right now. Your words and thoughts are wonderful tools."

Smiles lit both of their faces as a warm silence fell upon them. Caleb drew near to Victoria and placed his hand on hers. With a gentle touch he brought her hand to his chest, covering his heart. "My heart is pure and my love is like a virgin forest. It's not to be ravished, scarred, or destroyed, but to be walked through, touched with care, and handled gently."

Victoria sighed. "Tell me more—tell me more about your love."

"Most men look at the forest and think how much money there is when the trees are milled. Some men look at the forest and see the beauty that will always be there if the trees are left standing. Some men look at women and think—what can this woman give me? Other men look at a woman such as you and think—how can I love this woman in the way she deserves? Men say they own this, or they own that—they possess. True love is not in possessing, but in enjoying what is given and what is offered in return. I don't believe you can really own another person."

Victoria understood what he said—she had felt owned by Mark for years, and her heart was never fully given to him. Her heart was flush with excitement as she listened to Caleb speak words she had longed to hear for a lifetime. They walked around the base of the tree stepping over Twin Flower; their feet crushing some of the blooms, making a fragrance rise and fill the air with sweet aroma. Victoria took a deep breath. "What is that nice smell?"

"Twin Flower—the white blooms on the ground—it's the most fragrant flower in our mountains."

"It smells wonderful, and it's so beautiful."

"Like love, it's fragile. The Indians use it in their wedding ceremonies as a head-band for the bride. The flowers come off long runners that trail on the ground. One stem comes off the runner and produces two flowers. The two flowers symbolize two lovers becoming one and the stem being attached to the vine symbolizes that love needs to be rooted to grow and survive. White is for purity, and the fragrance is for the joy that the two will share. It's a beautiful thing that nature has created."

"Having never loved a woman, how do you know so much about love?"

"My grandfather taught me a lot about love, and Rose speaks of love. Nature tells us about love and life, if only we would look, listen, smell, and feel. The Song of Solomon in the Bible tells a lot about love. We all long for love, no one is exempt. I just believe that some people don't really know what love is. I've questioned it myself."

"Do you think that you could love someone like me?"

"I remember the first time I saw you so many years ago. I was walking back from Mount Vernon and you were standing by the creek. You look just as beautiful now as you did then. The sun was shining in your hair and I thought that you were the kind of woman that I would someday like to be with."

Victoria reached for Caleb, and he welcomed her advance. Embracing each other under the giant trees, standing in Twin Flowers trailing through the deep green moss, their lips met, sending tingles through both their bodies. Mist rose from their feet as the kiss lingered on. A beam of light from the sun shone upon them as though God was giving his blessing. Caleb ran his hand up her back into her long hair, running his fingers through it saying, "Your hair is soft and falls gracefully just like waterfalls flowing from our mountain meadows."

He drew her closer, kissing her lightly, the way she had always dreamed of being kissed, softly, passionately, and with lips full of love. She leaned up against the giant tree as his hands held onto her waist. He kissed her again, and then looked into her eyes. "Up on Cultas Mountain in the meadows, the waters are brown from the soil and peat mosses that grow in the area. The ponds they form are deep in depth and deep in color. Your eyes remind me of that—inviting me to swim in the depths of your soul."

She leaned her head back, giving him access to her neck. "Swim in me, Caleb."

He slid his lips over her neck, kissing from the front to the sides to the back. His hand traced her spine upwards to the base of her head. His fingers massaged the back of her neck while he continued to kiss her. She raised her hands up to her chest and started to unbutton her dress down to her waist, exposing her breasts. Caleb cupped her breasts in his hands as he continued to move between kissing her neck and her lips. He looked down at her breasts. "Just as Solomon said to his lover—your breasts are as graceful as two fawns that are filled with excitement—and your nipples stand erect taking in all the sounds, feelings and sensations."

He leaned down and put his mouth on the top of her breast, kissing it. He took her nipple in his mouth letting his tongue roam, then pulled up and again kissed her lips sending chills through her body. Sliding his hand from her breast down to her waist, touching her skin all the way. "Your skin is smooth and warm like the lake when it's calm in the afternoon summer sun, soft like the clouds that float in the summer sky."

He put his lips back on hers as she started to undo his flannel shirt, revealing a muscular chest above a flat stomach rippled with strength. Her hands ran across his chest, feeling every movement of the energy that this encounter was producing in his body. He slid her dress off her shoulders and it fell around her feet. Goose bumps covered her body as Caleb took in the full view of Victoria. He kissed her lips, and then started kissing her neck moving down to her breasts. She tilted her head back as he gave her light angel kisses down her stomach. She reached out and took hold of the back of his head and slowly raised him up as he kissed her entire body. Back at eye level, she smiled. "Caleb, make love to me— make love to me here in this forest—make love to me here on the moss with the Twin Flower—make love to me!"

Her hands found his pants and she undid the button. He stepped out of his pants, revealing a muscular body that was toned from years of hiking and working in the mountains. She let out a sigh of approval as she longed for his body to be next to hers. He held her as he gently laid her down on the deep moss, not for one moment ceasing his kissing of her. He was erect with passion, standing bold as the big trees in the forest. He moved over her. "The limbs of the trees are our canopy—the sun our star—the moss and flowers our bed. Let me give you my love—let me into the depths of your soul—be with me."

She pulled him into her, feeling his vigor move smoothly inside, as waves of pleasure overcame her whole body. They touched each other and felt all over each other's bodies. Their bodies were in rhythm and it seemed the world surrounded them. All their energies were spent on each other in one great climax like neither had experienced before. Caleb's body merged into hers as he kissed her. "We're like two rivers flowing from distant lands that have finally met, forming the waters of experience that we two will share."

Time passed as they held onto each other, lost in a wild forest they had found in each other. Neither one wanted the day to come to an end. They heard the distant sound of the whistle signalling that the train would be leaving in thirty minutes. They quickly dressed and headed back to the top of the incline and then down to Camp Four where Victoria met her girls and sister. Caleb went to get on the train with them when Lowland walked up. "You didn't come on the train, and you won't leave on the train."

"There seems to be plenty of room and from what I read on the poster in town, the ride was free."

"Free from the town, but from here you must pay."

Lee Lowland figured that Caleb didn't have any money on him, and he was right. Caleb gave a kiss to Victoria. He left heading over the mountain toward town. It would take him about four hours, he figured. He wanted to make it back in time for the dance that was going to be held at the Skagit Club that night.

Lowland climbed up onto the connect and laughed. "I don't think he'll be making the dance tonight."

Victoria shook her head. "Oh, I think he'll make it there."

"There's no way he can walk that far in that short amount of time. Besides he's not welcome at the dance. He's a troublemaker—helping those radicals of the IWW and starting up that crazy save the trees movement. He should be taken care of just like the others."

"What do you mean by that?"

"You know that radicals aren't welcome here—the men in the company take care of such men."

"Murder?"

Silence fell upon the whole connect as every ear was turned to hear Lowland's response. He smiled. "How foolish to think that any man in our company would ever do such a thing. The radicals were just sent away. The man you fancy is a murderer."

"You can say what you want people to believe, but I know your heart and your deeds. Even at this time you're trying to destroy Caleb, but know that there are people coming to help him save the big trees left on his property."

Lowland didn't respond. If this were true, then he would have to make plans to deal with it.

Lowland called Hammer and a few others to his office upon arriving back in town. It was two hours till the dance started and he wanted to make sure that if Caleb showed up they would be ready for him. Seven men sat around a table as Lowland paced around the room. "Our good friends down in Humboldt County in Northern California have been having problems with radicals. Not the radicals that want to unionize the workers, but the kind of radicals who want to save trees."

The men laughed as Lowland continued. "Can you imagine someone wanting to save a tree?"

The laughing continued.

"Anyway, Caleb Cultas is in the same category as those radicals—he wants to save trees for a park. He doesn't want his way of life to change. I'm sure if he had his way he would stop all our activities now and forever, but we're not going to let that happen. He must be taken care of once and for all lest others start to believe like him."

"Will that do us any good?" Hammer asked.

"I see a future where people such as Caleb try to stop anything from happening in the forest—radicals bent on destroying our way of life. This must not happen—we need to destroy him first."

"Won't that only further their cause and make him a martyr?"

"No, it will stop it. After the dance tonight we'll call a special meeting to deal with this matter. I'm asking you men to spread the word to the others."

There was nodding of heads and smiles. All of them, in one way or another, wanted to have Caleb Cultas out of their way. Lowland still wanted Victoria and he had lost Rachel as well. Hammer hated men that didn't work a normal job. Caleb was a bum in his eyes, and some of the men in camp thought that Caleb had gotten away with murder. There was jealousy in each of their hearts as they cherished the thought of being the one to cut Caleb down. Word quickly spread among the men about the meeting after the dance. It was of supreme importance to the livelihood of the company, they were told.

Caleb cut across the ridge of Cultas Mountain. He looked at the sun and knew that it was taking him longer than he planned. Entering one of the many meadows, he saw three horses grazing on the grass. They didn't run when they saw him. He calmly walked up to the horses and petted one on the neck. He touched her belly and then slowly put his hand over her back. She didn't spook at all. He grabbed her mane and jumped up on her back. With a slight squeeze of his legs, the horse started off. He would make it to town in time for the dance.

Victoria thought of ways to bring the idea of a woodland park to the woman's society. It would be a good thing for the community and for the children. When all the big trees were cut down in Western Washington, people would come to Clear Lake to visit the park. They would bring money to spend in the stores, and some people might even choose to live here. She was determined to get Caleb's message out.

Almost everyone who attended the company picnic came to the dance. Victoria waited outside for Caleb to show up. She wasn't going to go in unless Caleb was her escort. Lowland saw her standing outside and walked over to her. "You may as well come in—he isn't going to make it down here on time, so come on in and dance with me."

"Even before today when you made Caleb walk all the way back to town, before I was sweet on Caleb, before the beginning of time—I would never dance with you!"

Victoria's words burned with anger inside of Lowland. He wanted to cut her deep. "Going through company records I recall before your husband died, he borrowed some money from the company bank. Because McMaster liked Mark, we never came after the money, but I think that you should think of paying it back."

Victoria shook her head. "If Mark had taken out a loan, he would have told me."

"Women know nothing about finances—so he probably never told you. I have the records down at the office. I maybe could forget the whole thing if you stay away from that uncouth Caleb. He's full of radicalism and other crazy thoughts."

"That man is more civilized than you'll ever be. He's a gentleman, a caring man, and something you'll never be, an honest man."

As they talked, Caleb came riding up on the horse. He rode right up to them and jumped off. Lowland saw the brand on the horse. "Where'd you steal the horse from?"

"I found it up in the upper meadows, and I've used it to ride here many times—the brand is of McMaster. I don't see Lowland anywhere on this horse. Besides, I'll turn it loose again—*Tyee* was looking out for me."

Lowland walked back into the Club. Caleb walked up to Victoria and embraced her, kissing her on the cheek. They stared at each other for a few seconds, exchanging words of happiness. When Lowland came walking out with a few men at his side and back, Caleb moved himself between Lowland and Victoria. Mr. Ramey, the company policeman, stood next to Lowland. Lowland pointed his finger at Caleb. "That's a company horse you've stolen—we're going to have to place you under arrest and have you sent to the county jail."

"Those horses have been free for years—not until I rode into town on one did you ever take concern for them. I've done nothing wrong."

"I bet you're the one who turned them loose."

"They were turned loose long before you owned the company."

Victoria looked at the horse. "It was Mark who set the horses free. He didn't want them to be killed for food."

"Well, since Mark is dead, that makes you responsible for his actions—an accomplice to this crime. I am sure he went against what he was told, and I am sure you knew, and that makes you just as guilty. I might as well have you arrested also," Lowland said, laughing. "Take them away, Ramey!"

Ramey reached for Caleb's arm to put cuffs on him and Caleb drew back.

"I'd advise you not to resist—it'll just make it worse for you."

Ramey turned toward Victoria and put a cuff on her wrist. Caleb stepped toward Ramey just as the rest of the men with Lowland jumped him. They hit him and kicked him, knocking him to his knees. A man gave him a hard kick to his side and he was out. Victoria screamed as she watched Caleb being kicked and hit. Lowland stood up and kicked Caleb as he tried to raise himself off the ground. Lowland turned away then turned back giving him one last kick. "Take them both away and lose them along the way to the county jail."

Ramey looked at Lowland as he walked toward a wagon. "Lose them?"

"Yes, take care of them, and make it so I never have to see them again. If you take them to the Sheriff he will turn him loose—for some reason the Sheriff likes Caleb."

Ramey nodded his head that he understood, and helped the others load them into a wagon. All but Ramey and another returned to the dance. They headed toward Mount Vernon. "I think we'll throw them into the Nookachamps Creek. Make it look like an accident—two lovers fooling around and they fell in the creek and drowned—how sad."

"Or maybe he tried to escape and they had to shoot him and she got in the way and they shot her by accident," the other said.

Ramey and the man laughed as they thought of how they were going to do away with them.

They arrived at the bridge where Victoria had first seen Caleb. She'd been crying all the way. Lying on her side with her hands cuffed behind her back, she'd been rubbing the side of Caleb's face with her cheek. He would moan and try to open his eyes, but they were badly beaten, being swollen shut.

They stopped and pulled Caleb out of the wagon and threw him over the railing. Victoria heard his body splash into the water, and she hoped that the shock of the cold water would wake him up. They grabbed her and walked her over to the edge of the bridge. "Why are you doing this?"

"You should've never rejected Mr. Lowland—he would have given you everything a woman desires."

"Like Lowland, you don't have any idea what a woman desires."

"Oh, I give women what they desire all the time. Even my daughters," he said with a disgusting laugh.

"You're a sick man—a very sick man."

Ramey turned her around and took off the cuffs. "Why are you taking the cuffs off? She might be able to swim to shore—I don't think it's too wise."

"Her dress will weigh her down when it gets wet. It'll weigh more than her and sink her like the *Titanic*. Then tomorrow we'll show up when the bodies are found and tell everyone what happened. Caleb tried to make an unwelcome advance toward Victoria, so she pushed him in the water, and he hit his head. She got scared and jumped in to help him and ended up drowning also. This is one sad tale of romance," he said laughing.

He started to lift her dress up. "Right now I'm going to give her what every woman desires—a little of me."

Victoria raised her arm and slapped Ramey across the face. He drew back shocked. "You bitch!"

With those words Ramey shoved Victoria off the edge of the bridge into the cold water. Ramey listened for the sound of a splash, then jumped back on the wagon and headed back to town. "I thought you were going to get some."

"Some women don't deserve the good things in life."

Victoria thrashed in the water, trying to kick her way to shore. She managed to keep her head above the water and saw Caleb floating face down in the stream. Thoughts of death filled her mind. She yelled for Caleb to wake up, but he didn't respond. She floated close to him and nudged up against him, hoping that would stir him. He still didn't respond, and she resigned her heart that it was the end for both of them.

She turned him over in the water, almost pulling him under from the weight of her dress. He coughed, but still didn't gain his breathing back. Then she heard a rushing sound like someone running into the water. Before she could make out what it was, there were hands grabbing and pulling on her and Caleb. They pulled them both to shore. She looked up at the faces of those who saved her and recognized Rose standing near the top of the ledge above the creek. Two men helped Rose down to where Victoria and Caleb rested. Victoria couldn't move. Rose knelt close to her as Victoria pulled Rose close to her heart. "I am so thankful that you came—but how did you know? How did you find out that we were in need of your help?"

"On the wind I heard the raven cry out Caleb's name. I was out by the salt water and I asked my brothers to come help. We followed the raven until he came to a rest in that tree over there. We made it to our old camp and waited. Then we heard voices and saw Caleb fall from the sky into the water and then you. We waited until they were gone and now you're safe."

"We're not safe—Lee Lowland thinks we're dead and will stop at nothing to make sure that we are if he finds out we're alive."

"He won't check Charlie's cabin—at least not for a while," Caleb said.

A sigh of relief came over Victoria when she heard Caleb's words. Rose's friends helped them to their feet. "We need to get out of here, and leave no trace—Lowland and his men will be down here looking for us. I want him to think we're dead, that some wild animals carried us off and ate us. I've some plans for him."

They started walking toward the cabin. "What about my girls?" Victoria asked.

"They'll be all right—I'll visit them and tell them you're doing fine," Rose said.

Rose headed for Victoria's house as the others headed up to Charlie's cabin.

CHAPTER 18

▼

SURVIVAL

"Caleb is out of our way. We've taken care of all the radicals that could cause us any problems. So now we can log the rest of his property without any problems. No union radicals and no tree lovers—what more could we ask for?"

Lee Lowland loved speaking in his office. He was the Mill. He gave life and took life. He felt as though he were God. "We may as well log the Southerland property also, since Victoria ran the same fate as Caleb," he said laughing.

"But what about the girls? What should we do with them? They're going to do nothing but cause problems for us. And what about her sister? What if the sheriff finds out about our doings?" Ramey asked.

"Put the girls on a train or send them out to the reservation. They're just stinking Indians anyway. They don't need to be in this good community, so get to it. It'll look like they left once they found out their mother died. I'll deal with her sister, and then the Sheriff. Nobody's to find out about this, everybody keep their mouth shut and our hands will be clean."

Ramey smiled an evil grin. "You wouldn't mind if we gave them some white blood before we send them off?"

"I don't care, do what you want, but don't tell me about it. I know nothing. Understood?"

"Yeah, we understand."

They left and headed up to the Southerland property. Ramey had a paper sealed with the Mill stamp to give to the girls, an order to vacate the property because it now belonged to the Mill.

Shasa was inside when she saw Ramey and the other men coming. She called for her sister and then went out on the porch. Nomi came out and took her place next to her sister. "What do you men want?"

"Your mother died sometime last night and now this place belongs to the Mill. It seems that some debt has to be settled. A decision has been made to make it easy on you girls and just take the property for payment."

The girls didn't move from the porch, and they didn't show emotions of loss, Ramey noticed. "Didn't you hear me? Don't you girls understand English after all these years? Your mother died last night and this property is no longer yours. So you best be off. The longer you stay around here, the greater the chance of bad things happening to you."

"We're not leaving this place!" Nomi said.

"I warned you—you should've listened. Give them some white blood, boys," Ramey said with an evil laugh.

The men with him moved for the girls and grabbed Nomi and started ripping at her clothes. Shasa ran into the house, screaming for help. Two men followed her into the house and caught up with her before she made it out the back door. They dragged her out to the front porch and put her by her sister. They ripped and clawed the girl's clothes off and then repeatedly raped them.

Ramey looked on with approval after he was the first to have both girls. He kept telling the men to give it to them. "Every squaw needs some good white blood in her."

Tears poured out of the girl's eyes. They tried to fight, but to no avail. The men were too many and too strong. As the men finished, Ramey spit on both of them. "Get up and get what you can carry. We're sending you to Seattle on the next train. We'd send you to the reservation, but that's too close. Maybe you can go sell yourselves down there just like your white mother who used to sell herself in this town."

The men all laughed, listening to Ramey. The girls cried, being prodded along and spit on by the men. They called them names as it gave them great pleasure. They put the girls on the train to Seattle. They knew that from there they'd be shipped to some reservation. Nomi held onto Shasa as they sat on the train. In her heart she felt contempt for the whites, yet she felt deep love for the white woman who raised her and Shasa.

Even though Victoria raised her, she was still looked upon as second class to any white person. Her skin would never be white. It would always be brown. She could speak perfect English; she dressed like white girls, yet she knew in her heart that she'd never be accepted as equal. She felt fortunate to have been raised by Victoria. It was better than growing up on the reservation as an orphan. She had seen the people living on the reservation when she had been in LaConner a couple of times. They had such sad faces as though they had lost their lives. It was a place she never wanted to be or to have her sister be. She would work hard to make sure that she'd never end up on a reservation. "We will return to our home, and become great women someday in this valley." Shasa said with conviction.

Mill productivity continued at an all time high. The ground lead system of yarding logs had slowly been replaced with the high lead method. A climber would climb up a tall, sturdy tree, cutting its limbs on the way up. At about three-quarters of the way up, he would top the tree. Thus the tree would become the spar tree. He would hang a few blocks to run the cables through. Using the same yarder that they did on ground lead, they would now have the cables high in the air. Yarding now became more efficient. The trees could come down and out of the forest faster.

Clear Lake Lumber boasted eight locomotives running the logs out of the forest, twenty-nine donkey yarders, and four active logging camps all complete with hot, running water, electricity and all the other comforts of home. The mill itself was the most modern mill in the United States with almost a square mile of holding yard, dry kilns, a nine-foot band-saw, other band-saws, cut-off saws, and two huge turbines to provide all the power the mill needed. In the mind of the mill there would never be an end to the timber or to what they could accomplish. It was the greatest.

Caleb left Charlie's cabin and climbed to the top of Cultas Mountain. From a rocky crag he could see the steam and smoke rising from the mill. The lake looked like a waste yard because so many logs blocked the view of the water. The water was no longer clear, but dark like the souls of the men who ran the mill. He sat there thinking of what he could do to save the life of the woman he came to love. He knew that Lowland wanted both of them dead, and maybe even her daughters. There were big trees left on her property that would be easy pickings for the mill.

He looked down on the property that he loved, the only place he had called home. The mill had its fingers running into his property. A few trees still stood their ground. They had been left for fear that an omen rested over the property. Some men even believed that Caleb's grandfather's ghost roamed the mountain.

The myth wouldn't go away. Caleb thought that maybe it was time to concede defeat to the monster, for its arms not only reached to Caleb's property but thirty miles upriver to Finney Creek, upriver to Day Creek, and up that creek to the top of Haystack Mountain.

From his vantage point, he could look to the south part of the mountain range and see the workings of the English logging company, running out of Conway up to Lake McMurray, up the Nookachamps Creek, and on past Lake Cavanaugh to Deer Creek. It wouldn't be long, he thought, before the whole range was logged and the camps would move further up into the Cascades. Across the Skagit River, he could see the workings of the Lyman Logging Company. Someday, he thought, every area would be logged. There were not many people interested in preservation. It was hard enough to scratch out a living, and who would want to waste their time trying to save trees?

The help from northern California never arrived, and he was at his wits end trying to find a solution himself. He realized that he needed to find any way to stop the madness. He decided that he would try one more time to bargain with Lowland. His first priority was Victoria, he decided that he would forever forfeit his rights to the disputed property on his side of Cultas Mountain if Lowland would let Victoria and her daughters live in peace on their property. He had fallen in love with Victoria and wanted her to have the place she had worked so hard to build and make into a home.

As for himself, he would always have the mountains to roam. He'd pick out a place way back in the depths of the Cascade Range and start the process of having it set aside for all future generations to see. He would talk to people, telling them of the need for having such a place. He would write letters to those in government in hopes that maybe he could find someone who would listen to him. He would need money to do this and where it would come from he didn't know, but he had to believe that it would appear some way.

CHAPTER 19

▼

LASTING LOVE

There was a knock at the cabin door. Victoria, her wounds healed, walked over to the door. "Who's there?"

"Shasa and Nomi."

She opened the door and became overjoyed at the sight of her daughters. They all wept as they held onto each other. Rose stood off in the forest watching as her heart warmed. The last of her tribe were being cared for by the woman who some of her people had called the mountain of fire, *Ha-lea-chub*. She could finally see that Victoria had erupted out of her misery and sadness to become a beacon of light and fire. She was no longer held down by the sorrow that had her in bondage, but filled with life. Even though at the present time she had nothing in material possessions and had lost the place she'd spent her life working on, she had joy that her daughters were safe and that a man whom she adored was in love with her.

As Caleb walked into town, people stared and talked to each other. "I thought he was dead."

"Doesn't look that way," a man said.

A few people took off running, thinking it was his ghost coming to deal out vengeance. He walked down the street to the main office of the company. He didn't knock, but walked right in to the surprise of Lowland and Hammer.

Word spread quickly that Caleb was still alive. It had been reported that he died along with Victoria in the Nookachamps, never to be found. A crowd gathered around the mill office to see what was going to happen.

There was silence as Caleb walked over to Lowland's desk. He sat down and picked up a pen from the desk then took a long look at Lowland. "What do you want?" Lowland asked, with a quiver in his voice.

"Thought I was dead, didn't you? Now everyone's thinking that maybe you had something to do with my demise—kind of puts things in my hands—wouldn't you think?"

Lee Lowland got up and looked outside at the people gathering around. Lowland took a deep breath as he looked at Caleb. "What do you want?"

"I want you to give Victoria the title to her property and to never bother her again. I want you to set aside some property where the big trees will stand and live. As for my property that you've tried to log—I'll leave it all if you follow my wishes."

Lowland again looked outside as more people arrived to see what was happening. "Anything else you want?"

"Yes, keep your men away from me and from my friends. Have Ramey hanged for rape along with the other evil men. Most of all let Victoria and her girls live in peace."

Lowland thought for a moment and looked out the window at the growing crowd and back again at Caleb. "You can have those things as long as you don't implicate me in what happened to you, and if you agree not to organize any radical protests against my company or against our logging of big trees. You and your friends have caused enough trouble for me to last a life time."

"It's you that has caused trouble—you brought it to this whole area. The sins you have created, and allowed will plague this area for years too come."

"I provided jobs for this town—yet this isn't the point—lets just finish this now and forever."

"Just one more thing—I want you to apologize to Victoria and her daughters in public. She has been accused of wrongs that she never committed, and your men violated her daughters. If this is not made right that you will be visited with wrongs ten times over from *Tyee Ma*. You've crossed over to the side of the dark spirits, and if things are not set straight, they'll have a home in this place for generations to come. It's you, Mr. Lowland, who can change the future—the choice is yours."

Anger showed on his face as he looked outside again. "Don't you realize who I am? I'm one of the richest men in America. I'm admired, even worshipped by some. If God were to come down and make his home…"

Caleb held up his hand for Lowland to stop. "Don't you think people are tired of hearing that? If God were to come down here he'd kick your ugly ass all over the place." As Caleb finished speaking Lowland picked right up. "I am the one that makes wealth—the one that provides a living to those souls gathering outside. I could have you killed and tell them that it's for the good of the town, and they would follow. Yet, I'll show you mercy and grant you what you desire—except that I won't admit to any wrong here or in public. I am Lowland, and I bow to no man."

"When Lucifer said he was higher than God, he fell to earth. You too will be brought low, brought down by the trees you fall. Now put into writing the things we have agreed to, and I'll be on my way."

Lowland sat down at his desk and wrote out the agreement. He handed the papers to Caleb. "No word of what was said in here to anyone or this paper is no good. I'll live up to my end of the deal as long as you do. If you cross me, you'll be sorry."

"I won't speak, for the trees will speak for me. The people standing out there will speak for me, nature will speak for me, and God will be my witness and will stand for me."

Caleb walked out the door and past the crowd. As he walked past the people, nothing was said. People stared and some cheered. He didn't understand why they were cheering, but he enjoyed it. He knew in his heart that he had stood up to a monster that many in the town feared. He had stood up to that monster and in his own way had won a giant victory. The Sheriff stood among the crowd and shook Caleb's hand, and then walked up to the office. He walked inside and looked at Lowland. "I'll be watching your every move."

Caleb gave the news to Victoria, and she returned to her home with her daughters. Things were strewn all over the place, but it wasn't long before everything was back in order. Caleb came over to help clean up the outside and to cut firewood for the coming winter. He visited with Victoria and shared with her his thoughts about his life and dreams. He listened to her talk of her desires, her dreams, and the things she wanted to accomplish. Victoria's sister had met a Russian worker from the mill at the dance, and was spending most of her time with him. Like her sister she had fallen in love with the land and wanted to stay. Victoria and her would visit often talking about their lives.

Caleb stacked the last of the cut firewood in the woodshed when Victoria came out with a glass of water. She sat down, watching him drink. "Where are you going to go this winter?" she asked.

"My home is destroyed and Charlie's cabin will be buried under deep snow. I may build a new place before winter comes."

"Where would you plan to do that?"

He sat down next to her and looked toward Cultas Mountain. The mountain was completely logged. There were a few snags left standing here and there but as for the tall trees, there were none left, only the rocky crags and the deep gullies of ancient streams and huge stumps showing the remnants of a greatness that was no more. He pointed at the mountain. "Things look ugly up there right now."

She nodded her head in agreement. "Before the trees were cut, you didn't really know what that mountain looked like. I didn't know all of it. Oh, I've walked all over it—climbed over many streams and over many rocks, but I never really knew what the mountain looked like without the tree cover."

"Lots of scars and wounds," Victoria replied.

"Yes, but it'll grow back someday. The land will heal over—the earth is like that, as you know. The seeds will sprout and become small trees and then grow into big trees. Some day a hundred years from now there will be new loggers logging new trees. I'll build a new home for myself somewhere up there, and who knows, it might even be there a hundred years from now."

They sat in silence for a while, contemplating the thoughts running through their minds. "Have you ever wanted a family, Caleb?"

"Oh, I've thought of that many times, but never went any further than thinking."

Again there was silence as they looked at each other. Caleb stood reaching his hand toward Victoria. "Come walk with me."

She put her hand in his and they walked toward town. From there they walked toward Mount Vernon with Victoria following blindly, not knowing where she was being led. They arrived at the Nookachamps Creek bridge. The old bridge was long gone and a new one was in its place. What was once a dirt road was now paved.

Caleb stopped in the middle of the bridge and looked over the edge at the water flowing toward Puget Sound. "Why are you stopping here?" she asked.

"Remember the first time you saw me? It was here in this place. There was a different bridge at that time, but it's still the place where we first saw each other."

"Yes, I remember. I was amazed at what you were carrying on your back. We laughed at you, but I was still amazed."

He looked her in the eyes. "This is also the place where we were dumped over the edge and left for dead."

Tears filled her eyes as she thought of being in the water trying to get Caleb to respond. He held her close and gently kissed her face where the tears were streaming down. "The place where we first met—the place where we were almost killed. The old bridge is gone, and a new bridge is here. This is our life. The old things have passed away—the new things are coming into being. Just as the clear cuts look ugly, in years to come they'll be beautiful again. It will become new. Underneath us the water flows, being ever new. So it can be with us—a new beginning."

"What are you saying Caleb?"

"I am that mountain, and I am this stream—you have brought so much new growth—so much understanding—so much love into my life."

They gazed into each other's eyes, holding on and never wanting to let go. Caleb kissed a tear running down her check. "Victoria, will you marry me?"

Tears flooded from deep within her soul. "Yes," she said.

They walked back toward the house talking, and making plans for the wedding. They felt like there was nothing in this world that could stop them from accomplishing the things they desired together. As they walked, Victoria thought wonderful things. "When we're married, we can make our home at the place I live now."

Caleb smiled in agreement, thinking he would gladly leave his mountain to live with such a wonderful woman as the beautiful Victoria.

*   *   *   *

Logging was taking place so fast in the Day Creek basin that Camp Four had to be relocated further up the mountain. Almost all of the good timber had been logged, and so the mill set it sights on another large creek basin further east.

The Finny Creek basin was another gold mine of big trees. Tracks were laid up the south side of the Skagit River another fifteen miles to reach the lower end of Finny Creek. One-log loads were soon rolling down the tracks to the mill from the Finny basin.

Jim could see the workings of the loggers from his canoe. He floated down the Skagit with all that he owned. He was getting on in age and knew his days were short, and for that reason he was off to find his friend Caleb whom he hadn't seen in years.

Seattle City Light had taken an interest in the upper Skagit. They had recently finished the first of three dams on the river, providing electric power for Seattle. He knew that before long his claims that he worked on the upper reaches of the river and various creeks would be under hundreds of feet of water. In his canoe he had all of his belongings, a few pans, an extra pair of jeans, a couple of well-worn shirts and four bags of Cascade mountain gold.

He pulled his canoe on shore next to the bridge that crossed the Skagit between Clear Lake and Sedro-Woolley. He waited for one of those new horseless carriages to come by and hopefully buy a ride into Clear Lake.

Caleb was in town and noticed a face he hadn't seen in years. Seeing Jim made him smile. He walked over and shook his hand. "You're looking good for an old man," Caleb said.

"Don't lie to me—I know I look like I've been mined out."

They laughed as Caleb helped him unload his things from the truck. "I'm glad you've made it for the wedding. You can stay at Victoria's house while you're here."

There was a nod of agreement as the two started off down the road. People watched as they walked through town. No one bothered them. A lot of people believed that Caleb was somehow protected supernaturally. "I've been really sick lately, the kind of sickness that takes away life," Jim said as they walked.

Caleb shook his head, understanding what he was saying. He put his hand on Jim's back. "I'll take care of you, my friend."

A moment of brotherly love filled the air, and if any one were near, they would have felt it.

On the day of the wedding, the sun was shining brightly, and Cultas Mountain had a fresh layer of snow. Rachel was Victoria's maid of honor, and Jim stood at Caleb's side. Rose sat with the girls and all were happy. The invited guest had arrived. It was a glorious day that no one would forget.

After the reception, they left for a trip to Seattle, then to the Big Four Mountain Lodge. Upon returning home, they found Jim sick in bed. Caleb went in and stood next to the bed. "You look like you're not going to beat this Jim. Can I do anything for you?"

"Yes, take me back up to Ruby Creek before I die, and bury me high on the ridge overlooking my claim."

"I'll do that for you, Jim. In the morning we'll head to the upper reaches of the Skagit. I'll stay with you and do as you ask."

"I want you to have something of mine. In those heavy bags under the bed—it's all yours."

"I can't have your gold. Don't you have any family that I can send it to?"

"I've no family—I only have you, and there's one thing I want you to do with that gold—I want you to do whatever it takes to save some of that land up in the Cascades from the faller's axes and saws. I'd like for generations to come to see my name up there on some trail saying that Jim once lived in this land. Have it say that I cared for this land, that I overcame many obstacles and lived a long life, but I don't want anyone to know where I'm buried, lest some evil men come and deface my grave."

"I'd be proud to do those things for you—every one of them."

Caleb held his hand, as they looked deep into each other's eyes, remembering all the things they had done together. They would remain friends into the next life.

On a sunny morning the three of them started the two-day trip up to Ruby Creek. Fall showed with leaves falling and snow resting on the mountain peaks. They traveled by train up to Rockport. From there they hired horses to take them to the old Davis ranch just below Diablo Canyon. The Forest Service had moved the Davis's out because of the dams. The rest of the trip would be on foot to Jim's cabin that sat back in the woods from Ruby Creek.

Once in the cabin, Caleb made a fire and Victoria prepared a meal. Jim sat down on the edge of his bed. "I wish I could live forever—I was born a slave, and I found my freedom up here in the high Cascades. Do you know what I'm talking about?"

Caleb nodded. "Yes, I understand what you mean."

"I should've taken myself an Indian bride, but they were more scared of me than I was of them," Jim said laughing.

"Jim, you wouldn't have known what to do with a bride. I'm sure that you'd have moved down to civilization if you had one."

"Yes, I know. I don't belong down there—this is the place I belong."

The next morning Caleb awoke to find Jim motionless in his bed. He passed during the night. They put him in one of his open shafts and slowly filled it in. They left no board with Jim's name on it. It was what he asked for, that he be left alone in peace with no one knowing his place of rest. They burned his cabin and then returned to Clear Lake.

Caleb and Victoria sat on the porch and talked about where they had come from. Caleb longed to learn about Victoria's old home, the land of Scotland. Victoria learned about Caleb's grandfather. They talked about how the town had grown and changed over the years. They talked of the big trees and the mill. Rose would stop by and visit and tell them stories of the early days of her life.

Rose became sick and Caleb moved her into their house to take care of her. One late night Rose called Victoria, Nomi, and Shasa into her room. "I'm about to pass to the next life. Come take my hands girls."

They came close to her bed and took a hold of her hands. She smiled, as she adored them. "You two are the last of our Nookachamps tribe. May your lives be full of children and love. May you prosper in this land. You will see the mill come to an end soon, and you will marry men that love the trees. Remember me in your thoughts, and never forget from where you came. I see that you will become great women honored among men. Great sorrow will come upon you, if you forget whom you are. Live right, do right, and walk in the light."

"We will do those things," Nomi said.

Rose then called Victoria to her side. Taking her hand she started to cry. "I saw you before you came to this land. I knew what would become of you. You shall be blessed in all ways, for your love and compassion are great. We shall meet someday in the after life and be united again."

They all watched as her spirit left. A calm wind moved through the house. They buried her out near where the old Indian camp sat up on the hill overlooking the Nookachamps creek. It was a calm afternoon with the sun shinning bright. Caleb and Victoria, and the girls said their goodbyes. As they left the wind moved through the trees. Caleb smiled and pointed to the moving branches. "I heard the trees whisper Lowland."

Victoria looked at Caleb. "I think I heard the same thing."

Victoria mourned for days. The girls would come and comfort her. Victoria dried her tears and held her girls. "Rose will live through your lives and through your children's lives."

Victoria had so much to be happy for and she knew her life was good. She walked out to the apple trees and saw that the blooms were pink instead of white. The trees were at their maturity. They had been weathered, pruned, and harvested over the years. "A picture of my life—a picture of Rose's life," Victoria said as she touched a pink bloom. "Her fruit and my fruit will go on."

There seemed to be no end to the growth of the mill. Year after year it had grown to remain the largest inland sawmill in the world. Three trains daily would come and go from Clear Lake. Automobiles were a common sight in town, being owned by the men who held higher positions in the company. Wealth was abundant.

Large logs were being milled and new tracks were being laid. The big trees were falling. The mill started to log the rest of Caleb's property. The fallers went into the tall trees and started to work. When they were deep in the forest they saw spirits floating through the trees, and their names being called out. They became full of fear and ran out to the tracks and all the way to town. Hammer and Lowland sat in the office when the men ran in. "There are ghosts up on Caleb's place!"

Lowland shook his head. "There are no such things as ghosts."

"Well, we're not going back up there."

Lowland slammed his fist on the desk. "I will go up there myself and show you that it's all a bunch of bull crap!"

Hammer stood up. "I'll go with you."

They went out to the rail yard and jumped in a speeder. They traveled up to Caleb's property and walked out into the big trees. They found where the fallers had left their saws and axes. They walked around a huge tree then stopped and listened. A slight wind moved through the trees. "Lowland, Lee Lowland."

"Who's there?" Lowland said.

He picked up an ax and swung it into the tree. "I don't believe in your fairy tales Caleb!"

He took another swing and a chip of bark fell off the tree. "Hammer."

Hammer searched the trees and looked at Lowland. "I think we should leave. That's not Caleb."

Lowland shook his head back and forth. "Who the hell's playing games with me?"

The wind started to intensify. It grew to a gale force and Lowland and Hammer took off running out of the timber. The wind blew a huge tree down a few feet in front of them. They stopped and turned running the other way. A second tree fell again blocking their way out. They ran back to the tree Lowland had hit with the ax and watched as trees fell all around them.

Hammer stepped away from the tree and looked to the sky. "Go ahead and strike me!"

A tree crashed down with a giant whoosh like a sword slicing threw the air. It drove Hammer down into the ground as if he were a stake. Lowland watched in fear. Sweat poured off of his forehead. "I'm sorry—don't hurt me!" he cried as he looked to the sky.

A bunch of fir needles fell out of the tree he stood under, knocking him to the ground. The tree cracked and moaned and with a thunderous crash it fell to the ground opposite Lowland. He crawled on the ground into a crater the fallen tree had left. "I am safe here, no trees can get me in this hole," he said.

The wind switched direction blowing a tree on the tree that had created the crater. Lowland felt the impact and heard the tree moan. The force of the tree hitting the downed tree broke it in half. "I'm going to be buried," he said as he tried to climb out of the hole.

As he crawled, the stump and root structure groaned and cracked, and the tree righted, standing back up as if it had never fell. The roots tore into Lowland's body and buried him under the soil with his hand reaching out of the ground. As the wind blew through the trees a voice was heard. "Justice is done."

When Lowland and Hammer failed to show up to work the next day they sent men to find them. The men walked out to the end of the tracks and found the speeder. They walked into the timber over all the downed trees. "What in the hell happened here?"

"Looks as if a mighty wind storm passed through. Lots of blow downs."

They walked over the downed trees and found the saws and axes, and Hammer half buried in the ground under a tree, but no sign of Lowland. All the ground was disturbed. They came to the tree that Lowland was buried underneath. They saw his hand sticking out of the ground from under the stump. "That's his hand—it's his ring."

"Yep, that's Lowland. The spirits got him."

They looked around and were overcome with bad feelings. "Let's get out of here before they get us."

*   *   *   *

The sheriff went up to Caleb's place. Caleb sat on the porch with Victoria as they watched the sheriff walk up the path. "What brings you here sheriff?"

The sheriff stopped and stood on the steps. "Hammer and Lowland were killed on your old property. Some think you are responsible."

Caleb rocked in his chair. "Must have happened yesterday or I would have heard about it."

"Yes, they were killed yesterday."

Caleb looked at Victoria. "We were in Seattle yesterday—didn't get back until late last night. We have our ticket stubs from the train still if you want to see."

"I believe you. I am just doing my job. I saw where they died—a bunch of blow downs."

"Do you believe I can make the wind?"

The sheriff laughed. "No I don't, but a lot of other people think you know the spirit world personally."

"I know them, but can never control what they do. Nature always has its own mind, and a hundred years from now men will still be at its mercy."

As Rose and Caleb prophesied, everything came to a halt. Lowland was gone and as if with one giant swing of the faller's ax, the mill began crashing down.

It had been four months since the death of Lowland. Men who were building a new trestle near Finny Creek heard the news that the company had gone into receivership and walked off the job. The trestle was never finished and it slowly rotted away. Two fallers heard the news and left a tree half cut through with just the undercut done. The tree lived three years until a large wind came from the south and blew it down. Logs were left on the carriage of the mill, and fresh-cut lumber sat on the green chain. The new Baldwin locomotive was repossessed along with twenty-five new disconnects. The mill was dismantled and all the equipment put up for sale at auction.

There seemed to be no apparent reason why the company lost everything except for the absence of Lowland. There was plenty of timber in the hills, and there were plenty of workers to run the operations, and no catastrophes from the forces of nature such as fire or bad weather. It was as though unseen forces brought the mill down. "Without the head a serpent will die," Caleb said.

People slowly started moving out of town. Houses were sold at any price that the owners could get. Some left with only the things they could carry or pack in an auto or wagon. It was exodus from paradise, and only a few remained.

Caleb didn't boast, for he didn't bring the mill down. A force much greater than him had brought it down. It was nature fighting in self defense. He just pondered all the events that led to the fall of the mill. Fate sometimes has a strange twist, he thought, like being killed by the tree you're killing.

The timber in the Clear Lake holdings would have a time of rest before someone else came to log it. English Lumber Company, working the Nookachamp basin to the south and Lyman Timber, logging the north side of the Skagit, were both going strong.

Rumors abounded as to why the company went into receivership. Nothing was ever officially said. The offices closed down and the company newspaper closed its doors. There were many broken dreams left behind, finding no rest for their weary souls.

Clear Lake looked like a ghost town as Caleb and Victoria walked to Beddall's store. "There is so much to do for the wedding of the girls. I'm so happy that they are going to marry finally," Victoria said.

"One of them is a good man, but I don't know about the other," Caleb said.

"I am happy for the girls Caleb. I'm just glad they both have found love."

"So am I."

Victoria held her mid-section. "I'm with child, Caleb—your child."

A huge smile raced across Caleb's face. Victoria and Caleb would go on and on. Their seed would be passed down another generation. They walked with pride for they were still here and the mill and others were gone. They were the big trees that didn't fall. Their love of the forests would leave a lasting legacy. Years later their vision would be realized.

In the late 1960's the North Cascade National Park was established, and today people can walk the mountains and valleys and view the big trees that will never be logged.

The End.

0-595-32508-4

Made in the USA
Middletown, DE
12 January 2021

31277964R00137